THE ROD OF LIGHT

Deepened into three-dimensionality. It took on a soft, fiery outline, indistinct hands, arms, legs, two booted feet. The head was oval and smooth, featureless, hatless. Quick as lightning, the figure flew across the room, passed Prime Cornelian, and drove itself into a far corner. In a moment there was another streak and the creature stood in its original position, holding a rodent's whiskered head, neatly severed, in its hand.

"Ahh . . ." Prime Cornelian said, scratching beneath his chin with a long metallic finger.

The Machine Master spoke slowly, in his voice. "They will fight anywhere, under any conditions, in any weather. They will do whatever needs to be done until that foe is destroyed. They cannot be stopped."

Prime Cornelian raised two of his hands and brought them together with anticipated satisfaction. "But will they *obey*?"

EXILE

THE FIVE WORLDS SAGA

Al Sarrantonio

A ROC BOOK

ROC
Published by the Penguin Group
Penguin Books USA Inc., 375 Hudson Street,
New York, New York 10014, U.S.A.
Penguin Books Ltd, 27 Wrights Lane,
London W8 5TZ, England
Penguin Books Australia Ltd, Ringwood,
Victoria, Australia
Penguin Books Canada Ltd, 10 Alcorn Avenue,
Toronto, Ontario, Canada M4V 3B2
Penguin Books (N.Z.) Ltd, 182–190 Wairau Road,
Auckland 10, New Zealand

Penguin Books Ltd, Registered Offices:
Harmondsworth, Middlesex, England

First published by Roc, an imprint of Dutton Signet,
a division of Penguin Books USA Inc.

First Printing, June, 1996
10 9 8 7 6 5 4 3 2 1

For Isaac Asimov,
Good Doctor,
Who Launched Me Forth:
With Gratitude and
In Memory.

1

An electric shock went through Dalin Shar, ruler of a world, at the moment of his first true-love kiss.

He opened his eyes and found himself looking straight into Tabrel Kris's eyes, which were open also. He knew at that moment that she had felt the shock, too. Her eyes were copper-brown, wide, oval as almonds.

Then Tabrel closed her eyes and Dalin did also, and their lips pressed deeper into the kiss, somehow sealing what they had felt.

"Well," she said, pulling back away from him, suddenly aware of herself.

"Well indeed," Dalin said. He had recovered himself, he thought—though his voice was somehow hushed.

Color touched Tabrel's cheeks, the hollow of her neck. She said, "This is no way for a diplomat to act—"

"Not unless she means it—" Dalin began, then stopped because he knew he was being foolish, playing a game that was expected.

Taking a deep breath, he looked straight into Tabrel's eyes and said, "*I* meant it."

Her cheeks colored even deeper, and she was suddenly flustered.

He rescued her from her embarrassment with a laugh, realizing that she was, after all, a diplomat, and the game *was* expected. Taking her arm, he continued their tour of the gardens, helping her step gingerly from the ancient wooden gazebo where they had paused, at first just to admire the flaming colors of the bloomed roses which were trellised around the structure like a blanket of perfumed scent.

They took one of the many paths leading deeper into the gardens. Above, the afternoon sky had begun to fill with fat white clouds, like cotton. Cotton was, after all, what they had come to talk about.

"So I imagine that your quotas will be filled without difficulty?" Dalin said, sensing that Tabrel would feel more comfortable returning to the initial subject of her visit.

"Oh, yes," Tabrel said, seemingly distracted. But the color of her cheeks had returned to its healthy normal hue, and her attention seemed to follow. "Prime Minister Faulkner has already made arrangements with your cabinet. I would say the talks have gone . . . better than expected."

He sensed her hesitation as something more than the lingering effects of his kiss.

"You're troubled by this?" Dalin asked.

Suddenly she stopped and faced him on the path, amid the buzzing of insects. Accountably, with the partial blotting of the sun by clouds, the spring afternoon had grown almost chilly.

She took his hands, and Dalin thought she meant to kiss him again until he saw the worry in her beautiful eyes.

"The negotiations went too easily," she said simply.

Dalin smiled. "And this is a bad thing?"

"Yes."

She had lowered her voice, which somehow troubled Dalin.

"Can we be heard here?" Tabrel asked abruptly.

Dalin shrugged. "I suppose so. If my guards are doing their duty. They are sworn to secrecy, of course."

"I wonder . . ."

Her frown was contagious, and Dalin could not help being annoyed at this sudden change in the afternoon's events. He thought fleetingly of the feel of her soft lips on his. An uncontrollable chill of pleasure rose up his back.

"Anything I can do to assure you . . ." he said.

"It's not that," Tabrel said. "It's not you. But Minister Faulkner . . ."

Dalin laughed. "Minister Faulkner has been with me since I was a child. He was my father's closest adviser, and I consider him indispensable."

"There are things you aren't aware of . . ."

For a moment Dalin grew serious. "If you'll confide your fears in me . . ."

"Not here," she said; and suddenly, as if she had

dropped that bit of business into a file and closed it, her face became relaxed again. Dalin noticed that she still held his hands in hers and that the deep color had returned to blush her cheeks.

"Perhaps later?" Dalin said, and only the hint of a frown touched her features before she nodded.

The rest of the afternoon, in Dalin's memory, was golden. Their walk through the gardens was verbally uneventful, which meant pleasant and playful, but the air had been charged with a growing electricity between them. Tabrel delighted him with her knowledge of fauna and flora, comparing the species of bees to those on Mars, as well as Martian flowers, which, she claimed, were larger and even more colorful than those in Dalin's garden.

"That I won't believe! I have the finest gardeners in Afrasia to tend these flowers—look at that specimen!" He took two quick steps forward to cup the huge yellow-gold face of a sunflower in his hands, turning it away from the sun to face her. "Do you mean to tell me you have anything to match *this* on Mars?"

"Certainly," she said. "They grow twice as tall, and the colors are deeper because the carbon dioxide content in our atmosphere is higher."

"You must send me one, then, to prove it to me."

She smiled. "It would be my pleasure, Sire."

He felt his own face heat with blush. "You must bring it to me yourself."

"I—"

And then they each took a step, Dalin's cupping hands slipping from the wide sunflower to cup Tabrel's face, as once again their lips met, in a longer and deeper kiss.

"I don't know how this could have happened—" Tabrel whispered, and Dalin had the feeling she was talking more to herself than to him.

"Shhh," he soothed, and held her close.

"But—"

"It happened because it happened," Dalin said, hoping greatly that he didn't sound foolish. In his heart he knew that if he only spoke the truth he could not go wrong.

"I don't know how, with one kiss, but I believe I'm in love with you," Dalin said.

"Yes," she said.

"And in my heart," Dalin went on, still holding her close, "I've always believed that once I fell in love, it would be forever."

He felt her nod against his shoulder.

"That means, Tabrel, we are united for all time," Dalin whispered. "No matter what happens."

"Yes . . ." she whispered, in return.

As if a switch had been thrown within her, he felt her giving body go hard. She pushed suddenly away from him, hiding her tear-stained face from his sight.

"Tabrel!" Dalin shouted. "What's wrong?"

"I cannot!" she cried.

"What do you mean?"

"Please let me go!"

"Tabrel, there are things we must speak of!"

But she had already turned away from him and was running off through the gardens the way they had come, back toward the Imperial Palace.

She paused once to look back at him before running on, and Dalin Shar had the chilling impression that she was trying to memorize his features.

"Tabrel!"

"I cannot love you!"

And later, when the Martian delegation, including both Tabrel and her father, Senator Kris, did not show up for a banquet in the Imperial ballroom—a banquet both in their honor and to celebrate the signing of the much-anticipated trade pact—Dalin Shar learned not only that would the Martians be absent from the banquet, but that their shuttle had departed abruptly, hours before, for Mars.

2

Staring at the fading glow of a pink Martian sunset, Prime Cornelian was disturbed.

It wasn't that his plans were not going well. They *were*, by any measure. The first and second phases of his campaign had just been completed, and in a few moments he would address the Senate and complete the third.

That was not the problem now.

There was the problem of Senator and Tabrel Kris, which was still unsolved—but it was not that, either.

It was something else, something at the very fringes of his brain, that bothered Prime Cornelian.

He ran the unnaturally long fingers of one hand along the sandstone ledge of the balcony he stood on. Below, the pink-red stone spread to either side in a graceful sweep; above, successive floors of the residence of the High Prefect of Mars, deceased not five minutes before of unnatural causes, narrowed to a single garret, topped with the Martian symbol of solidarity, the sickle within a circle of black iron.

It stood as a symbol for something whose memory Prime Cornelian was now ready to rejuvenate: the ancient, vicious battle for the planet Mars, fought in the middle of the twenty-first century between what had been then the Two Worlds, Earth and Mars. It was during those times that Martians had evidenced a bloodlust like none ever seen on any of the worlds, a bloodlust which had, in the end, gained them their independence.

Prime Cornelian's own great-grandfather had died in that conflict; and now Prime Cornelian was ready to elevate that symbol to an even higher place, by once again filling all of Mars with a hunger for war and savagery that would even outstrip the ancient one.

Soon, perhaps, the pink sickle within the iron circle would fly on all of the Four Worlds.

And also the Fifth.

"Ahh," Prime Cornelian said to himself, knowing at last that he had come to the edge of the problem that bothered him.

The Fifth World.

Venus.

As one of his long-fingered hands continued to lightly stroke the sandstone of the railing, two others managed with the Screen he held. Almost reluctantly, he activated the viewer and watched as a series of pictures flashed inside the three-dimensional area. They were the latest from Venus orbit; and as Prime Cornelian viewed them, once quickly and then again slowly, one at a time, with great care, the tiny area of uneasiness he had felt began to blossom within him. This was not something anyone else would ever see—but Prime Cornelian knew that what he was looking at was the one vulnerable area of his plan.

"Sir?" the timid of voice of Pynthas squeaked behind him.

He turned his insect's head without moving the rest of his body and regarded the intruder with all the interest of a biologist studying a bacterium in a culture dish.

Pynthas, his human body quaking, bowed at the waist, not looking up.

"I'm sorry, sir."

"Sorry for *what*?" Prime Cornelian snapped. He despised the man's inability to say what was on his mind, even more than he despised the man himself.

"I only wanted to tell you, sir, that there's been an update on the transmissions you requested. If you'll press—"

"I know how to use the machine!" Prime Cornelian roared. In a smooth motion accompanied by the soft tickings and whirrings of his inner mechanisms, he swiveled the rest of his body around to face Pynthas. His fourth hand slid from the balcony, the long metal fingers wrapping with the other three around the body of the Screen.

His vertical blue-black eyes regarded Pynthas silently for a moment, and then he turned his attention back to the Screen as the new pictures came into view.

"Damnation," Prime Cornelian swore beneath his breath.

"I'm told it's not as bad as the photographs seem to show," Pynthas said in a hopeful whisper.

"Don't patronize me!" Prime Cornelian said angrily. "It's that bad and worse! They're arming the terraforming equipment as quickly as they can—*as quickly as they can*! Do you know what that means? It means they don't care if they die! They'll martyr themselves along with the equipment!"

Breathing heavily, Prime Cornelian turned his attention back to the new information. On the screen the hazy green-orange orb of Venus swam in a haze of thin yellow cloud. Near the poles, the budding whites of ice caps stretched tentative fingers past their boundaries. Pockets of lush darker green dotted the landscape here and there; and in two spots on the planet's visible surface—the huge canyon Aphrodite Terra and Alpha Regio—shallow pools of standing water glistened like silver, surrounded by fringes of vegetation.

And here and there on the planet were the sites of future formations: where terraforming stations now stood, and where, after the detonation of the plasma blast equipment now being erected, would instead exist the blasted craters of man-made explosions hundreds of miles wide.

Making a disgusted sound, Prime Cornelian switched to the final transmission, a close-up of a station in the process of being armed, the long sleek blue tanks of the detonators clinging like leeches to the massive blocklike terraform stations.

"But sir—" Pynthas began.

Filled with rage, Prime Cornelian reared back one long-fingered hand and hurled the Screen at the toady, driving him back and knocking him to the sandstone floor, where he lay trembling, eyes closed, not daring to look up.

For a moment Prime Cornelian studied the sharp tip of one finger, which seemed to be covered in thickly drying blood, but was merely smeared with viscous oil.

Ignoring Pynthas, Prime Cornelian swiveled his body back to stand at the balcony ledge and stare out over the now darkened horizon. The lights of the city were winking on below, even as the stars spread out in the sky above. At the horizon, the pink glow turned with a departing flash of orange to blackness.

"Something will be done," Prime Cornelian said to himself.

Even deeper inside his brain was another problem, even more troubling, that he would not as yet even admit existed.

But one problem at a time.

Gliding close by past the still cowering Pynthas, his six long-jointed limbs, the front four bearing his hands, making ticking sounds like dog claws on the smooth sandstone floor, Prime Cornelian said almost as an afterthought, "Alert the Senate that I am coming."

Pynthas, groveling, not daring to even open his eyes, nevertheless nodded vigorously, rising from the floor only when he was absolutely sure he was alone.

3

In the Senate Chamber of the Grand Assembly of Mars, Senator Cray-Pol was given the floor.

The old parliamentarian shuffled slowly from his seat to the podium. Though his face was wrinkled and his walk lethargic, those who knew the old man understood by the look on his wizened features that he was boiling with anger. The strength of his voice was legendary, as was the depth of his wrath when riled. He had often been compared to a dune snake: sleepy and shade-driven when left alone, but when poked with a stick or dragged into harsh sunlight, all sharp tooth, fiery eye, and poison.

The membership waited for the old man to reach the dais, which he now did with aid. He did not turn in his customary way to thank the Senate page, which in itself gauged his displeasure.

Pushing back the arms of his crimson velvet robe, Cray-Pol gripped the top of the lectern and aimed his fierce stare out at his compatriots. The eyes below his shock of unruly white hair were bottom-less with ire.

For a moment he did not speak, the gathering storm taking shape in his ancient body. But when the words finally broke from his lips they were of a force and stentorian level that had not been heard in that deliberative body for decades—since Cray-Pol himself, as a much younger man, had denounced from this same podium the High Prefect's road-usage tax of 2411.

"This is outrageous!" Cray-Pol shouted into the depths of the pink Senate chamber. For a moment his voice lingered in the high recesses of the domed ceiling, like a bird circling and reluctant to fly away.

From the silence of the gallery came a few mumbled ayes.

"Outrageous, I say! To think that we have been dragged from our supper tables at the whim of one man! That the august body of the Senate of Mars should be treated in this fashion is indefensible! What crisis could possibly warrant such behavior? No one, not the High Prefect himself, warrants the authority to treat this assembly in such a manner. I move that we adjourn at once and that a writ of protest be filed! Whatever this mysterious crisis is, it can wait until morning!"

Cray-Pol pounded on the lectern. Though the strength of his hand in no way matched that of his voice, the murmurs of assent now rose to a clamor from the nearly filled half-circle of seats in the gallery.

With a dismissive wave, Cray-Pol turned from the

podium and accepted the help of the Senate page in descending.

Amid a chorus of talking and rustling, the Senate members, remembering their dinners and other activities, rose as one to depart.

"Not yet, gentlemen!" came a voice from the rear of the hall.

Startled, Cray-Pol paused halfway down the final step from the lectern and now, on beholding Prime Cornelian's insect body filling the back doorway of the Senate chamber, indicated to the page that he should be helped back up to the dais.

With a collective sigh, the senators settled back into their seats. One, the incongruously (for a Martian) stout Kol-Fan, produced a ripple of laughter with his lament of, "My roast goose!"

After what seemed an eternity, during which relative silence returned to the chamber, Cray-Pol resumed his spot at the rostrum, pushed back his robe's arms, and gripped the top of the lectern once more. Now, his eyes filling with even greater fury, he shouted, one palsied finger leaving the desktop to point the length of the gallery back at Prime Cornelian.

"How dare you enter this chamber! You are not allowed here! Haven't you caused enough trouble in the last months with your red-shirted ruffians running wild in the streets, your talk of war? You may have fooled some of the Martian people—and even the High Prefect—with your phony nationalism and your call to the old, warlike heritage of Mars, Cornelian, but you haven't fooled me!"

Cray-Pol's words echoed and faded. Absolute silence descended on the Senate chamber. A few heads swiveled to regard Prime Cornelian, who stood unmoving in the open doorway.

"Sentinels!" Cray-Pol shouted. "Remove that . . . *thing!*"

Before the two festooned guards at the sides of the chamber could react, Prime Cornelian, in a voice even stronger than Cray-Pol's, said, "I bring you sad news . . . of the death of the High Prefect."

A collective gasp rode through the gallery.

"No!" Kol-Fan, settling weakly into his chair, whispered, all thoughts of dinner gone.

"We must stay in session until a new High Prefect is chosen!" came a voice from one side.

"Where is Senator Kris?" came another. "Let us elect him new High Prefect!"

At the podium, Cray-Pol seemed stunned, unable to speak or move.

"May I speak?" Prime Cornelian said courteously.

When Cray-Pol still made no move, a voice cried out, "Let him speak!" seconded by, "Yes!"

Cray-Pol, at a loss for words, mumbled, "This is . . . highly unusual. . . ."

"Give Cornelian the podium!"

In the back, Prime Cornelian waited patiently.

Cray-Pol, mustering his strength, said, "We must put this to a vote. All those in favor . . ."

Nearly every hand, save for Cray-Pol's and that of Kol-Fan, who had fainted, shot into the air.

"Very . . . well . . ." Cray-Pol said.

The old man turned away, leaning heavily on the page, and was helped down from the dais.

An electricity of anticipation built as Cray-Pol was helped to his seat and was lowered, shaking, into it.

Only after the old senator was seated did Prime Cornelian make his way up the center aisle. He seemed oblivious to the fact that those senators seated on the center aisle shrunk away from his form as it passed. His six insectlike limbs climbed the platform in a fluid motion and he turned to regard the assembly with his slitted eyes.

He spread his front hands in mock sadness, tilting his head to one side.

"He did not die in his sleep," Prime Cornelian said with a sigh, "nor peacefully."

He made a flicking motion with one needlelike finger.

Instantly a detachment of Martian Marines filed in through the rear doors, spreading like red ink around the perimeter of the chamber.

"Sorry about the, ah, security," Prime Cornelian said mildly, "but one can never be too careful."

In his seat, Cray-Pol began to recover and sat regathering his wrath.

Marines continued to file in, completely ringing the chamber. Now with another flick of Prime Cornelian's finger the heavy rear doors of the chamber were slammed shut with a hollow sound.

"I could say you are a captive audience—but we'll dispense with the levity," Prime Cornelian said. "The bald truth is, the High Prefect was murdered, by myself. As was General Korvin. They were both unreasonable men and refused to believe in the coming crisis. General Korvin, whose underlings seem more inclined to my views, has been replaced by . . . myself, and the High Prefect has been replaced by . . ." here he turned a sharp metal fingertip to point at his chest, "myself."

An uproar welled through the chamber. It was quickly silenced by the raising of two hundred Marine raser rifles.

Prime Cornelian held up his hand for silence—which nearly ensued, until Cray-Pol, his face a deep shade of angry red, pushed himself, shaking, to his feet.

"*If Kris were here you would dare not—*"

With a sigh Prime Cornelian said, "Kris is not here. In fact, aside from the few of you miserable lizards in this room who are still his friends, I have already eliminated any of his allies I could find, in the military, in the cabinet, hiding behind chairs—wherever I could find them." He made a motion to one of the Marines, who sighted his raser and fired. A ruby line pierced the old senator's upper body.

With a shocked gasp, the wrath, and life, left Cray-Pol's body. He collapsed into his chair, a knuckle-sized blackened hole showing completely through his chest cavity.

Tomblike silence descended on the chamber.

"And now," Prime Cornelian said, "I'm afraid that I must insist that the Senate be dissolved. All in favor?"

Prime Cornelian help up a hand, glaring at the assembly.

All hands in the gallery, save that of Kol-Fan, still mercifully unconscious, rose trembling into the air.

One brave voice, that of the young Senator Fel-Pen, called out, "What crisis do you speak of, Cornelian?"

Prime Cornelian waved a digit in dismissal. "It's no concern of yours. After all, you won't be around to be bothered by it."

"But," a frightened voice called out, mixing with others voicing similar pleas, "we are dissolved!"

Prime Cornelian gave indication to the ring of Marines, who now sighted their weapons as one, training them on the mass of senators, caught like fish in a barrel.

"You can't do this!" one voice cried.

"We'll go quietly!"

"We're dissolved!"

"We'll side with you!"

"We hate Kris!"

"Did I say dissolved?" Prime Cornelian smiled. "I meant . . . liquidated. You're much too dangerous as a deliberative body. The people will follow me much more readily if you aren't around to . . . interfere."

His jointed limbs carried him smoothly from the platform to the aisle, toward the back of the chamber. As he passed, those senators on the aisle seats who had shrunk back from his passage now reached out to grab at his body.

"Don't do this!"

"The people of Mars will never let you get away with this!"

"We have wives and children!"

"Kris will stop you!"

"We'll help you!"

Prime Cornelian pushed past them. In the midst of a phalanx of Marines, he strode through the chamber doors, which opened ponderously on their ancient hinges.

As the two Marines manning the doors began to swing them shut, Prime Cornelian stayed them.

"Leave them open a little," he said. Onto his insect's face came something resembling a smile. "I want to hear the . . . deliberations inside."

There was a clamor of voices from within the chamber, protestations drowning out beggings. Then one high whine sounded as a single raser began to fire. It was immediately joined by a multitude of others until a sound resembling a high-pitched organ chord drowned out the screams of the senators.

Soon there was only the sound of the raser rifles. Then silence.

Prime Cornelian sighed.

"Such a waste," he said, moving off with clickings of his machine limbs. "I always liked that chamber. Now it will have to be cleaned before it can be used again."

Filled with a sudden thought, Prime Cornelian stopped, turned, and returned to the doors.

"Open them," he snapped.

The rigid Marines obeyed immediately, swinging the doors back to reveal the carnage within. Already, the great majority of the soldiers were stacking the dead corpses in one corner of the giant hall; Prime Cornelian noticed the incongruously rotund body of Kol-Fan on top of one pile, and was mildly annoyed that the fat senator, who was such an anomaly among the generally lean Martians, had never regained consciousness to feel the raser fire burning through him.

Prime Cornelian made his way to the front of the chamber, mounted the steps to the dais once more, and looked out over the assembled, sightless dead.

"It occurs to me," he said, noting with pleasure that his Marines did not dare to pause in the work, but continued on obediently, "that I did not give the Senate the courtesy of answering Fel-Pen's question: namely, what crisis has prompted me to do this. That is an easy enough question to answer.

"The answer is this: *We are going to war!*"

4

Alone in his room, brooding like only a young man in love can brood, Dalin Shar heard a second knock at his door.

He ignored it, as he had the first. He knew who it was, and he did not feel like speaking to Prime Minister Faulkner at the moment. In fact, he did not feel like speaking to the prime minister ever again—or anyone else, for that matter.

The knock came again, more insistent.

"Go away, Faulkner! If there's any business to be taken care of, take care of it yourself!"

"But Sire, I *must* speak with you!"

"I said *leave me alone!*"

"This is a matter of the utmost importance!"

"What is it—cotton? Has the price fallen again? Or is it the wheat lobby in the West, clamoring for more favor? Are the North American nomads threatening colonies with their plagues, as they did two years ago?"

"Sire, I must insist!"

"Leave me alone!"

"It concerns the Martian delegation!"

Instantly, Dalin's interest was piqued.

"What of it?" he shouted, through the still-closed door.

"Sire, open this door at once!"

Now Dalin's interest was further heightened by the note of anger in the minister's voice—a rare, actually unknown, element. Dalin Shar rose to let Faulkner in.

The prime minister bowed from the waist on confronting Dalin face-to-face.

With impatience, Dalin snapped, "Come in and tell me what you know."

Faulkner straightened to his height of six-foot-five, smoothed his immaculately pressed tunic, and followed Dalin stiffly into the room. He stood while the king threw himself facedown onto the bed.

"Speak," Dalin Shar said morosely. "Tell me what you know of Tabrel Kris and her father." He sighed. "Forget her father—tell me what you know of Tabrel."

In measured, serious voice, Minister Faulkner said, "Very little, in fact, Sire. The senator and his daughter are on their way back to face a crisis on Mars. Their shuttle engaged its phase drive soon after passing beyond our Outer Defense Shield."

Idly, Dalin said, "Did you check to see if they stole any silverware, Minister?"

Confusion washed across Faulkner's face, and then he said, "That was a joke, Sire?"

"Yes, it was." Dalin sighed. "Tell me what you know of Tabrel Kris."

Faulkner said, "There are more important things to discuss. It seems we have a crisis here on Earth, too." The minister turned to the far wall and gave a command. Instantly its paintings melted away into a depthless Screen.

"Forty-four, twenty," Faulkner said, and the deep black filled in with an aerial, three-dimensional view of a blackened section of Earth.

Dalin did not look at the wall, but kicked his legs languidly against the bed, his chin resting on his fists.

"Sire, *please*," Faulkner said.

"Oh, all right," the King said, sitting up to face the screen. "If it will make you leave any faster."

"What you see—" Faulkner began to lecture.

"What I see is part of the Americas," Dalin Shar said, utilizing a bored, singsong voice. "If my dreadful geography lessons serve me, it is the main portion of the Lost Lands, stretching from what used to be the middle Atlantic States of the United States of America down through the Amazon Basin. It is an area nearly devoid of ecological activity. The acid content of the rainfall in the area is . . ."

Dalin's rote memory failed, and Minister Faulkner immediately spoke up:

"Thirty point nine, by the Rhemer scale, deadly to most plant and animal life. The area is inhabited by cockroaches and mutant mammal life . . ."

Faulkner's voice trailed off as he noticed that the

king had abandoned his viewing of the screen and once more lay on the bed, this time on his back. He stared at the ceiling.

"Sire?"

Dalin Shar yawned. "What is it, Minister Faulkner?"

"Please bear with me!"

Blowing his breath out, Dalin dragged himself up to a sitting position once more.

"Is there a point to all this, Faulkner? I've seen these pictures a thousand times, as well as the blackened areas of Europe, the Lost Lands in Australia and lower Africa. I know all the facts about mineral depletion and natural resource scarcity. I know that Afrasia is all we have left on what used to be blue little Earth, and I know that outside of cotton and a few other commodities that won't grow anywhere else, we have very little that the rest of the Four Worlds wants or needs. I know about our little colonies on Earth, and our two colonies on the Moon. I know all the geography, meteorology, climatology, agronomy, and, for that matter, literature, music, history, languages, cultural differences, tact, diplomacy, and games theory that I will ever need or ever want to know. So what, Minister Faulkner, is the point of all this?"

Prime Minister Faulkner's eyes hardened for a moment—this was another reaction that Dalin Shar had never noticed in the man before. The look seemed to say, *Stupid boy,* and it was not one that Dalin relished. Instantly his own manner changed, from peevish young pup into inheritor of the throne of Sarat Shar, First King of Afrasia and Ruler of Earth.

"Get to the point, Prime Minister."

Faulkner himself obviously noted the change in the air, and immediately became more conciliatory. He turned and indicated an area along the coast of the Gulf of Mexico, where a fringe of green made a stark contrast to the bleak brown and black areas inland.

"As you know, Sire," he said, "this perimeter of land was reinhabited twenty years ago by a group of colonists sponsored by your father. The colony is called New Texas, even though the strip of land touches on what used to be parts of the United States, stretching to Georgia, all the way around the gulf into former Mexico." To the screen, Faulkner commanded, "Zoom."

The picture widened, so that the strip of green curled around the perimeter of the screen.

"Zoom again."

The screen was filled with green, the lushness of trees and greenery of which not even much of Afrasia could boast. And in cleared-out areas, one large one in particular, stood clearings dotted with man-made structures, in the Indo style of the twenty-fourth century, when the Indian peninsula had been the seat of Earth's government before much of it, too, succumbed to ecological ruin and became Lost Lands.

"It is here," Faulkner said, "in a town called Sarat,

ironically named after your father, that a rebellion has broken out."

"A *rebellion*?" Dalin Shar said, his eyes widening.

The minister did not turn around, but nodded curtly.

"Yes, Sire. And I have reason to believe that it has already spread to the other colonies along the American coast, and even into the Far Colonies in the Pacific."

"What kind of rebellion, Prime Minister?" Dalin said, still not sure of what he was hearing. "What could these people possibly want?"

"They want to bring down your government, Sire."

Suddenly Dalin laughed.

"But that is preposterous!"

"They are getting outside help, Sire."

Silence hung between them for a moment, and Faulkner turned around to face the king. "They are being funded, and encouraged, by certain factions on Mars."

"But why?"

Faulker paused before answering. "Because, I believe, certain factions on Mars believe it would be better to take from Earth than to trade with it."

Dalin Shar shook his head. "This is incredible! We just signed a new trade pact with Kris—"

"Senator Kris had nothing to do with this. I believe he was sent here to get him out of the way. We have garbled reports that there has been a coup d'état on Mars. It seems Prime Cornelian has assassinated the High Prefect and is now in charge. If that is so, everything that's happened makes sense, since Kris was the only man who could have stopped Cornelian. I also believe that Cornelian has been in contact with these rebellious colonists and is supporting them." He hesitated. "I'm . . . also fairly certain that Cornelian has gained alliance with one or more members of your own government."

"Who?"

"I'm not certain, Sire. But I'm very worried."

"I don't believe any of this! It's too fantastic!"

The prime minister turned back to the screen and issued a series of commands. The view of the Sarat colony disappeared, and a procession of intercepted communiqués flashed across the screen, messages from Sarat to Prime Cornelian and vice versa.

"That's enough," Dalin Shar said, raising his hand.

"There's much more evidence," Prime Minister Faulkner said.

"I've seen enough for now. I must think on this."

Again, Faulkner hesitated before answering—always a sign of his disapproval. "There are things I would like to do, Sire. Measures we can take now, in your name. Time is precious—"

"I must think on this, as I said."

Faulkner bowed. "As you wish, Sire. But might I suggest that we meet in the morning to go over a course of action?"

Distractedly, Dalin nodded.

The prime minister bowed again and turned to

the Screen. After a word, it blanked and pulled back into the wall of paintings it had been before.

Faulkner walked to the door, opened it, and turned to bow again.

"Until the morning, then, Sire."

"Prime Minister?"

"Yes?"

"Tell me something. In your research, what is it you know of the senator's daughter, Tabrel Kris?"

"I know that she grew up on Mars and attended a private school in Wells until a year ago. Her mother died when she was very young."

"Is that all?"

Prime Minister Faulkner stood in the doorway for a moment, regarding the young man. "There is one other thing I am aware of about her, Sire."

"Well?"

"I . . . hesitate to tell you, Sire."

"Must I order you? Out with it!"

"It seems," Prime Minister Faulkner said uncomfortably, "that she is betrothed to a diplomat's son on Titan."

Dalin Shar stood motionless.

"I believe," Prime Minister Faulkner said gently, before closing the door, "that the marriage is to be within the Martian year."

5

A mere hundred thousand miles from Mars, Senator Kris called his daughter to his side.

The home planet was framed in the shuttle's window. It hung in space like a claret ball, its shroud of atmosphere greatly softening its surface, still rusty even three hundred years after terraforming. Only the fragile, wide patches of green, the sustaining, oxygen-giving plains, fed by the aquifers which led down from the highlands, where it occasionally rained, and from the polar caps, where frozen water now ruled, made it appear any different than before man had tinkered with it. Indeed, it now looked much as Percival Lowell had described and drawn it in the late 1800s, after carrying Giovanni Schiaparelli's vague description of "canali" to preposterous lengths of scientific delusion, turning channels into man-made canals.

Now there were man-made canals, and the green of seasons that Lowell had also, in his tame dementia, so assiduously described.

Even so, it hung before Senator Kris a planet changed, overnight.

"Tabrel," the old man said, drawing his daughter near, "I'm afraid it's time for us to go separate ways."

"What do you mean?" Tabrel said with alarm.

Nodding toward Mars, the senator drew a deep breath and said, "I must return home and attempt to stop Cornelian."

"But how—"

The old man's lined face now turned to his child. "There is a chance that the people, if they are not too lost in Cornelian's delusions of war-glory by now, will side with me. If I can get that to happen, the army may follow. It is a slim chance, but one I must take."

Tabrel clung to the old man.

"If I fail," Senator Kris continued, "it means war throughout the Four Planets, and on Venus also. It means a return to dark times for Mars."

"I'll go with you, then," Tabrel said.

"You must not be allowed anywhere near Cornelian. You know that, Tabrel."

"But he'll kill you!"

The senator paused before saying, "I've never lied to you, daughter. We both know how probable that is. You will be safe on Titan, at least for the time being. The outpost there is secure. Jamal Clan is waiting for you."

"Jamal Clan . . ."

The senator paused before saying, "There is . . .

another matter I wish to discuss with you. I have become aware of your . . . attachment to King Dalin Shar. I am also quite aware of your betrothal to Jamal Clan."

"Whom I have never seen."

"True. This marriage was arranged long ago, in the best interests of both Mars and Titan. Since at the moment it would mean little to Mars, I would feel secure in releasing you from the vow, if you so wish."

"Are you sure, Father?" Tabrel said.

"There . . . would be certain diplomatic hurdles should this happen, of course. The Titanians might not be as sanguine as I about dissolving this arrangement." He smiled wanly. "But I have no doubt my daughter could jump those hurdles."

"Thank you, Father."

"And who knows? You may find Jamal Clan's charm overwhelming nevertheless!"

Tabrel smiled.

"I've . . . not often spoken of such things," the senator continued, "but I want you to know it has not been easy for me raising you alone. Since your mother's early death I've often felt . . . inadequate to the task. But looking at you today, I feel as if this, at least, was a victory in my life."

Senator Kris gently cupped his daughter's chin with his hand and looked into her eyes.

"I want you to be strong, daughter. With the strength I know is in you."

He waited until she nodded.

"I'll be strong, Father."

"No matter what happens?"

Again she nodded. "No matter what happens."

"I must go back," he said, his voice low and gentle. "Greater evil will come to Mars if I don't."

Tabrel clung to her father.

Senator Kris, standing stiffly, looked with tired eyes to his attendant standing a respectful distance away. He made a motion and the robot deftly approached. Gently it tried to pry the clinging Tabrel from her father.

Senator Kris said, "I've arranged for you to leave immediately, Tabrel. I felt it was best."

The firm hands of the attendant pulled Tabrel away from her father. Suddenly she stepped back on her own and said, "I understand."

Her father looked down at her and smiled sadly. "Good-by, dear daughter," he said.

"Good-bye . . ."

Before long, the senator, still standing at the window, hands clasped behind his back, watched as the coffinlike pod of the lifeboat was jettisoned. It moved serenely away from the shuttle until reaching a distance of two kilometers. Then its rocket ignited, throwing it sideways in the senator's vision away from the shuttle, on its way to rendezvous with the Titanian craft waiting another hundred thousand miles distant from Mars.

Taking in a deep breath, the senator let it out slowly.

"Good-bye, dear daughter," he said. "Forever."

Five hours later Senator Kris's shuttle was in
Mars orbit. An hour after that it had been given
clearance to land.

Prime Cornelian himself patched into the communications line and came on screen.

"Senator!" Prime Cornelian crowed. "How nice of
you to return!"

"I feel no joy about it, myself," Senator Kris said,
refusing to look through the front portal at the red
planet rushing up at them. He knew how safe shuttles were but declined to put himself through the
roller-coaster plunge of their landings.

"Nonsense!" Prime Cornelian said. "You and your
lovely daughter will be my guests of honor on
your landing!"

The senator smiled inwardly at the inclusion of
Tabrel in the statement.

"After all," Prime Cornelian continued, "you are
the only specimen of the Martian Senate left in
existence! Perhaps we'll put you in a zoo!"

Senator Kris said, "I demand an immediate plebiscite on your usurpation of power. If you refuse,
you'll be challenging the most ancient tenet of Martian government. I don't think even you could get
away with that."

"You wish to have the people choose between you
and I?"

Kris nodded solemnly.

"A parliamentarian till the end, eh, Kris? Very well. You shall have your plebiscite."

Trying not to show his surprise at Cornelian's answer, the senator said, "And I demand safe passage at landing, and immunity from harm until the vote. Agreed?"

Cornelian's metallic visage was unreadable.

"Agreed," the insect man said finally, cutting off communication before the senator could say anything else, leaving Kris wary, but vaguely hopeful.

They were on the ground soon enough, on the farthest pad of Lowell Port. Immediately the shuttle was surrounded by Martian Marines, as was the senator when he alighted the ship.

"Prime Cornelian cannot *wait* to see you," Pynthas Rei said, pushing his way through the soldiers to stand before Kris. He moved his hands one over the other in a constant, annoying motion. He looked up at the senator from his hunched-over position with his bulbous eyes. He smiled lopsidedly and reached out a thin finger to stab at the senator.

"Cannot *wait*!"

"Remove your hand from me, Pynthas," the senator said. "I'm not a fowl ready for plucking."

"We'll see about *that*!" Pynthas hooted, poking at the senator's tunic again.

Senator Kris's attendant immediately pushed its way between Pynthas and the senator.

Pynthas stumbled back, then fell down on the tarmac.

"Destroy that machine!" Pynthas screeched.

The order was ludicrous, because attendants were inanimate objects incapable of real harm to humans, and also because the command had come from Pynthas Rei—a life-form not much higher on the evolutionary scale than an attendant.

Nevertheless, to Senator Kris's surprise, a Marine immediately raised his weapon and fired a line of destroying fire at the attendant.

With a final, calm "Sir—" the attendant froze where it stood. Then its limbs collapsed and it fell to one side, smoking from a hole in its innards.

"Was that necessary, Pynthas?" Senator Kris said, trying to keep both anger and fear—fear that a man such as Pynthas should have the power to do such a thing, or to do anything at all, for that matter—out of his voice.

"*Yes!*" the toady said, rising from the ground to look with lopsided satisfaction at the ruin of the attendant.

"Prime Cornelian awaits," the red-suited Marine who had shot the attendant said dispassionately.

"I wish to be brought to a neutral location," Senator Kris said. "Until the plebiscite is held."

Pynthas's attention immediately returned to Senator Kris.

"Of course!" he said. "My orders are to take you to a neutral location—as soon as you see Prime Cornelian!"

"I do not—" Kris began, but the Marine turned

his weapon on the Senator, indicating the first in a line of waiting transports, whose door stood open.

"Shall we?" Pynthas smiled unctuously, leading the way. He stopped only to kick ineffectually at the now inanimate robot.

A broken length of metal shot out of the machine, hitting Pynthas, nearly knocking him down again. He whimpered, scuttling sideways, before scrambling into the transport ahead of everyone else.

Staring out through raser-proof glass, Senator Kris tried to keep his mind blank.

When that didn't work, he watched the landscape scrolling by outside.

This was a beautiful, if bleak, world. Those who were born on Mars loved it because they were of it; those who had settled here from other places—as Farman Kris had done as a boy, when his parents left a sick Earth to start a new life on a new planet—came to cherish it with an even deeper love.

It was not a perfect place. It never would be. In many respects the Terraformers, as the pioneers who had settled and then set about to change Mars in the 2200s were known, had failed in their experiments. There was an oxygen atmosphere that constantly needed replenishment, because the few plants successfully engineered to thrive on the planet's meager resources were not numerous or fertile enough to do the job by themselves. The problem was water. Though surface water had once existed on Mars, billions of years ago, it stubbornly refused

to exist now. Even with all that the Terraformers
had been able to accomplish—the thickening and
oxygenating of the atmosphere, the subsequent in-
crease in surface pressure to the point where human
blood did not boil, the formation of a pencil-thin
ozone layer to deflect the Sun's lethal UV rays, the
cultivation of scant crops and hybrid mammals—
even with all this, they had not succeeded in making
water flow on the surface. And though Mars' polar
caps and fairly abundant underground aquifers had
proved relatively rich in water, the size of the caps
and the depth of the aquifers (which ranged from
fifty to two thousand feet below the Martian surface
soil) were just not sufficient to nourish an entire
planet. When it rained—and it did rain, infre-
quently—what scant moisture reached the parched
ground was soaked downward by thirsty soil, or upward by instant evaporation. There was an occasional dusting of snow to play in, but for Martian
children, there were no lakes to swim in, no streams
to sail paper boats in, no puddles to jump in.

So a sort of hybrid had eventually emerged, half
original Mars, half new Mars.

For those who loved it, there was no other place
to live.

Like their planet, Martians were not perfect.
Their cities were permanent, beautiful, and cultur-
ally resplendent, with abundant water for their regu-
lated populations. Martians were a hard people,
capable of sealing themselves in their habitats for

months at a time when a global dust storm raged, capable of living like camels when an aquifer dried up or collapsed and water rations went into severe effect. Over the centuries, genetics had turned the original Earth settlers into a wiry, tall, and for the most part lean people; their eyes were large in their gaunt faces, their fingers long and delicate, their skin shades of brown ranging from a deep mahogany to a light pinkish tone.

Their imperfection evidenced itself in their history of self-government. Their War for Independence with Earth had been savage, and some of this savagery had persevered in the Martian character. It had been said that no Martian was more than one insult away from a fight. That a form of democracy had persevered for the last hundred years, in the form of a High Prefect presiding over a Senate elected by the people, was, to Kris, next to remarkable. He had often argued with his colleagues, to little result, about the fragility of their own freedom; sometimes he had felt that he was the only man on the planet who understood that they were only one madman away from barbarity.

And now that madman, in the form of Prime Cornelian, had come—and unless Kris, with his own weak voice, could reverse the process that Cornelian had set in motion, Mars would once again show its malevolent side to all the worlds.

And yet, Farman Kris loved this planet. Here on the road into Lowell, the senator beheld two of his favorite sights: at the edge of the road, a cluster of impossibly fat sunflowers, feeding off some errant rise in the local aquifer, their faces pointing flatly toward him like suns; and, at the farthest edge of the horizon stood the towering caldera of mighty Arsia Mons. Even at this distance, it seemed to bite a wide, high hole out of the pale pink sky. In front of it, miles of highlands led down to the Syria Planum, where Lowell lay. As a younger man, Kris had attempted to climb Arsia Mons with two college friends; and though they had given up after a week, carried down more dead than alive by rescuers, it had been one of the ecstasies of his life, as, for a scant moment, he had stood nearly at the top of his world, only the sky and a single ridge between himself and God. . . .

"Enjoying the view, Senator?" Pynthas Rei tittered beside him. "It may very well be your last view of anything, you know."

"I'm aware of that," Senator Kris said idly, trying unsuccessfully to bring back that vision of Mars spread out below him like a rusty red ornament, as he spun in the thin air, a victim both of rapture and hypothermia.

Pynthas tittered again. "I imagine it won't be long before you see nothing at all." The vile man cocked his head sideways and laughed, the corners of his mouth twitching.

Senator Kris turned to stare at him.

"Being dead and all," Pynthas added.

"Yes," Senator Kris said, staring levelly at Pynthas, easily remembering the man as he had been before Prime Cornelian took power. He had been more than a janitor and less than a court jester. His main function had been to carry tidbits of gossip to Prime Cornelian, and his fool's status had been in plain view. Apparently some of those tidbits had been valuable to Cornelian.

And now this reptile was . . .

"What exactly *are* you, Pynthas?" Senator Kris said.

Sitting in the cab of the truck, Pynthas Rei nevertheless tried to preen himself up to full and inadequate height. "I am *important*!"

"What I mean," Senator Kris continued in a serious vein, "is what makes a man like you? How does an individual surrender his soul to another individual—sell himself to a devil, in effect? Why would one man become less than himself, and give himself to another, evil man?"

The senator turned away from the confused but angry Pynthas Rei and contemplated the scenery again. They were almost to the city limits of Lowell. The sandstone spires of the city were rising into view ahead of them, giving the desert form.

"It's a question we humans, since our early times on Earth, have not answered," the senator mused to himself, while Pynthas beside him suddenly found his voice, deciding that he had been insulted, and spewed forth invective, which was not listened to.

* * *

Their entry into the residence of the High Prefect of Mars was not a grand one. The convoy, five pink camouflaged Marine trucks, slipped unobtrusively into the rear gates of the building, down into the depths of the parking garage beneath.

Senator Kris listened to the funereal clang of the metal doors closing behind him. Men like Pynthas Rei were used to entries like this. But to the senator, this was a new experience. Like all new experiences, it sparked his interest. He noted, for instance, how well armored the underground area was with precious steel walls. That steel had been imported from Earth. The steel-making process had never been perfected on this planet. He imagined these walls dated back to the War for Independence, when more than one Martian landmark had been destroyed by sabotage. Remembering his Earth history, Senator Kris recalled that the Martians, too, had had their Tories.

"If you *please*?" Pynthas Rei said sarcastically, waiting for the senator to exit the vehicle, whose door had been opened by a Marine.

Senator Kris climbed out. Once again, a phalanx formed around him as they walked to an elevator tube nearby. The tube hissed to a halt and the senator was escorted in.

As it rose, Senator Kris studied the design of the tube's interior. This, too, seemed to date from the war, with ornate designs reminiscent of ancient Earth's art deco period. The floor was inlaid with green marble—another luxury not often found on Mars.

"Tell me, Pynthas, do you know anything regarding—"

The tube arrived at its floor and hissed open.

"*Out!*" Pynthas Rei shouted, shoving Senator Kris through the phalanx of Marines and nearly into the insect arms of Prime Cornelian.

"*Pynthas!*" Prime Cornelian screeched.

Instantly the sychophant began to tremble.

"That's no way to treat our guest! Now get out—and take these men with you!"

The Marines turned as one, reboarding the elevator, with Pynthas Rei scrambling into the tube behind them, stumbling and then falling as the doors hissed shut. The end of his tunic caught in the closing mechanism, and the doors flew open again, revealing Pynthas on the floor, mumbling to himself, trying to crawl farther into the elevator's cage.

Striding forward on his ticking limbs, Prime Cornelian kicked at Pynthas as the doors once again sealed.

With a faint hiss, the tube lowered.

Prime Cornelian turned his head without moving his body and gave his slit-eyed insect's smile to Senator Kris.

"How nice of you to come! I trust you enjoyed your journey home?"

"It was pleasant enough," Senator Kris answered. "Until I landed."

Prime Cornelian maneuvered his body around to face the same direction as his head.

"More pleasant than the last—or should I say final—session of the Senate. You missed quite a meeting."

"I demand to know when the plebiscite will take place."

Prime Cornelian ignored the challenge, moving past the senator to the depths of the room. At the far end, the wall from ceiling to floor spread out in a magnificent window showing a panorama of the city of Lowell below; nearly to the edge of the field, sandstone structures dotted the landscape, while down the center, between the High Prefect's residence and the dome of the Senate chambers a mile distant, spread a mall of pale green grass. Continually fertilized, a soft fescue completely unlike the tough stiff native grasses, it was the only bed of its kind on the planet. Citizens flew kites and picnicked on that expanse; and occasionally it was the site of protest to various government measures—though this day not a protester was in sight.

Prime Cornelian stopped at the window, took in the vista for a moment, then turned to face the senator.

"What news have you from Earth? Did you gain the trading pact the late High Prefect sought?"

"We both know you have no intention of honoring that pact."

Cornelian shrugged, an eerie gesture. "Soon there will be no need."

"I've warned Faulkner of your designs."

"No matter. There is nothing he can do. This is a resource-poor world, and we have been polite about getting what we need long enough. That will change."

"With war?"

Cornelian smiled thinly. "You remember that Mars was the god of war, Kris. You forget the wars that were fought here long ago."

"Those were foolish times, and we've tried to banish that spirit from Mars."

"Tried, yes. But succeeded? I don't think so. You yourself have watched the people recently. At first they thought me a circus freak. So did the High Prefect. They listened, smiled, and then went back to their daily lives. But in the last months my word has started to take hold. They've begun to listen. As shortages began to affect them—less Earth sugar for their coffee, less Titanian metals for their jewelry—their ears have pricked up. They look around at the other of the Four Worlds and say, 'Why don't we have that? Why must we pay so much for that?' And soon they will be ready to say, 'Why don't we just take that?' "

"You'll never get them to follow you blindly, Cornelian."

"We both know how wrong you are, Senator. The amount of unrest following the Senate's and High Prefect's departure was surprisingly small. I crushed it, of course. It also helped that I blamed the High Prefect's assassination on Venusian agents. The

Senate was wiped out by agents from Earth, of course."

Senator Kris barely held in his boiling anger. "They won't follow you into war."

"Oh, but they will. They want someone to lead them, to tell them what to do. A little terror may be necessary, of course—but in the end they'll follow gladly. Already the old war spirit is resurfacing. Enlistment in the Marines is up thirty-five percent!"

"Once again I ask you: When will the plebiscite take place?"

Prime Cornelian's eye slits narrowed. "I notice that your daughter did not come up with you. Is she resting?"

Senator Kris said nothing.

"Did she proceed to your residence to refresh herself after the journey? I trust I'll see her this evening?"

"She's not on Mars, Cornelian."

For a moment Prime Cornelian was visibly stunned.

He quickly recovered. His nails clicking on the stone floor, he walked slowly over to stand beside the senator.

"Did I hear you correctly?" he hissed, his metallic breath warm on Senator Kris's face.

With effort, Senator Kris retained his composure. "She's not on Mars. I know what you want from her, and I've taken steps to assure that you never receive it."

For a moment there was nothing but the hot, oil-scented bellows of Prime Cornelian's breath on the senator's face.

"You were very foolish to do this, Kris."

"She's my daughter."

"Yes, but she would have been—will be—much more!"

"I could not allow that to happen."

"She will go through *that* with or without you! Who do you *dare* to think you are?" One metallic hand, fingers splayed and locked, drew back and came across Senator Kris's face, cutting deep across the cheek and knocking him to the ground.

"You *dare* to oppose me? *Your daughter belongs to me!*"

"Not if I can help it," Kris said through pain.

Prime Cornelian moved forward to stand over the fallen senator; straddling his body, his head ratcheted down to stop inches from Kris's own. Kris could hear the whirs and tickings within Prime Cornelian's corpus; could smell the faint scent of plastic, metal, and lubricants.

"Listen to me very carefully," Prime Cornelian hissed. The slits of his eyes had become thin and sharp as knife blades. "No one ever disobeys me, Kris. No one."

Prime Cornelian lowered his metallic torso to rest upon the prone body of Senator Kris. Sudden fear rose into the senator's eyes, and he stared straight into the huge elongated quartz orbs of Prime Cornelian.

With a faint humming sound, Prime Cornelian's

body began to descend, like a shop press toward its lower plate. The senator's body began to feel pressure, and he found it hard to breathe.

"Comfortable, Kris?" Cornelian purred.

Prime Cornelian's body continued to lower in precise increments.

Senator Kris gasped, and suddenly two ribs in his chest cracked with a muffled snap, followed by two more.

"Cornelian—for the love of—God!"

Cornelian's face split into a smile, even as the rest of his torso continued its inexorable lowering.

Another rib cracked, and another, and now Senator Kris's face began to go blue with lack of oxygen. The red gash on the senator's face showed deep purple.

"Cor . . . nelian!"

There was another chorus of breaking ribs, and then Prime Cornelian suddenly pulled his body up and away from the gasping senator.

Senator Kris fell into unconsciousness, then rose out of it to find himself being dragged across the floor toward the elevator cage by two burly Marines.

He tried to gasp out words, but they would not rise through the pain he felt.

"Don't worry, Kris—you'll live, at least for a while. Look on this as an example of what is to come. I very much wanted to kill you a moment ago. I could have lowered myself until your body had turned to jelly. Besides being messy, though, it occurred to me in the middle of that plan that it would be best to let you live—although in a rather reduced state.

"By the way: I lied about the plebiscite."

There came excruciating pain in Senator Kris's chest as the Marines dumped his body on the floor of the elevator.

The senator floated down toward unconsciousness once more, hearing Prime Cornelian's final words:

"You're alive because you'll make wonderful bait to catch your daughter!"

6

It is strange how one's perspective changes with morning light.

Despite his heartsickness, Dalin Shar slept well. And when he awoke, with the sun streaming through his open window and a soft breeze wafting the curtains, it seemed as if the events of the day before had happened to someone else.

He was not quite himself again, to be sure. But now it seemed like his interlude with Tabrel Kris had been a pleasant afternoon spent in a dream. *That* Dalin Shar, who had given away his heart so quickly and so freely, seemed somewhat distant now, somewhat foolish. After all, how could one tell, from a single brief meeting, that one had met the love of one's life? How could a king, ruler of a planet, declare true love with his heart before his head had had time to be brought in for consultation?

After all, Dalin Shar had known love before. There had been other meetings in that garden, other gazings into various eyes, of blue, of hazel green, of

violet—yes, he particularly remembered those violet
eyes, set in the perfectly chiseled bronze face of the
daughter of his Nubian governor. Hadn't *that* been
an afternoon to remember! And hadn't the rest of
her body proven to be as perfectly sculpted as her
face. . . .

But something tugged at the corners of Dalin
Shar's memories of these other garden meetings,
seeking to push them aside to inconsequence. Yes,
there had been kissing involved, and groping
limbs, but—

A measure of the misery Dalin Shar had felt the
night before, on learning that Tabrel Kris was betrothed to another, returned like a wave through
him. He suddenly felt sick in his stomach, short of
breath, a pain no doctor could treat moving through
him from head to toe—

"*Damnation!*"

He ran to the window, sought to draw the fresh
morning air into his lungs, feel the warming sun on
his face, sought to forget—

But no, there was her face, in his mind, in his
heart. Burned there as if by raser fire. He knew that
he would never be able to burn it out without tearing his own heart and brain from his body. It was
as if some hideous disease had taken hold of him—
hideous and wonderful at the same time—and he
would always, from now on, be beholden to this
parasite within him.

From the window, he looked out over the beauty
of the royal grounds, the topiary sculptures of ex-

tinct animals—lion, elephant, tiger—bordering the
perfectly clipped lawns, the rolling hills of verdant
green, the bloomed flowers in riotous colors in the
mazed garden—and once more, all he could see on
this beautiful day was her face. . . .

"*Damnation!*"

Concurrent with this oath came a brisk knock on
the door, and Dalin Shar turned his attention to it
rather than bask in his present anguish.

"Come in!"

The door opened, revealing his valet, the manlike,
chromed length of his body bedecked in a crisp
black and white servant's uniform. The smooth oval
sphere of his head, eyeless and bald, turned in Dalin's direction as the valet rose from his bow.

"It is time for you to dress, sir. And eat. Have
you showered yet? Shaved?"

"No . . ." Dalin said absently.

"May I serve your breakfast then, sir?"

"Yes . . ."

Instantly, another robot, not more than a table
with wheels, rolled in around the valet and stopped
by Dalin Shar's side. An arrangement of covered
dishes smoothly slid their silver covers off, revealing
a perfect slice of deep green melon, steaming scrambled eggs, a neat row of bacon.

Absently Dalin reached down to pick up a slice
of bacon; absently he chewed on it while he turned
his attention to the breezy day outside the window.

"Valet, has Minister Faulkner arrived yet?"

"Funny you should ask, sir. He has arrived and is awaiting you in the conference chamber."

Dalin Shar absently chewed on his bacon, staring toward the gardens.

"Valet, do you know anything about love?"

Behind him, the valet straightened. "What is it you wish to know, sir? I can access anything you desire." The valet's even voice retained its flat demeanor. "If you mean physical love, there are precisely two hundred and fourteen positions between human female and human male—"

"That's not what I meant, valet," Dalin Shar said. "I was speaking of being *in* love."

"Ah. I can, of course, access love poetry, or other classical allusions to the subject, such as Mahldeen's *Chasteness of the Lair* or Shakespeare's ancient play *Romeo and Juliet*. I can—"

"Never mind, valet."

"I presume you are in love, sir?"

Dalin almost laughed at the placid preciseness with which the valet's words were delivered.

"Oh, yes, valet: I am in love."

"Congratulations, sir."

This time a laugh broke from Dalin's lips, and Dalin's morose spell was broken.

He looked down at the slice of bacon he was eating and at the rest of his breakfast, and realized he had an appetite after all.

"All right, valet," he said, "that's enough of love for now. You may fetch my clothes."

The valet bowed. "Very well, sir."

*   *   *

Tabrel Kris was sick of starlight.

She used to think, when she was a girl, that starlight was for lovers. But now she was not so sure. With little else to do during the trip and little space to do it in the Titanian freighter that had picked up her life raft, she had spent most of her days wedged between pallets of goods in the cargo hold, staring out the single porthole. The crew—two androids and a lecherous old salt who had spent as much of the first few days regaling Tabrel with stories of his life on cargo ships as he did eyeing her bosom— had proven inadequate company, and she had at first found solace alone with only perpetual night as her companion.

But that companionship had proven as inadequate as that of the crew, and, when she wasn't worrying about her father, she found herself thinking more and more of that first startling kiss with King Dalin Shar of Earth.

She had never felt anything like it before—and knew in her heart that she would never feel anything quite like it again. It had been like putting a hand into a wave generator: a shock one was not likely to forget.

And she was sure he had felt it, too.

She wondered what Dalin Shar was doing now. Her first impressions of him—too young, callow, insulated, and inexperienced—had proven in many ways to be correct. She had known, going into that garden with him, that he would try to kiss her; she

imagined he had done such a thing many times before. She had entered into an agreement with herself that she would let him play out his game, since
at the very least it would be a diplomatic thing to
do—but when the kiss finally came, she knew it had
been like a bolt of lightning to both of them.

Is this how true love comes?

Once again, staring idly at the wash of passing
stars outside her window, she wondered what he
was doing now, if he was thinking of her.

Such foolishness, but so much time to do nothing
else, unless she wanted to worry about her father.

There came a bang and creaking sound which
announced the opening of the cargo bay's old hatch.

"Missy, you in there?"

Where else would I be, you old lecher? she
thought—but out of inbred politeness she said,
"Yes, Captain, I'm here."

"At your old porthole, eh?" Captain Weens cackled, making his appearance between two lashed pallets of tall crates. He put his hands on his hips,
and once more his one good eye strayed down to
her bust.

Tabrel crossed her arms over her chest to thwart
his stare.

"You require something, Captain?"

"Just company, deary," Weens said. "I gets tired
o' scrapping with them two metal heaps up front.
They don't want to hear 'bout nothing save the
truth." He cackled again, leaning closer to Tabrel.
"Did I tell ye about when I was a younger man, on

the crew o' the *Abilene,* when the whole aft section o' the ship got blowed away by a meteorite?" Weens shook his head. "Oh, that was a sight—"

As politely as she could, Tabrel interjected, "Yes, Captain, you told me."

Weens stood up straight. "Oh. Then did I tell you 'bout losing me eye?" He flipped up his black patch to reveal, for the tenth time, the charred crater of his socket. "Took a raser shot right in the looker, I did. Would o' burned me brain out if my retina hadn't deflected it portside." He pointed to a scarred round section on the same side of his temple. "Shot came out right there, it did. That's when they named me Popeye—"

"Captain, if you don't mind, I'd rather be alone."

"Oh. Well, then, I guess I'll be delivering my message and returning up front. Wouldn't happen to have a crowbar, would ye? There's a little score I'd like to settle with that heap o' junk metal pilot."

Smiling indulgently, Tabrel shook her head.

If he would just stop staring at her chest. . . .

Weens rubbed his chin and said, "Well, then, I'm to tell you that we'll be on Titan within the day, and that Jamal Clan will be waiting for ye. Sounded mighty eager, he did, too. Would've been there sooner, but we've had to do a little dancing to avoid them Martian patrols. Their cruisers out this way are few and far between, but they've gotten mean as hornets the last week or so. You'll be safe once we gets down to Titan, though. Tough bunch, them Titanians."

He rose, but his eye lingered on Tabrel's breasts. He rubbed at his chin again. "Say, you wouldn't by any chance be interested in an old farter like me, would ye?"

Before Tabrel could answer forcefully in the negative, one of the ship's robots had appeared at the cargo bay doorway and announced in a flat tone, "We are being boarded, Captain Weens."

"*Boarded!* What in hellation—"

There came a loud clang to the fore section, and the entire ship shuddered. Weens fairly ran from the cargo hold, pushing the retreating robot out of his way.

"Let me up front, y' waste receptacle!"

The navigator righted itself and followed after the captain.

From her porthole Tabrel could see nothing. Again the ship shuddered, and Tabrel followed the other two up front, where a loud commotion had commenced. Yet again the ship shook violently, and Tabrel noticed that the airlock light on the fore entryway was green, indicating that the outside door had been breached.

"Pirates!" Weens shouted, wrestling the controls from the pilot robot, who sat placidly in the captain's chair. "What in Mormon's hell is wrong with you bolt-holders! Can't ye see we're being attacked by pirates?"

"It is not in our nature to resist," the navigator, back at his post but doing nothing, answered.

"Resist this, y' sheet-metal moron!" Weens said,

picking up the nearest loose object, which proved to be a data card, and flinging it at the robot. It bounced harmlessly off the navigator's gleaming shell.

"Away we go!" Captain Weens shouted, punching the ship's accelerator and pulling at the stick.

The cargo ship veered sharply. Instantly the sounds at the airlock ceased. Tabrel went to the copilot's window and now saw their adversaries: a makeshift ship, a hundred yards long, seemingly made up of parts of various other vessels. Standing in free space with nothing to hold on to were two space-suited creatures bearing tools, their faceplates turned blankly in the direction of Tabrel's ship.

"Hoo! Ditched 'em, we did!" Weens shouted.

But as Tabrel watched, the two space-suited figures returned to their ship, disappeared into its airlock, and the lumbering jerry-built craft turned its nose in their direction.

"They are following, sir," the navigator said from his position.

"So you're good for somethin' after all?" Weens spat. "Well, keep your instruments on 'em, ye talking toolbox!"

"Yes, sir," the navigator said.

"And you, pilot!" Weens shouted. "Fly this box crate while I empty the crapper in our wake and give these fellers somethin' t' contemplate!"

On passing Tabrel, Weens put a hand lightly on her arm and managed to look kindly into her face while ogling her breasts at the same time.

"Not t' worry, darlin'," he said. "I've been this route before. We'll ditch 'em for sure, we will."

Hooting, Weens ambled off in the direction of the cargo hold.

Tabrel returned her gaze to the window and saw the pirate vessel falling behind.

But now there came a massive bang that seemed to emanate from everywhere throughout the ship at once.

Instantly Weens was back, his face drained of color.

He said, "What in blazes was that?"

The navigator said calmly, "We have been locked, sir."

"Locked! No way in—"

The power systems in the ship faded as one, leaving its occupants in sudden darkness.

Weens pressed his face to the pilot's window, looking back at the pirate craft, still far behind.

"It ain't them bast—"

"There is a second craft approximately point oh two parsecs to our stern side," the navigator reported evenly.

Ween's eye swiveled madly to the other side; to Tabrel it looked as if it would pop out of his head, it widened so much.

"Bejesus in paradise!" the captain swore.

Tabrel looked in the same direction and felt her heart stop for a moment.

"We are being pulled, sir," the navigator reported.

"No bloody lie!" Captain Weens said. "It'd be an amazement o' God if we weren't!"

There, filling the window and growing more massive by the second, approached a ship which dwarfed anything Tabrel Kris had ever seen: Its endless cone shape, widening from its pointed snout to where it overflowed the window ports with its bulk, was as smooth and chromium-shiny as any robot. At first Tabrel could make out no portholes or markings of any kind; but then, as the vessel grew ever nearer over them, she began to detect a faint long line of round windows which traversed the craft from bow to stern. They were like tiny black dots—fleas on the body of a behemoth.

"I know that ship," Captain Weens said in awe. He turned to stare, still pop-eyed, into Tabrel's face. "This is either very good news or very bad."

In partial answer, there was a blast of plasma energy across the bow of their ship from the very tip of the huge craft; it cut close, but they were not its target.

Captain Weens and Tabrel once more turned their attention to the pirate ship, which was in full flight.

The beam of plasma caught the pirate vessel in its stern and, like a raser cutting a metal can, opened the pirate ship from end to end.

Amid popping lights of system failures, the pirate vessel split languidly into two halves. Tabrel saw tiny struggling forms flailing between, but soon all had been turned into space debris and all was silent.

Weens whistled. "Well, I'll be! Never saw anything like tha' in all my days! Never even lied about anything that grand! Whoo!"

"We are still being pulled, sir," the navigator reported. "We will be in the hold of the adjacent craft within two minutes."

"Thankee, ye fool!" Weens replied, reaching back to strike at the navigator with his hand. Outside, the window was now filled completely with the massive craft, and Tabrel could make out an open bay door, toward which they were doggedly being drawn.

Captain Ween turned his attention to the pilot, which had remained nearly motionless in its seat through this entire episode.

"What about ye, ye hunk o' crap? Anything t' say for yeself?"

"There is nothing to say, or do," the robot replied implacably. "At the moment there are no piloting functions to perform—"

"Shut up, will ye! Just shut up an' be still!"

"Yes, sir," the pilot responded.

The cargo door over them widened; and then they were inside a cone of yellow light. Temporarily, they were blind.

"Leave me m' good eye at least!" Weens complained.

As if in answer, the light dimmed, went out. They were left in soothing shadows, bathed in a low amber luminescence.

"Oh, yes, I know who's behind this, all right."

"Who?" Tabrel asked.

"Someone who doesn't like to be spoken of," Weens said cryptically. "Someone—"

"Depart your vessel!" a cold, very loud voice commanded. It sounded the way a robot might if given the ability to speak feelings. If the laws of robotics were disobeyed, this was what a robot would sound like.

"Better do as he says," Weens said, moving for the aft airlock.

"I think I'll wait here," Tabrel said. "After all, I have diplomatic immunity—"

"Not wi' this fellow, you don't," Weens said. "Nobody's got tha' with this 'un. Best to come along."

"I'll stay here," Tabrel said defiantly.

"Please, lassie—" Weens begged, but when he saw the look on Tabrel's face, he shrugged and hobbled to the airlock, opening it and going quickly through. "If I can't change ye mind, it's yer own funeral," he said.

Tabrel, her heart fluttering, noticed that the two robots sat unmoving at their posts; by the look of the indicator lights to either side of their heads, they had regressed into standby.

Faintly, Tabrel heard Weens give a shout of alarm somewhere outside; then there was silence.

A presence descended on the ship as if a giant invisible foot had leaned its weight invisibly upon it.

In the dark interior, Tabrel felt the air around her darken.

"Anyone home?" a voice called out cheerily.

The dark feeling became oppressive and close and impossible to escape.

And then Tabrel felt nothing but her own darkness descend upon her, as the world went away and she spiraled down into a place where only dreams and remembrance dwelled, and nothing more.

7

"Report," Prime Cornelian demanded from his bed, casually.

Pynthas had never been so frightened, and approached with quaking knees. He had eaten not an hour before and felt his stomach about to give up its contents. He found that when he attempted to open his mouth, only a dry rasp came out.

"Speak up!" Prime Cornelian said. One slim metallic limb fell languidly from the side of the tank, dripping lubricant onto the blindingly reflective floor. The deck, octagonal walls, and sectioned, domed ceiling of the sleeping chamber were covered in mirror: this in itself, without the aid of bad news, made Pynthas ill whenever he entered. He felt as if he were inside a kaleidoscope, with blue, green, and red bits of Prime Cornelian hovering around him like vicious bees.

"Well?" Prime Cornelian said, moving a slitted eye to stare at Pynthas from a thousand vantage points.

Pynthas felt dissected.

"Bad news, High *Leader*," Pynthas croaked out.

"Really? Why don't you let me be the judge?"

Pynthas knew that the only thing going in his favor was the fact that the High Leader was still groggy from his rest. Floating like a June bug in his huge tub, which resembled a halved sphere on a rodded pedestal, polished to high brilliance, Prime Cornelian would still be under the effects of his lubricant bath, which renewed and sustained him while he slept. Pynthas had never seen the High Leader eat, but without his monthly rest and renewal, Prime Cornelian would tighten and lock like a rusty hinge—as well as go mad.

"Yes, High Leader," Pynthas managed to force out hoarsely.

"I rather like that term—don't you Pynthas? High Leader sounds so . . . *high*."

Prime Cornelian chuckled listlessly, pulling his leg back into the bath and now stretching out all his limbs, which squeaked and hissed.

"Ahhh, that feels so good!"

Once more the High Leader opened an eye to stare at Pynthas from a hundred-times-ten vantage points.

"Report!" Prime Cornelian suddenly snapped, his harsh voice bouncing around the room like light.

"Yes!" Pynthas said, finding his voice. But still his knees knocked and his hands shook.

"Riots have b-broken out in Bradbury and Schiaparelli," Pynthas stuttered. "P-parts of W-Wells have been . . ."

"Yes?"

"T-taken over by government loyalists."

"Is that all? I expected that. What about response?"

"Marines have restored order in most areas, but last night there were bombings in many places. The central police station was destroyed in Schiaparelli and fifty-nine policemen killed. A Marine detachment was ambushed in—"

"Is that all you have to tell me? What about Venus?"

"Things have been quiet on Venus, High Leader. Our contacts on the ground there are monitoring the situation closely. They'll let us know of any change."

"Good."

"But the Terraformers have finished arming their plants and have threatened to destroy them at the first sign of trouble on the planet."

Prime Cornelian was silent for a moment. Pynthas closed his eyes and wished he were anywhere else on the planet—or better yet, on another planet.

But an explosion did not come. There was only the lap of lubricating fluid on the sides of the tank, the occasional drip of a rogue drop onto the polished floor.

Pynthas opened his eyes and saw a thousand slitted orbs regarding him from every corner of the room, making him feel like a bug under a lens.

"And do you have word of Senator Kris's daughter?" Prime Cornelian said, very quietly.

"No, High Leader. You realize how . . . difficult it is to get word from that sector. Wrath-Pei—"

"Wrath-Pei will talk to me, if he has her. Of course, *I* will have to call *him*. But the call will be worth the temporary denigration of my pride." Prime Cornelian sighed, shifted in his bath to stand up.

Pynthas nearly gasped in fright at the horrible sight of the insect-man towering nearly to the ceiling as he stretched, golden sheets of oil flowing from his carapace, and the entire monstrous scene reflected hundreds of times—

Pynthas's breakfast rose into his throat, and he gagged it back down.

"For heaven's sake, man—get yourself something to eat!" Prime Cornelian ordered.

"Y-yes, High Leader."

"And hand me a towel before you leave."

"Yes, High Leader."

Swallowing his regurgitated meal, nearly swooning, Pynthas reached to take an oil-slicked cheesecloth in the vague form of a robe from a rack next to the door. He walked through slick puddles of lubricant and handed it up to the High Leader, all the while wanting to faint.

"Thank you," Prime Cornelian said.

Pynthas nodded.

"Summon the provisional governors to my chambers, and also the various military heads. Perhaps they're not aware of what my instructions meant.

It's very important that we make this look like a domestic squabble—at least for the moment."

"Yes, High Leader."

"And if there is any news from Titan, I want it immediately."

"Yes, High Leader."

"That means *immediately,* Pynthas. No matter what I'm doing."

Head bowed in sickness, Pynthas mumbled, "Of course, High Leader."

"Pynthas, look up at me."

Stifling a groan, Pynthas lifted his gaze to look at the shrouded High Leader. The robe now covered Prime Cornelian's husk and had soaked the oil away like a sponge.

Prime Cornelian climbed from the tub like a spider, his six limbs keeping the rest of his body from reimmersing itself in the oil bath. He stood on the mirrored floor of the room and continued to dry himself, two limbs at a time working along the length of his other parts.

He paused and looked at Pynthas—his gaze, now mingled with Pynthas's own, locked in reflection around the room.

"You really should try it sometime," Prime Cornelian said, nodding his head toward the tub, which at that moment slopped a wave of sickly scented lubricant over the side to splash on the floor.

Pynthas stumbled from the room, the harsh bleat of the High Leader's laughter ringing in his ears.

8

"Tabrel?"

It was a fairy-tale voice she heard. No one had ever spoken her name like that before. It was like musical chimes, like singing, like a breath of sweet wind telling poetry. It almost didn't sound like her name, but like someone else's—someone magical, worthy of song.

"Tabrel?" the minstrel's voice came again.

"Yes?" she heard herself saying, trying to sing, rising up out of her sleep.

She opened her eyes.

There was the minstrel standing over her.

She knew his face, though vaguely. He looked older than the picture she had of him in her mind, though he was still young. He had the face of a troubadour, from pictures she had seen of long ago.

But his eyes looked troubled.

"Tabrel, can you hear me?"

She could hear him, and tried to nod, but could not. She was slowly rising out of another place. There had been no dreams she could remember. It had been more like being unalive than asleep. She felt groggy and weak.

"You'll be all right," the troubadour said.

"Jamal?" she said weakly, and he nodded.

"Yes!"

"Ohhhh . . ."

She tried to rise on her elbows and swooned back. His hand was behind her head, helping to ease her back down.

"Now you must sleep," Jamal said. "When you have had real sleep, you will feel better."

Again she tried to rise, but it was pushing against a world weighing down on her.

"But my father and the others . . ."

His cradling hand, so soft on the back of her head, lay her gently down.

"Shhh, now. Go to sleep."

She nodded, already closing her eyes.

"Tabrel," she heard him say again in his singsong voice, and he sounded so pleased. . . .

She awoke, from real dreams.

Startled, she sat up.

She was in a bed of sorts, and the room was dark. There were curtains, and a window opening out onto a soft evening. The curtains rustled with night breeze, which reached coolly to bathe her face.

She rose from the bed and walked barefoot to the window, feeling carpeted floor beneath her.

Above, there were stars, and something bright and startlingly close cutting at the western horizon like a scythe. Against this yellow light was outlined a skyline of trees and faraway structures.

As she watched, the massive yellow edge moved down from view, as if a clockwork were in motion pulling it away below the world.

In the sky, stars spread like an overlay, and there were two tiny round worlds, with phased faces.

In the near distance there was a body of water, and close by, a line of trees and a wooded hill; closer yet, a group of buildings close to the ground, grouped like a compound.

The coolness of the night felt good against her face.

Far off, an animal barked, sounding like a dog, and then there was another animal sound, like an Earth cock crowing.

The sky, she saw, was lightening in the east, but the stars still shone overhead, though less brightly as the distant Sun now rose, a small yellow orb, looking cold and inaccessible.

"Daylight on Titan," Tabrel whispered to herself, and now saw that lights were coming on in the distance, around the perimeter of the lake, which shone with silver brilliance; around the cluster of nearby buildings and at the horizon's skyline, where their massed luminescence washed out the stars overhead and made the edge of the world glow.

There came a soft knock on the door behind Tabrel, and the troubadour's voice sang her name.

"Tabrel?"

The door opened, and she beheld Jamal Clan,

who entered the room tentatively, as if afraid to intrude.

"May I come in?" he asked.

"Of course," Tabrel said, aware suddenly that she was dressed in a diaphanous nightgown and that the soft lights brightening the window behind her might outline her body through it.

Jamal stared at her, then looked away, which proved to her that this was true.

"There is a . . . robe in the closet," he said with embarrassment.

"And where is the closet?" Tabrel asked, amused at his reaction.

"It's . . ."

He reached behind him, fumbling for a switch—and then the room was flooded with light and they were both blinking.

Still blinking, Jamal Clan fumbled along the wall and found the crack of a door. His hand found the switch and the door slid smoothly open.

"In here, I think," Jamal said, pushing clothing back and forth on a rack before producing a dressing gown nearly as diaphanous as what Tabrel already wore.

"Oh . . ." Jamal said in consternation, holding it out for her inspection and making her laugh.

He was not as dreamlike or perfect as her first impressions had led her to believe. He was rather short; and he was burly in the chest and his hands were small. But his smile was beguiling, and his voice nearly as melodious as her stupored state had presented it to her.

"It's all right, I'm not cold," Tabrel said, turning back to the window."

"They turn on lights here during the day?" Tabrel asked.

"Oh, yes," Jamal said, daring to move closer to her. He still bore the dressing gown, and Tabrel turned to take it from him and put it on, to put him at ease.

"I should welcome you," Jamal said, standing by the window with her; outside, the world had come alive, with people leaving buildings to make their way from one end of the compound to the other. Out on the waved water a few sturdy-looking boats had set out, sails unfurled; in their midst a sleek powered craft shot over the waves, pushing water aside in a deep trough, becoming a tiny dot at the distant shore in a matter of moments, while in the sky the two Saturnian moons, now joined by a third, moved languidly among the lighter wash of stars.

"It all looks so . . . peaceful," Tabrel said.

"For now," Jamal answered, a note of despondency entering his voice. "These are unsettled times, Tabrel. The people of Titan have many grave decisions to make. The Four Worlds are facing a serious crisis. With the changes on Mars—"

As if waking from a dream, Tabrel turned to regard him.

"How did I get here, Jamal? And what happened to Captain Weens?"

Jamal looked at her blankly.

"There was a navigator, and a pilot also, on the ship that was taking me here—what became of them?"

"I'm afraid I don't know what you mean," Jamal answered.

"How did I get on Titan?"

"Wrath-Pei brought you to me; he said you had been adrift in a derelict after an attack by pirates—"

"That's not true! There were others with me!"

With a sincere look, Jamal shrugged and said, "I'm afraid I don't know."

"Then I must talk with this Wrath-Pei. My father entrusted me to Captain Weens, and I have an obligation to see that he's all right."

Jamal frowned. "That is not something you would be wise to do."

"Then you must help me. And I wish to have news of Mars—and of my father. I claim these rights under diplomatic privilege."

Jamal studied her for a moment. Tabrel was not sure that he liked what he saw; she had the feeling that he was about to speak to her the way a parent speaks to a headstrong and foolish child.

"Tabrel," he said softly, in his beautiful voice, "you and I are betrothed. We are to be wed. Though I never laid eyes upon you until three days ago, I already feel close to you. Please listen to me when I tell you this: There is much about Titan that you do not know. We are an insular people, peaceful when left alone, fierce when stepped upon. Though

originally of Mars, Wrath-Pei is . . . indicative of the
Titan personality, only more so. He is larger than
life, if you will. But one does not bother him. He
comes and goes as he pleases; he does not bother
us, we do not bother him. This is a tacit
agreement—"

With barely contained fury, Tabrel said, "He is
a pirate!"

Jamal took a deep breath. "Not a pirate, exactly.
More of a free spirit. In fact, he has been very help-
ful with our pirate problem. In return we . . . leave
him to his own devices."

Tabrel's anger had not flagged. "Do you pay him?"

Jamal Clan's manner suddenly resolved itself in
Tabrel's eyes: He was acting like any diplomat in a
tight situation. This Tabrel understood.

"Not in coin, so much . . ."

"What does he take, then?"

Flustered, Jamal threw up his hands and said,
"Pretty much . . . anything he wants."

"So he rules Titan!"

Splitting hairs, Jamal said, "I . . . wouldn't say
rules. After all, that is my job. And my mother's. I
would say rather that he . . ."

Again he shrugged.

"Leave me alone," Tabrel Kris commanded. Suddenly her diplomatic aura dissolved into frustration
and disgust. "Get out of my sight! You are a coward,
coming to me like this! I wouldn't marry you if you
were the last slug on the underside of the last rock!"

"Tabrel . . ." Jamal Clan said soothingly, his melodious voice suddenly sounding slick, unctuous. "You must understand the way things are done here—"

"I cannot believe I was betrothed to you! My parents must have been insane when I was born! The marriage will never take place!"

Jamal brought himself up to his full height and put a stern look on his face.

"Oh, we will definitely be married, Tabrel. Even if this union means little for Mars at the moment, it means a great deal for the future of Titan to have our two houses joined."

"Never! Our pact is hereby void!"

Jamal's face turned red. "It is very much in effect," he said coldly. "Only by decree of your father and my mother could the betrothal be broken."

"My father has already given his decree in this matter: He made the wedding my choice."

"My mother will never consent. The wedding will go forward."

As Tabrel searched desperately for something to throw at him, Jamal Clan turned and strode from the room, closing the door after him.

Too late, the dressing gown Tabrel had torn from her shoulders, wadded up, and thrown, hit the door.

When Tabrel Kris tried to open the door herself later on, the switch was inoperative, and she realized that she was, for all intents and purposes, a prisoner.

9

Targon Ramir, leader of the Engineering Corps, highest guild of the Terraformers, and therefore de facto ruler of the planet Venus, hated the mantle that had been thrust on his shoulders. He refused to wear any badge of office; insisted, as he had since his first day on the planet fifty-one years before, on wearing his plain drab uniform of dun overalls and waistshirt tucked in. It was out-of-date garb, even for a Terraformer, and Terraformers were a group not known for their sartorial sharpness. More than one younger Terraformer had made comment, but never in front of Ramir himself—not out of fear, but out of respect.

Respect was something that Targon Ramir believed in earning, and he had earned it each day of his life. He had grown up literally on the streets of Calcutta on Earth, in the blackest days of the Rolfus Plague. The true tale he had heard was that his mother had lain writhing in death throes during his birth, the pain of the disease—which froze the central nervous system, sending out wild signals which made the body jerk and tremble, earning the disease the nickname "Puppet Death"—even greater than that of birth.

His had not been a happy childhood. Though the Puppet Death had run its course a year after his birthing, he knew no father, and no public house which took him in was able to keep him for very long. Those were tumultuous times in what had once been called India, for the Afrasian Empire was in its own birth pangs. Tribal and multinational wars were rife, and it was only when Targon was nearly thirteen that Sarat Shar was able to unite the various parts of what was left of Free Earth into a cohesive whole.

Though the political nature of Earth settled when Targon Ramir was a teenager, his own life never really settled. He was a thief at nine, a caught thief at ten, twelve, and fourteen. It was only through the intercession of a member of his last jury, an apprentice of the Guild of Terraformers, barely twenty-one himself, that Targon was saved from the exile to the Lost Lands that awaited any three-timer. But during the brief trial the apprentice with the antiquated name of Carter Frolich saw something in Targon Ramir's nature to make him beg clemency for the young man. Without even realizing what he was doing, he found himself promising to take Targon under his own wing and train him in his own profession.

"Do you realize what this means?" the judge, a

stern woman with little patience and whose black
tunic made her look spectral, had said.

"I do," Frolich had answered.

"This boy will be your responsibility from now on!
Are you *sure* you want that?" With harshness, she
added, "And you understand that if *he* fails, *you* will
pay for his next crime?"

Hardly believing it himself, Carter Frolich had
found himself saying, "I understand."

"Very well," the judge had said, having done her
duty and quickly losing interest. With a shake of
her head she had struck her gavel and called,
"Next case!"

And Targon Ramir had suddenly found himself
with an older brother.

At first Targon was suspicious as any child of the
streets would be. But Carter Frolich would brook
no foolishness, for his own burning ambition had
no room for it.

Soon that burning hunger—an infection as rapa-
cious as Puppet Death but infinitely more grand—
had been passed on to Targon Ramir, and there
were two earthlings whose dream it was to terraform Venus.

"It can be done *now*!" Frolich said. "Look at
Titan! Every technique needed has been successfully tested on Titan! *Every single one!* Forty years
ago Titan was a smoggy mess, the air a choking
noxious orange mix of sulfides and organic garbage.
The surface was no better, a nitric swamp with
burning patches of land unfit for habitation.

"But look at it now! It's habitable! The colonists can see the stars at night, can walk outside their habitats with little more than an oxygen clip on their noses!" Carter enthusiastically waved a data generator under Targon's nose, made him watch a series of before-and-after photos of the moon.

"In another twenty years they won't even need oxygen and they'll be swimming and fishing in the oceans!

"And we could start now on Venus! All we have to do is make everything bigger! Drop the first units down on parachutes in titanium tube clusters—one every three hundred square kilometers would do it. Then we work on the atmosphere from above at the same time, start poking holes to let the clusters do their job! I'm telling you . . ."

Targon Ramir had spent most of his time in those early days just calming Carter down. And there had been a lot of calming down to do, since Frolich, even at that early age, had shown no patience for fools and no tolerance for bureaucracy—though he had grown better at it over the years, learning, like any dog needing a bone, that it was better to lick the master's hand than bite it.

And now . . .

Targon Ramir sighed, letting all the years slip away from him until he was left in this time. In this office, on this planet that Carter Frolich, with Targon's help, had begun to turn into the dream they had both shared all those young years ago.

Now they were two old men, and one of them

was responsible for possibly destroying all the work that they had devoted their lives to.

Targon sighed again and finally said out loud, knowing that his secretary, Ms. Garn, would hear what she had been waiting to hear in the next room, "All right, Fion, I'll take that call now."

The floor-to-ceiling windows in front of Targon melted away, showing the floor-to-ceiling worn face of Carter Frolich.

"Targon," Carter said. He looked ill, even worse than the last time Targon had spoken with him.

"Carter," Targon said, nodding his head in greeting and respect.

"I'm told that plasma generators are now in place at each facility," Carter said simply.

"I'm afraid they are, Carter," Targon said.

With a pang, Targon thought that Carter was going to break into tears. He looked such a broken man, so old.

"I'm sorry," Targon said.

Carter Frolich slowly shook his head.

"I'm sorry, too, Targon," he said. "And I don't understand how you could do this."

"Carter, I've explained this to you before," Targon said. "There's more to this than the dreams of two men now. I have this planet to think of, and the future of the people on it."

Now red anger replaced Frolich's sadness. "Venus doesn't belong to you!"

"It doesn't belong to any of us, Carter." With another pang, Targon remembered his early days as an apprentice, how their heated arguments had gone well into the night then: Even though he had been younger and more inexperienced, the basic philosophies of Targon Ramir and Carter Frolich had been in place then, and hadn't changed now. "The fact is, I can't let this planet fall into Martian hands. And I won't."

"Prime Cornelian has vowed to let our work go forward! He has promised not to interfere with the completion of what we've started, Targon!"

Carter's naïveté in political matters was astounding and always had been to Targon. Though Carter could woo the last dollar out of a governor's wallet, he still could not believe that anyone could possibly possess anything but the same purity of intention that he held about his Venus; to Carter Frolich, any other view was not only heresy, but fiction.

"Prime Cornelian will tell you whatever you want to hear! But the plain fact is that his plans call for the domination of this world, as well as the Four Worlds."

"That's nonsense, Targon! The Martian war is a civil war! A squabble among Martians!"

As often as he had been lectured by Carter Frolich in other matters, Targon found it bizarre that he was the lecturer when it came inevitably to turning their eventually finished work over to mankind. To Carter, that concept had been an abstract one; to Targon Ramir, it had been not only inevitable but more important than the terraforming itself.

How could one make a beautiful object and then not protect it?

"The Martian conflict is anything but domestic, Carter," Targon explained. Why couldn't the man see these things? "When Prime Cornelian consolidates his power at home, he will attack the other worlds."

"But why would he do such a thing?"

"Resources, Carter! How many times must I tell you? Mars is a resource-poor planet! It has relied on trade for its survival since the day the Terraformers gave up on it two hundred years ago! To a man like Cornelian this is not acceptable. Why should he trade for the things he needs when he can take them? This is what he will do!"

"Prove it to me, Targon!"

Targon threw his hands up in frustration. "Just open your eyes! Has he not fomented trouble on Earth already? Have the streets been safe there in Cairo the past couple of weeks?"

Carter made a dismissive motion with his hand. "More domestic troubles. A band of rebels has been nipping at the empire's heels. It is nothing—"

"It is everything! The beginning of the end! One way or another, Prime Cornelian will have his way on the Four Worlds. But I won't let him have this planet!"

Carter's weariness returned; he ran his hand through his thinning gray hair.

"And you'd rather destroy Venus than let him take it."

"Not destroy it; just stop our work in its tracks. Cornelian knows that the terraforming equipment on this planet would take decades to replace. More than anything, he wants work to continue here. He wants Venus the way you and I wanted Venus, Carter—green and blue, wet and fertile. He'll never need anything else in the Solar System if he gets what he wants here. And I won't give it to him."

"For God's sake, Targon! You can't—"

Suddenly the transmission was cut; Targon watched a deep black screen which returned to depth a moment later, giving him back the puzzled visage of his mentor and friend.

"Targon, are you there?"

Targon spoke in the affirmative and was startled at first to see Carter give no response. Then, after a number of seconds, his friend said, "I can see you now, Targon, but we seem to have been cut from phase transmission."

After the ten-second delay, Targon answered, "Yes."

After another ten seconds, Carter heard his voice; before he responded, Carter looked to one side, leaned that way, and spoke, "You tell me they're outside the building now?"

Targon waited; his heart clutched in his chest before his old friend turned once more to him and said, "I must go, Targon. It seems there is some trouble in the streets outside. Some sort of disturbance." Wearily he added, "I'll speak with you soon."

Targon Ramir immediately voiced his concerns for Carter's safety; but by the time the transmission had reached Carter, the old engineer had risen and gone, and Targon heard his words echo in an empty room fifteen million miles away.

10

Dalin Shar did not precisely understand what was going on.

Despite the counsel of Prime Minister Faulkner and a half dozen other advisers, despite his close monitoring of the news broadcasts, it seemed that his empire was crumbling around him. From the shores of the Black and Red seas to the Bay of Bengal and the South China Sea, civil unrest seemed to have risen up like a nest of sores from everywhere at once. Even on the far outskirts of the empire, in places like Athens and Manchuria, riots had broken out over food and work conditions. These in turn had given birth to further riots over government attempts to control what little stores had not been hoarded or destroyed in the rioting.

But still, after weeks of escalating trouble, Dalin was loath to use the iron fist.

"Your father would have done so without hesitation!" Minister Faulkner counseled, with the mixture of mild exasperation and calm reserve that characterized him. "It's obvious that rebel cells have been at work within the various governorships—you must let the army do its job!"

There had been, that morning, a bomb scare in the palace itself, and this meeting was being held underground, in the lower chambers Dalin's father had had built during the early consolidation of the empire, when threats had been a daily occurrence. Dalin vaguely remembered playing down here: the hushed, tense voices around him while he ran from dank room to dank room with toy soldiers clutched in his fist.

The present room was little different than it had been in those days; the years of disuse had inspired disrepair, though, and there were dusty paintings on the dented walls and stacks of abandoned and broken furniture in the corners. Dalin's advisers had had to sift through this mess to arrange a table and chairs for Dalin and his ministers to occupy.

Somewhat to his chagrin, Minister Faulkner discovered that the ancient wall Screen, an early and small model, did not work at all, depriving them all of the minister's ever-present data—a development which did not bother Dalin in the least.

"You must *not*, under any circumstances, use the army, Sire!" Defense Minister Acron shouted, red-faced. "It would only make you look like a tyrant!" Acron was a man who almost never acted calmly, and Dalin had tried to keep him away as much as possible, which had been impossible lately.

"I disagree with Minister Acron utterly," Faulkner said.

"I had no doubt you would," Dalin answered.

Acron's face reddened to deep ruby. He pounded his fist on the table, which shook on its three good legs, the fourth being propped on a stack of old aluminum cartons.

"There *is* no rebellion as Minister Faulkner keeps suggesting! Merely a bit of civil unrest in reaction to the events on Mars!"

Minister Faulkner shook his head at this last suggestion.

Down the short table, Minister Besh nodded.

"I agree with Minister Faulkner," he said quietly. "There is more than enough evidence to prove that Prime Cornelian is behind the Afrasian uprisings. I believe the military should be used without delay."

Acron turned on the new voice with sarcasm. "That is why you are finance minister, Besh! Tend to your ones and zeros, please!"

There were a few titters, but mostly silence.

Besh said, "And how have we handled the current shortages in food and supplies?"

This last question was directed at Labor Minister Rere, a stout man with a deep voice, who now cast a malevolent glance at Besh and said, "I authorized a discreet holding back of certain items to prevent hoarding and further rioting. This is standard practice."

"Is it standard practice to ration water and wheat?" Besh said.

Rere turned his hands palm upward. "When necessary—yes!"

"Where did the rioting begin?" Dalin Shar asked.

Minister Faulkner answered, "In Canton, Sire. A week ago yesterday. As you know, there was an attempt on the governor's life, followed by a general labor strike. This led to shortages and then Minister Rere's attempts to bring those shortages under control."

"What prompted the labor strike?"

Minister Faulkner hesitated before answering. "We had . . . certain information that rebels had infiltrated many of the guilds. This influence has spread. That is why I believe that immediate military measures—"

Dalin found his anger level beginning to rival that of Minister Acron, though he was able to keep it under control for now. "Am I correct in concluding that this was not brought to my attention earlier 'for my own good'?"

There was silence at the table, and not a few downcast eyes. Only Minister Besh looked at Dalin Shar and nodded. "This seems an altogether fair charge," the minister said.

Minister Acron suddenly stood up, his face nearly purple, his finger pointing at Dalin. "This . . . *boy* is not fit to rule! He is not old enough nor wise enough!"

Instantly Prime Minister Faulkner rose and turned to the imperial guard standing by the doorway. "Remove Minister Acron and place him in detention. As of this moment he is under house arrest."

Two guards, burlier and taller than Acron, approached and took the defense minister by either arm, pulling him up out of his chair.

"Let go of me!" Acron demanded, but the guards, at Faulkner's motion, took an even firmer grip and dragged the beet-faced, shouting man from the room.

"I apologize, Sire," Faulkner said, bowing toward Dalin Shar.

Dalin said, "You have much to apologize for, as do the rest of my ministers." Dalin let his anger build slowly, and let Faulkner and the others see it. "Why do I seem to know nothing of what has been happening in my own kingdom?"

He pounded on the table. "*Why?*"

Minister Faulkner looked calmly down at his nails for a moment and then looked at Dalin Shar. "Do you wish the truth, Sire?"

"Of course!"

Minister Faulkner said quietly, "Because for the last weeks, it has seemed like you have been behaving like a lovesick puppy, incapable of action."

Dalin Shar's face reddened, not in anger but in embarrassment. He began to shout in protest but then held his tongue, chastened for the moment.

Minister Faulkner continued quietly, "I apologize to you, Sire, for speaking this way, but you did demand the truth from me."

Choking on his mortification, Dalin Shar studied the faces of his ministers and saw by their aversion to his gaze that this was true.

"All right," he said finally. "Be that as it may. What, then, can we do?"

"We should follow our present course of controlled shortages," Labor Minister Rere said without hesitation. "And we should allow Minister Acron's . . . replacement to take military action against the colonies—and in the cities, if necessary."

Still red-faced, Dalin began to speak, but then Faulkner caught his eye with a well-known glance that said, *Speak with me. Alone. Now.*

"I . . . will think on this and make my decision as soon as possible," the king said.

The meeting was adjourned.

The Imperial security detachment advised that the upper levels of the palace had been cleared of danger; no explosive device had been found.

Dalin thought he would be asked to accompany the prime minister to a conference room, where his cherished wall Screens and data could be put to use; it therefore came as a surprise when Faulkner asked to walk in the garden with the king.

"You? Outside?" Dalin said with amusement. "In all my years I don't believe I have seen you in sunlight, Prime Minister."

Faulkner tried not to look sour. "It would be a welcome change," he said unconvincingly. "And besides . . ." the prime minister motioned with his hand as if they should proceed to the garden now.

When they reached the rose trellises—in fact, when they stopped at the precise spot where Dalin had first kissed Tabrel Kris—Faulkner said, "There are things I wish to tell you that other ears should not hear."

"Do you mean the palace is not safe for speaking?"

"Not these days, Sire."

"I see."

Faulkner allowed slight impatience to creep into his voice. "You are a burden to me, Dalin Shar! I have never known when you are not being frivolous. I have tried my best to counsel you in all things these past years. But your attitude . . ."

Dalin allowed a bigger grin to cross his face. "I have made you angry! It has been my life's work!"

"Please, Sire! Let me speak of these things!"

"Go ahead. But you know very well we are being watched and listened to here as well."

"Yes, but by people loyal to you."

Dalin's manner immediately sobered. "Has it gotten that bad, then?"

Faulkner drew a weary hand across his face. "Sometimes you vex me, Dalin. Your father was not like this."

"You miss him, don't you?"

Faulkner seemed mildly startled. "Yes, I do."

"I didn't know him very well myself. A bounce on the knee, a pat on the head. And then he was gone."

"He was a good man. A great man."

"As are you, Minister Faulkner."

Again Faulkner seemed startled. "Perhaps . . ."

"Tell me, then, of these plots and intrigues. As

long as I can remember we have had plots and intrigues."

"This is different. This may mean your life. I'm afraid Acron was only the beginning. I'm not even sure of his part. At the least he is a pompous fool who needed airing out. At worst . . ."

"Tell me, Faulkner. As I told you in that meeting, do not treat me like a boy."

"But you *are* a boy! And you act like a boy! Acron was not wrong with that."

The prime minister pointed to the riotous colors of the roses surrounding them; their bright reds and pinks made the afternoon air thick with perfume.

"I, of course, witnessed what happened here between yourself and Senator Kris's daughter on that afternoon three weeks ago."

Anger began to fill Dalin, but Faulkner held up a stern hand. "Hear me! It has been my *job* to watch over you since your father's death; it has been my *existence*."

"And have you watched my other assignations in this garden?" Dalin hissed. "Have you peeped into my most private moments like a lewd voyeur with sweaty hands? Is everything recorded on a data card?"

Dalin's hands were balled into fists, but the hardness he now witnessed on the prime minister's face—iron beneath the surface which he had only beheld a rare glimpse of before—made his fists relax and made something like fear crawl into his gut.

This was a man who, Dalin Shar was suddenly sure, had killed before, possibly in his, Dalin's, name.

"Listen to me," Faulkner said, with a coldness Dalin had never heard from either the minister or anyone else; he realized that he was seeing a man on the edge, at the limits of himself.

Dalin managed to keep his composure and summon a measure of courage. "All right," he said. "But I tell you that no one has ever spoken to me like this, and I will not forget."

Faulkner spoke between gritted teeth. "I have *watched* you, yes, King Shar. I have watched nearly your every move since you were still soiling your underclothes. On the day your father was butchered, I lifted you from your daybed and hid you in my cloak, while murderers passed by me with bloodied knives. I hid you in a place no one knew about, not even your father. Did you know he was tortured before he was slaughtered? They wanted *you*, Dalin; they wanted to end your father's line and destroy his empire. But *I* saved your life."

Faulkner's face belied an inner rage, a cauldron that must have been building for years. "*I* saved you, when I could have let those dogs have you that day. And every one of those traitors I tracked and brought down. For your father. For you.

"And in the years since, while you grew and frolicked and fancied yourself becoming a man, I pulled the strings for you in this government, because you did not yet seem ready for that mantle to be placed upon you. I would be lying if I said I did not welcome rule by proxy; it is what I do best and what gives me most pride.

"But all these years, through all the crises, the trouble, the petty insurrections and betrayals, I have managed for you, I have waited for you to flower not with manhood, but with your father's capacity for rule. I have steeled myself, waiting for the day when I could see your father in yourself.

"And that day has not come."

Suddenly there was more than just rage in Faulkner's words; there was sadness and resignation. "I fear it may never come."

"I am sorry I disappoint you, Minister Faulkner."

"Disappoint! That is a stupid word! A useless word! There is a burden, a . . . *weight* . . ."

Suddenly it seemed as if Dalin could see that burden which Faulkner had carried; the weight of an empire bearing down on his stiff shoulders, the weight of years and rule which was not rightly his own, and which he would gladly dispense with.

"And now," Faulkner said, his voice filled with weariness, "when the biggest crisis has come and you are needed most of all, you choose this time to fall in *love*."

Dalin was about to explain himself when the minister suddenly placed his hands on Dalin's shoulders and looked deep into his eyes. Here, then, was the root of the man, shown in those recesses behind even the iron.

Back there, Dalin saw fear.

"It is beginning now, Dalin," Faulkner said. His

hands were like talons digging into the king's shoulders. "And it will come swiftly. There will be a move against you, very soon. And I don't know who it will be. What I did with Acron was merely a feint; the fact that no one protested my action worries me greatly. At most Acron is a co-conspirator, an affordable loss; but the real master remains hidden. I could have Acron tortured, but I doubt he even knows who is pulling the strings; he is stupid enough to think he is pulling them himself. *And I don't know who it is.*

"Listen to me, and very carefully. Trust no one, from this moment on. For the past two weeks, while you sulked, I have used every power I have to find out who has plotted against you and, if that plot was enacted, to give you a back door to pass through. I have failed in the first enterprise, and now I fear we are very close to an attempt on your life. There are very specific things you must do, if and when this attempt comes. And you must not think of me if it happens."

Faulkner removed his grip from Dalin's shoulders and sat the young man down on a nearby bench. "Now listen to me very carefully. . . ."

There followed hours of discussion. When Dalin looked up, he saw that the stars and a sickled moon had risen above the trellises and that it was now night air that was scented with the sweet, languid odor of roses. At times he thought Faulkner had gone mad and was ranting with fever; but finally the discussion ended and the prime minister took his leave.

In the faintness of moonlight, Faulkner's face looked ghostly and pale; he seemed a diminished man, unburdening his strength along with his plans and advice.

"Take care, my king," Faulkner said, melting into the night. "With another meeting I have this hour, we may know who is friend and who is foe."

The prime minister was gone then; and Dalin, suddenly aware of the chilled night, felt as if he should have said good-bye.

It did not come as a complete shock, then, when Dalin Shar was awakened deep into the same night, with the sliver of moon edged down the west, to be told that Prime Minister Faulkner had been found that night murdered in his own chambers, his eyes and tongue cut out, his severed head still resting upon his pillow but robbed of all but eternal sleep.

11

"It makes little difference to me, you understand," Prime Cornelian said languidly, "but I really would like to know where your daughter is."

As he spoke, the High Leader took lazy pulls from the hookah borne by a rolling assistant. The machine had been designed expressly for this purpose and no other; it was, in effect, a hookah on wheels with a primitive brain. As Cornelian slowly circled the upright field where Senator Kris was held tightly suspended—so tightly that the yellow light of the field protruded not a bare millimeter from his crushed chest; his chest produced great pain each time the senator breathed, which was not that often. The field commenced a bare meter off the ground and held the senator in a suspended state with no movement possible. The room, in one of the higher towers of the residence of the former High Prefect, gave a stunning view through its open window of much of the Arsia Mons region in the distance—though Cornelian had made sure that the senator, when placed within the field, had been facing the bare opposite wall.

"Oh, do talk, Senator!" Cornelian chided, taking another pull and letting the smoke out in precise O's, which floated through the field and made Kris cough painfully. "I'll find her nevertheless, and it would be so much easier on you for me to let you die today—think of all the pain to come tomorrow and the day after, otherwise!"

Kris, through torment, muttered, "You know I won't tell you."

In the middle of another string of smoke O's, Cornelian said, "Correct! That is why I should tell you that she is safely on Titan, a guest of my good friend Wrath-Pei, and that she will soon be on her way back to see you!"

Kris sought to struggle within his confines, gasping, "He said he would protect her! Wrath-Pei promised—"

Cornelian hooted, "A *promise*? From Wrath-Pei? Did you really think you could believe anything that monster told you?"

Kris abruptly stopped struggling and let the pain subside before he panted, his eyes steady, "Wrath-Pei won't return her." Something like a smile came briefly to his lips, before the agony in his rib cage wiped it from his face. "I don't care what he's told you, he won't let her go. She's too valuable to him politically."

The senator hissed in pain as his ruined heaving chest pushed out against the steel-like wall of yellow light. "And . . . not because of her union to . . . Jamal Clan."

Moaning in pain, Senator Kris fainted away in his upright cage.

Prime Cornelian stood tapping one long digit against his cranium in thought.

"You're wrong, of course, Kris, but as always, your political instincts are in the right place. That's what made you so valuable to me as a tool. I must think on this."

Prime Cornelian passed through a soft shaft of afternoon sunlight, which played across his angled body like a caress before hitting the far pink wall again after the High Leader's passage.

On his way from the room, Cornelian paused in his thoughts long enough to tweak the containment field a fraction tighter; Senator Kris immediately came back to consciousness, fighting for breath and groaning in discomfort.

"You realize, of course, Kris, that Tabrel will return for your sake?"

A long moan escaped the senator, which followed the High Leader happily from the room.

A demonstration had been prepared in the city of Shklovskii, in the Acidalia Planitia, in the northern hemisphere. Though bored with the trip, Prime Cornelian relished the destination.

Pynthas, who had regrettably been put in charge, had the shuttle pilot fly high enough so that he could ogle the Tharsis Montes ridge; to the High Leader, they were dead cones on the ground, of no importance. A thin salmon haze at the edge of the world was more interesting to Cornelian; in his mind, he thought that if only they could find a way to punch selective holes in that haze, which represented the tenuous atmosphere of the planet, then none of these other, messier methods would be needed. Just extract a neatly sliced area of atmosphere—including, of course, all the oxygen, like cutting a cylindrical wedge from a melon—and *voila!* no more problems in the city below.

"Look at Tharsis Tholus from this angle—ohhhhh!" Pynthas said, straining his unnaturally large eyes to look below as the shuttle made its turn east. Below, the volcano lay wide, high, and majestic, one side of its shadowed caldera filled with frost.

In his enthusiasm, Pynthas turned from the window, grinning, and sought to pull at one of Prime Cornelian's appendages to make him look; but he shrunk back in horror immediately at the High Leader's harsh gaze.

"Dead mounds of dirt," Cornelian said, in response to which Pynthas began to bob his head madly.

"Of course, High Leader—of course!"

"How much longer?" Cornelian called up to the pilot, who immediately replied, "Not twenty minutes, High Leader."

"Very well."

The High Leader snorted, seeing that Pynthas had once again turned to the window to gaze wide-eyed and openmouthed at swirls of sand, spare forests of pale green, and bits of rock below.

*   *   *

At Shklovskii, Prime Cornelian's interest picked up, even as Pynthas's waned. For the final ten minutes of the journey there had been little sight-seeing to do: only a vast plain of unsheathed rock, vestigial craters, and intermittent desert. Vegetation was sparse, and only when the shuttle lowered toward the nearing city was any life visible on the surface. They might be on any habitable desert area anywhere, except that here the brush grew taller than a man, the flowers were wan shades of blue and yellow, and the sands were some of the darkest on the planet, a deep rust approaching red.

"*That's* Shklovskii?" the High Leader sniffed, as a ragtag cluster of bland two-story sandstone buildings ringed by water tanks came into view below them. At the northern perimeter, the ugly quarry cuts of a sandstone mine did nothing to brighten the picture.

Pynthas said eagerly, "It's one of the reasons it was picked, High Leader. No one will miss it."

His eagerness for landscape had been replaced by his equally unattractive eagerness to please.

"Where are the nearest towns?"

"Mutch and Sagan, fifty and a hundred kilometers away."

"And you're sure there'll be no spillover into those communities?"

"None."

As if sensing that Prime Cornelian wanted con-

firmation, General Ramsden, who had sat thus far
silently in the copilot's seat up front, turned and
said, "No possibility, High Leader."

"Good. I would hate to see anything happen to
that museum near . . ."

"Chryse Planitia, High Leader," the general said.
His eyes were as blank as his tone, his leathery thin
face impassive. Through experience, Prime Cornelian knew that the man's reptilian qualities were
only skin deep; otherwise, he would not be alive.

"Good. You may proceed."

"Very wel—"

"One more question. You're sure this will be
seen live?"

General Ramsden said impassively, "Every Screen
on the planet, High Leader. With an appropriate
message condemning Shklovskii as the center of
civil disobedience and a rebel stronghold. I believe
the message will be clear, High Leader."

"It's not necessary for you to believe anything,
General. The fact that there is no rebel resistance
on Mars is no concern of yours. Proceed."

"Very well."

General Ramsden spoke a few words, and the Marine cruiser which had been following the shuttle
pulled overhead and in front of them. As it did so,
a bay in its sleek golden belly opened, revealing a
glint of brilliant light within.

"May we get closer to the ground?" Cornelian
asked.

Pynthas began to say no, but General Ramsden cut him off and said, "Of course, High Leader."

The shuttle lowered, leaving the hovering needled length of the cruiser above and ahead of them.

"Is this all right, High Leader?" the general inquired.

They were three hundred meters above the city; at this height, Prime Cornelian could see the thin upturned faces of the curious citizens who had come out into their yards and into the single paved street that ran the length of the town to look at the wonders in the sky over them. At this height, Cornelian could see the whirls of dust devils caught in various dry yards and open lots.

"Do they know?" Cornelian asked.

"No," the general answered. "We thought they would flee into the desert if they were warned."

"Of course. Tell them now."

"As you wish."

General Ramsden again spoke, and there was a momentary lack of action. Below him, Cornelian watched as the citizens of Shklovskii seemed to cock their heads as one, listening to others who had listeners or Screens.

Before long, the High Leader had the response he wanted, as more citizens rushed from their homes, some comically carrying belongings, others bearing children.

"They look like . . . insects, don't they?" Cornelian said, which brought dead silence in the shuttle.

"You may proceed," Cornelian said, chuckling.

General Ramsden spoke a single word, and the Marine cruiser opened its bay doors wide, letting out a startling light. It seemed not so much a ray as a fall of blinding sunlight, which dropped into the town below.

There was a snap of sound, like air too suddenly being let out of an overinflated device; and when the eye cleared of blinding light it beheld human skeletons caught in a rapidly expanding and flattening bubble, a kind of smoke ring of bright pressure that blew out from the center of Shklovskii to beyond its farthest edges. At the inside perimeter of the sandstone mine the edge of the expanding circle dipped to conform to the landscape; a bare moment later it climbed rapidly out the other side and resumed shape, even as it began to dissipate.

In a matter of ten seconds it was over, and Shklovskii was a circle in the desert, brushed clean of everything.

"My!" Prime Cornelian said. "I'm impressed!"

"Sam-Sei thought you would be pleased," General Ramsden said, his tone never changing. "Of course, the weapon has its limitations."

"Doesn't everything?" the High Leader said, almost gleefully. "It will be a wonderful instrument. We must play with it again soon. And now," he said, boredom creeping suddenly into his speech, "I'd like to go home."

"Of course, High Leader," General Ramsden said.

*   *   *

On the journey back to Lowell, Prime Cornelian's mind was so occupied that he heard none of Pynthas's catcalls of pleasure as one dead rock or another was flown over.

12

"Tabrel, you must speak with me!"

From behind the door to Tabrel Kris's room came silence.

Jamal Clan struck the door with the flat of his palm.

"The wedding is three days away, and you must begin to act like the princess you will be!"

Still: silence.

"Tabrel—listen to me!"

Angrily, Jamal unlocked the door and strode into the room toward Tabrel, who sat calmly regarding him from a straight-backed chair. Suddenly he drew his fist back—but, unable to strike her, stood frozen, tears welling in his eyes.

"Tabrel, please, you must do as I say!"

Her eyes, copper-brown, filled with depths of so much else, looked unblinking at Jamal.

"I have told you a hundred times, Jamal Clan: I am Tabrel Kris, member of the Martian diplomatic legation, and I demand to be treated in accordance with all laws and tenets of the Four Worlds Diplomatic Treaty of 2448; such laws forbid the unlawful detaining or improper treatment of a member of any diplomatic legation of any of the Four Worlds. My treatment is in clear violation of this treaty."

"But if you would just *listen* to me!" Jamal stood helpless before her, tears streaming down his face.

"That is not the way a prince of the house of Clan acts," a calm, chilly voice said from the doorway.

Jamal, startled, sought to compose himself before turning to face the figure in the doorway.

"As usual you are right, Mother," he said.

Kamath Clan gave a slight, imperious bow. Her girth was dwarfed by her height, which made her appear not stout but imposing. There were those on Titan who, speaking in corner whispers, called her Black Widow—and claimed that she had eaten her husband—or that he had at the lease died from fright at that expectation.

"Did anyone see you act this way?" Kamath Clan asked.

"No, Mother. At least I don't think so."

Kamath entered the room and closed the door.

"What I have just done, a simple act of closing a door, can do wonders toward avoiding such problems." She stopped to look down at Tabrel, who stared impassively ahead.

"It can turn a foolish act into a necessary one," Kamath continued. Her face was as impassive as Tabrel's. "How many times has she tried to leave this house?"

In frustration, Jamal said, "Every time I've left the

door unlocked. Once she nearly made it to a shuttle at the freight depot. Another ten minutes and she would have been offworld. She will not believe me when I tell her that we have no news of her father. When she is not trying to escape, she sits reciting that diplomacy nonsense."

"Have you tried striking her?"

Flustered by his mother's presence, Jamal said, "No! I cannot hurt her! I only want to make her listen!"

"There are other ways to accomplish that," Kamath said. "Soon she will have lost enough weight that it will be necessary to treat her. It is then that certain . . . medicines can be administered."

"I don't want you to hurt her!" Jamal said, his melodious voice rising in frustration. "I don't want anyone to hurt her! She is . . . beautiful!"

Kamath studied the young girl's face.

"That she is," Kamath said. "But she is also an embarrassment. The betrothal is valid as long as I refuse to dissolve it. But we obviously cannot count on Tabrel Kris's cooperation."

Jabal balled his fists. "I will not let you at her! I will make her see that this marriage must be accomplished and will be a good one!"

At this last remark his mother raised an eyebrow. "A good one? That doesn't matter."

"It matters to me!"

His mother studied Jamal impassively for a moment. "You have fallen in love with her?"

"Yes! And I want her to love me!"

"There are potions for that, too. . . ."

Jamal's face filled with fear. "No!"

His mother shrugged. "For now, you may try your own methods, Jamal." She turned to leave. "When I have closed the door behind me, you may hit her."

The door closed, and Jamal was left alone with Tabrel Kris, who sat staring straight through him.

"Why can't you just love me?" Jamal sobbed out, reaching out a trembling hand, daring to touch her face. Another, longer sob escaped him, sounding like incongruous music. "Why?"

Kamath Clan had other stops to make. In the Ruz Balib section of the Sacred Grounds, after passing down the central walkway of the tree-lined quadrangle bordered by dominion buildings, pedestrians moving aside at her approach, she mounted two flights of stairs in one particular building, disdaining the lift, and traversed a short hallway colored drab green. There were two doors at the end of the hall, to left and right, and without knocking she entered the right door, closing it behind her.

At the desk sat a clerk who did not move to stop her from entering the inner sanctum of the office. Again she opened and closed a door and towered now above the desk of Commander Tarn, chief of defensive operations on Titan. The inviolability of Titan's near-space defenses was, in effect, in the hands of this man, who now gulped. He had once bedded Kamath Clan, to attain position, when her

husband had been alive, and had avoided ever since
the possibility of a second tryst.

Tarn bowed his head and rose; the Titan greeting.

"My queen."

"You may sit, Tarn. No, stand for a moment."

Gulping once more, Tarn stood straight.

"Turn for me. Slowly, with your arms out."

Praying to any gods who might exist or ever had
existed, Tarn did as he was told.

"No, it is not right. You may sit."

"Thank you, my queen."

Inwardly, Tarn cheered, having failed the test.
But there would be others to warn: that the queen
bee was in search once more for a bedmate.

"How may I help you, my queen?" Tarn asked,
recovering some of his official composure now that
the crisis had passed.

"I want to know just how impenetrable our defense shields are," Kamath Clan said. In her
shadow, Tarn briefly thought himself a small man,
though he stood above two meters.

"It is the best system possible," Tarn said, but
immediately saw that she did not crave generalities,
but specifics.

"It is point eight impervious, which means that
no plasma charge yet devised could pass through it."

"Might Wrath-Pei pass through it?"

"He . . ." Tarn suddenly realized that much, including his well-being, might hinge on this question.
"He has been allowed to, of course."

"I mean, if he weren't allowed to?"

"We could . . . defend Titan from him, my queen. If necessary."

"Very well. You are sure of this?"

"Of course, my queen."

The mountain looming over Tarn nodded. "Then if we were to decide that Wrath-Pei were . . . let us say, deemed *unworthy* of our company, he could be prevented."

"Anyone could be prevented, my queen. You are thinking perhaps of the troubles on Mars and Earth at the moment?"

"Beyond that, Tarn. Much beyond that." She had been looking inwardly, but now she turned her gaze on Tarn again.

"And our ground defenses?"

"The best and toughest of all Four Worlds!" Tarn said proudly.

"I hope so. Even so, I would like you to order a state of heightened alert. In the event . . ."

"Yes, my queen?"

"Never mind, Tarn."

Again her gaze sharpened and became more interested in Tarn.

"Stand again, Commander."

Tarn drew a breath, but did as he was told.

"Turn for me, arms akimbo."

Tarn turned.

There was an approving sound, which made Tarn's blood freeze—but it was followed by a resigned sigh.

"I was right in my first estimation. You may sit again."

"Thank you, my queen," Tarn said, not able to hide his relief.

"Though I may be back for you," Kamath Clan said, without a trace of humor.

She departed, leaving the door open, and leaving to Tarn's clerk the remarkable sight of the commander himself, wan and trembling, fumbling for his communication console to warn those who should be warned.

There was one other stop for Kamath Clan to make. Up through the bright glare of Titan's day lights, the late afternoon Sun shone like a distant warm coin. Kamath thought briefly of her birthplace, so much nearer to that Sun, and so much warmer. Not in temperature, for the same omnipresent lights that flooded the streets and valleys and even the hills of Titan with light also fed its plants and, along with the core reactor deep in its bosom, gave it warmth. But it was in many ways a bland, clinical warmth, unlike that of Sol.

On Earth, Kamath had played once, at the age of three, in a meadow under a bird-blue sky with the warmth of Sol, hanging like a ball in the air, on her skin. The toasty feel of that warmth was like nothing else she had felt since, and its loss was the great loss of her life. When her parents fled the consolidation of Sarat Shar's power, they tore their daughter not only from her birth home, which became the eastern governorship of Shar's empire, but from the rest of her life as well.

The warmth of Sun on skin . . .

In dreamy rumination within her hard shell, Kamath Clan found that her feet had taken her unheedful to her destination. There were no pedestrians to move out of her way here, for this, the most backward and dangerous of the city's streets, was deserted at any time of day or night. And anyone wondering at her visit here would keep such thoughts to themselves.

A day of doors. She stood before another door, opened and closed it behind her. It always felt damp to her touch, so out of harmony with the thing that brought her here. Inside, it was dark as any midnight.

"You have come again, my queen?" his voice, a little frailer than the last time; as it had been frailer last time and the time before that. "You have come to see old Quog again?"

"I have come," Kamath Clan said.

"And is it the same you seek as before?"

"As always," Kamath said.

"Very well."

He emerged from the darker shadows of the room into mere shadow. He was indeed a man, of sorts. He had told Kamath that first time, the one time when he felt obligated to explain himself, that he had once been a handsome specimen.

"But the Puppet Death," he had said, "changed all that. It twisted and turned me and pulled me every which way. It danced on me, all right! Oh, I was dashing before the disease, my queen. I was straight-backed and black-haired and had good hands and feet; I could dance, and could make things with my delicate fingers. But afterward, my wife left me and my daughter shunned me. But I took a bit of what I was and came here."

It was then that he had shown Kamath Clan what she had come to see. And it was what he again showed her now.

"Soon I will be gone, my queen!" his frail voice said. The sideways appearance of his arm-thin face, like a melted substance, plastic or cheese, one layer over the other, never failed to startle even Kamath Clan. In the midst of this visage were his organs of sight and smell, pressed to mere slits, and his mouth, a vertical oval hole.

The rest of his body was sloped sideways, also, though not as severely as his face and head; his walking was of a shuffling kind, baby steps by deformed feet.

"Hard to believe I've been this way since I was eighteen!" Quog said. He moved closer, giving the queen, with her unwavering stare, a good look at him; this was part of a ritual of cruelty and trade they had worked out long ago.

"Think you would have gone for me then, my queen?" Quog whispered breathily through his mouth hole.

"I think not," the queen said.

"Nor I you! Ha!" Quog said.

Trying not to show her need, which was a useless thing with this man, Kamath said, "You will provide me."

"Of course! Have I ever denied you, my queen?"

He waited for her response; which was, "No."

"But before long, when these soft bones are in the dust heap, you will be denied, eh?"

"Perhaps."

"Perhaps?" A trace of irritation entered the old man's panting words. "Do you think there are others like me?"

"Not like you. But what you have—"

"Can be duplicated?" Now he was angry. "Do you think so? Do you think I am so foolish as to think you haven't tried? You who have a chemical, a potion, for everything? Have you *tried*?"

His slitted eyes were as wide as they ever grew; within the vertical, flesh-flapped cavities the queen saw tiny fierce eyes, red with rheum.

"I have tried," she said.

"Of course you have! And failed! Ha!"

The queen waited; as did the old man, who stood panting tiny breaths through his mouth.

"You will apologize to me, Queen," Quog said finally.

There was silence.

"You will apologize immediately or get out of my home."

Kamath Clan turned her towering body away from the twisted old man.

"You will not take a step toward the door," Quog

said. "I know your needs too well. What you will do is turn and beg this thing of me; get down on your knees, Queen, and beg me!"

The old man was huffing in agitation—either anger or satisfaction.

Kamath Clan stood still.

"*Now!*" Quog spat. "*Or be forever banished from my house!*"

A moment ticked by, and then Kamath Clan turned slowly and lowered herself to the filthy floor; laying her hands flat upon the boards, she crawled forward, eyes downcast, and lay her forehead on the old man's deformed, sandaled feet.

"Kiss them!"

Kamath Clan lifted her head slightly to kiss the feet, one and then the other; his toes were like gnarled knuckles.

"Lick them! As a dog licks!"

The queen did as she was told.

"Very well," Quog breathed, satisfied. "You may rise."

Head still bowed, Queen Kamath Clan slowly brought herself up to her full height and stood impassively.

Chuckling, Quog said, turning to shuffle into the deeper shadows of the room to the shelves on which rested pots and metal containers and some ancient glass carafes of dark colors, green and red, "You know well, my queen, that all power resides with those who have what is desperately wanted. This," he said, still chuckling weakly, "is the *only* definition of power."

"Yes."

"Ha!" He lingered over various vials, knowing that such action was drawing out her torture.

"Cruelty," he said, the levity gone from his voice, "is something to be learned, though."

Abruptly he chose the canister he sought all along, a nondescript metal tube, one among a few, with one end sealed tightly.

"Two," Queen Clan said.

"No. One now, and one again tomorrow. I want you to return."

His deformed hand held the single slim container out from the shadows to her. Eagerly she took it.

"I will return tomorrow."

"Yes, you will."

As she exited, closing the door, this time, behind her, he said, breathing from the shadows, "I was not . . . always cruel. . . ."

13

"I'm sorry to report I have no idea where he is," Finance Minister Besh said in an even tone. In this case distance produced boldness, and Besh was well aware that if High Leader Prime Cornelian were standing beside him at this moment instead of sixty million miles away, his unsightly visage a mere image on a wall Screen, Besh's voice would be anything but level.

"I'm sorry to hear your report, Besh," the High Leader said, though he sounded not nearly as interested or upset as the finance minister had thought he would. "I imagine your people are out scurrying about trying to find him?"

"Of course, High Leader," Besh said.

"Good. Let me know if he turns up."

Before Besh could even bow, the Screen went dark, leaving the finance minister with salutations and such dryly stuck in his throat.

Strange, Besh thought, mildly irritated; he was the kind of man who liked praise for a job well done and considered dressing down appropriate otherwise.

Minister Acron, seated at the conference table behind him, was not quite so contemplative.

"The pup will be found, and when he is I will strangle him myself!" the florid-faced defense minister, newly released from incarceration, shouted. He raised his fist to pound the table, but held it frozen at Besh's request.

"Please," the finance minister, stroking his chin, said. "I must think this through."

"What is there to think through? The King must be caught and dispatched with! There is no greater danger to us!"

"That is true," Besh said, lowering his lanky frame into the nearest chair, "but there are other factors to consider. For instance, who has facilitated his escape?"

"Faulkner, of course!"

Besh waved a hand in dismissal. "I mean besides Faulkner. The boy could not do this alone. It is obvious that Faulkner foresaw his . . . present circumstances and alerted the king to their possibility. It is reasonable to suppose that the prime minister also provided the king with a plan of escape and a method to effect it. You say he was told when of the prime minister's demise?"

"At one-thirty in the morning," Acron said impatiently. "One of the bloody assistants alerted him."

"It was Faulkner's machine, no doubt?"

"Yes." Acron's ill temper was growing. "The machine was torn to pieces by my men. It saw nothing. Obviously it was programed by Faulkner to check

on his well-being every fifteen minutes or so. When
it discovered—"

"Yes," Besh said, continuing to stroke his chin.
"It then went immediately to young Dalin. It was
very clever of the prime minister. But now . . ."

"But now what? *Where is he?*"

"There were no obvious clues, I'm afraid, Acron.
He seems to have vanished into thin air." Besh con-
tinued to rub his chin. "But there are always clues,
Acron. Always."

Even in death, Prime Minister Faulkner continued to surprise Dalin Shar with his knowledge.
Dalin had spent his entire life sleeping in this particular bedroom—yet he had never had even the
faintest knowledge that there was a secret passageway built into the wall next to his bed. It had been
put there, Faulkner informed him, by Dalin's father
during the same period that the underground rooms
had been built in the palace.

Faulkner . . .

When the door from his bedroom closed behind
him, leaving him in a dark corridor with only a slim
handlight for guidance, a fear went through him
like he had never known before.

For the first time in his life, he felt truly alone.

When his father had been murdered, Dalin had
been young, and there had been constant attention
and diversions. There had been nursemaids, and
there had been . . . Faulkner.

It occurred to Dalin now that the prime minister

had always been there. Always. From the very beginning, Faulkner had been ever-present, as tutor, adviser, confidant. Never could Dalin recall a time
when the prime minister had been unavailable or
too busy to listen to whatever petty grievance or
problem the king found himself in the middle of. A
broken toy, or a nuance in diplomacy—these had
been equal things which Faulkner had dealt with in
appropriate ways. Though stiff, fussy, punctilious,
and often imperious, the prime minister had . . .
always been there.

And now he was gone. . . .

Gone forever.

A pang of something like panic went through
Dalin. Even now he could hear the entrance of
someone into his bedchambers not twenty inches
behind him. Beyond that wall, there were shouts
and angry recriminations.

They were looking for him now. No doubt to
kill him.

But his panic was not a matter of fear for his
own life.

It was that he would have to face what came
next *alone*.

Without Faulkner.

As the shouts grew louder in the bedroom, Dalin
Shar took one step and then another, the pencil
beam of his handlight illuminating the dusty, nar-
row passage before him—and he resolved in his
mind that the men who had taken Gorlin Faulkner
away from him, who had murdered the man who

until now he had not realized was the most valuable friend he had ever had, would pay for what they had done, and pay dearly.

The remainder of Dalin's night was no better than it had begun.

The passageway, which seemed to go on forever, cut first sharply right and then sharply left, narrowing to a seemingly endless series of steps downward before becoming even narrower and continuing its zigzag course. Dalin passed behind many rooms throughout the palace and was able to identify some of them by the sounds without: the frightened chatter of the cooks in the galley, gathered from sleep with the news of the murder within the palace; similar buzzing from the secretaries and clerks, in their separate offices; and, most telling, the angry cries of the Imperial guard being put under arrest to prevent their presumed dedication to Dalin's well-being.

The passageway finally did end, though, and in the spot that the prime minister had told him it would. Dalin emerged in the cellars they had so recently used for offices; immediately, he sought a second passage, easily found though just as well hidden as the first, and just as dark. This one was also possessed of a rank, wet smell, and the habitation of at least one rat, which scurried, red-eyed, away from the handlight's beam to splash off into the darkness.

This passage was wider than the first and pro-

ceeded straight for a good way before ending
abruptly at a wall, which was inset with footholds
leading up through a kind of well.

At the top of this hole Dalin shouldered up a
hatchway, and pushing aside dirt which had covered
the opening and which now spilled down on top
of him, he climbed up into the world outside the
palace grounds.

He was just within a stand of fir trees blocking
the view from the palace of the city beyond; through
the tree line he could see the palace, lit as if for a
ball, the lights of its spires making it appear magical
against the night's starry blackness.

But there was nothing magical about the shouts
of soldiers or the occasional line of raser fire pencil-
ing the night sky like an angry insect's flight—

"You are the one I was sent to meet?"

The voice sounded so close by Dalin's ear that he
started violently. But already strong hands were on
him, covering his mouth and pulling him deeper
into the woods.

"Do not struggle," the voice whispered fiercely.
"I will set you free in a moment. But you must
be quiet."

Dalin ceased his struggling in time to see a column of armed guards file close by the spot they had
just vacated, but still outside the tree line. Their
spotlamps brightly lit the ground before them in a
precise, mowed swath.

When they had passed, the voice said, straight
and clear into Dalin's ear, "We have little time. They

will be back within minutes. We have to hide your passing."

The strong hands let him go, and Dalin tried to make out the features of his companion as the two of them scurried back to the site of the tunnel portal; but the light was bad and he dared not shine his handlight.

Impatient with Dalin's attempts at cover, the other finally pushed him away and expertly brushed dirt, pine needles, and leaves over the spot; soon it looked as it must have before.

"They will not see it," the stranger said, nodding in satisfaction. He looked quickly at Dalin, who saw sharp features.

"We must go," the stranger said.

Dalin followed the other deep into the woods, trying to keep up in the near dark. They proceeded for perhaps a kilometer before the stranger stopped, laying his hand on Dalin's chest to check his progress.

"All right," the other said, his whisper a bit louder. "It is time for you to change."

Bending to study the bole of a tree, the stranger produced a bundle of clothing which he thrust into Dalin's hands.

"Do it quickly, and give me what you have on." Seeing the king's hesitation, the other said, "*Quickly!*"

Dalin stripped in the darkness, pulling on an uncomfortable ensemble, of whose nature he had not a clue. He could be dressed as a jester or mountaineer, for all he knew of the baggy pantaloons, large blouse, and other strange items he was being forced to don. When finished slipping into a pair of odd boots which nonetheless fit him, he gathered his original clothing and put it into his companion's hands.

"I feel like a circus performer!" Dalin said.

The other laughed. "Worse than that, my friend," he said, pushing something into Dalin's hands that felt like the pelt of an animal. "Put it on."

"Where?"

"Your head!" the other said, laughing, and dropped Dalin's clothing to help him adjust the wig to his cranium. In a moment, the truth had dawned on the king.

"I am dressed as a girl!"

"A woman!" the other said with a laugh. "And though I can't see you very well, I'd say you're a mighty ugly one at that!"

"I will not—" Dalin blustered, moving to remove the wig—but the stranger's hard grip held him fast.

"Listen to me once," the stranger said. "If you do not wear it, you will die. And not by my hand, but by those of your own people. If you do not follow my every instruction, that fate will befall you. And before the sun has risen. Do you understand?" the stranger spoke fiercely, giving a slight twist to Dalin's arm.

Dalin let his breath out slowly. "Yes," he said.

"Good." The stranger nodded. Then, in the darkness, Dalin made out a grin on the other's face.

"My, but you *do* make an ugly woman." The stranger laughed before gathering Dalin's clothing into a new bundle and dropping it where the other had been.

When they left the small wood, Dalin's real fear began.

Here was a place he did not know. These were his people, and yet he knew little of them and little more of their city. From the palace, Nairobi was a colorful place, steeped in four thousand years of history, a blending of the ancient and the modern, one of the few tourist meccas left on earth. Its zoos, brilliant arboretums, and ancient African ruins made it a must-see place for any visitor; and its financial institutions made it the money capital of the planet. Most of Afrasia's economy was centered in Nairobi; its governors met in session in its Grand Capitol building, a monument of modern architecture which Dalin's father had built only forty years before. Its polished dome, grand colonnades, and sweeping arches recalled an earlier time on Earth and never failed to provoke comment in visitors accustomed to clear tall spires—or, in the case of Martian visitors, the wan pale tones of sandstone and pyrite.

Nairobi's opera was the finest on the planet and rivaled only that of Lowell for dominance on the Four Worlds; its symphony was only bested by those in Cairo and Peking, though the recent signing (some said stealing) of the Cairo Philharmonic's

great conductor promised that in the near future
the Nairobi Symphony might hold that crown.

But it was a place unknown to Dalin Shar.
Though he had visited the opera house and symphony hall, though he had toured the Goodall Zoo
and the last animal preserve left on Earth, the
Zambire Range—where two lions still roamed free
and the last rhinoceros, artificially conceived twenty
years ago, splashed its bulk through its own watery
grounds—Dalin knew nothing about the streets of
the city. He had never been *on* the streets of Nairobi, traveling always in small shuttles from palace
to destination point, then back again.

And here he was, at the edge of it.

What struck him at first was the smell. As his
companion led him out of the trees and then quickly
over a small stretch of open parkland, past a quaint
set of children's outside play toys—including an ancient steel swing set and a contraption with a ladder
leading to a smooth corkscrewing slider—and
through an entry in a low chromium wall, Dalin was
struck by the city's particular smell. It smelled like
. . . dirt and life. At the palace, surrounded by roses
and fresh trees and, in the colder months, the scent
of pine and spruce trees which had been planted
hundreds of years before and now grew in a thick
ring around the grounds, the odors of the faraway
city never penetrated. Dalin's entire life had seemed
perfumed; even the human sweat from a game of
old rugby or ten shot would be washed away almost

instantly in prepared baths of rose petal and jasmine.

But here there was no rose smell, no jasmine— only the raw smell of human sweat and work. Even at this deep hour of the night there was traffic, both human and machine; tens of pedestrians hurried between buildings in walkways or down on the street; and road walks and the occasional brightly lit closed tram were occupied by scattered passengers.

"Is it always this crowded?" Dalin asked in wonder.

His companion's features now became apparent for the first time. Under the night lights of the city, his face was shadowed and sharp: a nose like a knife blade; slitted, careful eyes; and a thin-lipped mouth that now turned up in a grin.

"In the daytime we would have to wait in line," he said with a laugh.

"I don't believe it."

The other said, "Believe it. And follow me now or we will be stopped. They are confining their search to the palace grounds at the moment, but that will quickly change."

And so Dalin Shar was given a quick night tour of his own capital city: streets like labyrinths, with buildings so close on either side that Dalin felt closed in; modern buildings side by side with ancient structures of brick and even wood; walkways so high they made Dalin dizzy looking up at them;

and the constant hum of activity and life, and the smells. . . .

"This is marvelous," Dalin said in wonder.

"Better for you not to speak," his companion said, tensing at a crossroads. He restrained Dalin with a hand; then, to Dalin's amazement, he slipped that hand around the king's shoulder and drew him near, pinching Dalin's neck from behind.

"Put your head down," he hissed.

Dalin did as he was told, briefly catching a glimpse of a caravan of police vehicles, sleek black silent machines, gliding in front of them; inside were vague dark shapes.

Through all this his companion acted in the oddest fashion, kissing the top of Dalin's wigged head, acting drunkenly and loudly proclaiming words of love.

When the procession had passed, Dalin was set free, and his companion gave him another sharp grin. "Why, you're not so ugly after all!"

Dalin scowled, but already they were crossing the thoroughfare and continuing their walk.

Eventually their feet took them into sections of the city where the streets were not so congested and the buildings not at all tall. The smells were even more repugnant here, the lights dimmer, the structures older and less well cared for. And, for the first time, Dalin saw rubble in the streets: an abandoned vehicle, its plastic shell pitted and scored with what appeared to be burn marks, its windows missing; an

open container of refuse, giving off a foul tartness
which overrode the other smells; pieces of broken
furniture piled in front of one building like so many
abandoned toys. Looking up, Dalin saw that the sky
was lightening; and, off in the distance, there was
the constant sound of sirens.

"We're there," Dalin's companion said, as if reading the question in his mind. They turned abruptly
into the doorway of one structure huddled in a line
of disreputable hovels. Dalin's escort pushed him
into dimness ahead, checking the street up and
down before following the king inside—

—where hands fell on Dalin, pulling him into a
deeper gloom.

"Is this him?" a screeching voice demanded. "Is
this really him?"

"There isn't time to talk," Dalin's chaperon said.
"Take him upstairs."

A handlight was abruptly shone in Dalin's face,
whereby the screeching voice began to laugh.

"Gawd! He looks worse than me, he does! What
have you done to him, Erik?"

"I did what had to be done."

"Girlied him up, you have! Gawd!"

The light beam was pulled away from Dalin's
face, leaving him blinking; it was shone deliberately
by the screeching person up into its own face.

"What do you think of this, Your *Majesty*?" The
screeching creature laughed.

Dalin's vision cleared, giving him a start: a face
that was not a face at all, but a metal bowl, scored

and scorched like the burned vehicle Dalin had seen outside—with holes through which two human eyes protruded whitely, and a mouth whose two red lips pushed out of the bowl altogether.

"Ho! Surprised, he is! Wait until he sees himself, then!"

Sighing with impatience, Erik turned on another handlight and said, "I'll take him upstairs myself!"

"Whatever!" The screeching creature laughed, pushing Dalin toward his erstwhile guide. "I've got to tend to the cooking anyways!"

Erik took Dalin firmly by the arm and escorted him to a stairwell against the near wall; the steps were planked with wood, and missing in spots.

"Watch your step," Erik said, urging the king ahead of him, tightening his grip when Dalin sought to step on a place where no stair existed.

Downstairs, Dalin heard the screeching creature singing to itself and banging metal against metal.

At the top, Erik held the king in place and shone the light to the right, down a hallway. The planking in the hall, at least, looked sturdy. There were three doors in a row on the left, all with ancient knobs, and Dalin was brought to the first one; Erik knocked lightly.

"Come in!" a voice called.

Erik opened the door and nudged Dalin in ahead of him.

"Ah! Here already! Any problems?"

There was dim light in this room, courtesy of dawn outside, which shone heroically through a sooted window at the back. In the room was a chair, a bedstand and a bed itself, from which rose a man naked but for a pair of briefs; he had been reading and tossed his hand Screen on the bed as he rose to shake Dalin's hand.

"Your Majesty! Welcome!"

He had the overabundant manner of a performer, and Dalin merely nodded, not taking the proffered hand; courtesy dictated that this lowly, undressed fellow had no right to familiarity with anyone such as Dalin Shar.

"Oh, well," the man said, not losing his smile. Suddenly he bent forward and kissed Dalin hotly on the cheek. "Where are my manners, anyway? A lady needs *kissing,* not hand-shaking!"

The undressed man laughed, and Erik suppressed a smile.

"Don't mind our friend Porto here, Sire," Erik said. "He is crude, boorish, often drunk, and always unchaste, but he will help you to stay alive."

Porto bowed, sweeping one hand in a gallant gesture. "At your service, my queen."

A new figured appeared in the doorway; a dour young man with hooded eyes.

"They're sweeping the nearby streets," he said. He glanced briefly at Dalin, and there was no friendliness in the look. "They found his clothing before it could be retrieved."

"Damn," Erik said. Quickly he nodded his head. "Very well."

Suddenly even Porto was all business. "Onto the bed, please, Your Majesty," he demanded.

"What—"

"Listen to him," Erik said, the fierce urgency his voice had assumed earlier in their relationship returning, "as you did to me. Your life depends upon it."

Dalin did as he was told, reclining on the bed as Porto thrust two pillows beneath his head. The performer stood studying the king as if he were a picture, before retrieving a third pillow from beneath the bed and propping Dalin's wigged head on it.

Porto fussed with the wig, and with Dalin's tunic—and then abruptly yanked the king's boots off, followed by his bloomers.

"How dare you—"

The King was given a warning glance from Erik, who had produced further objects from beneath the recliner, including a battered metal case and a protuberant thing with straps.

The young man with hooded eyes reappeared in the doorway. "I'd hurry," he said. "You have twenty minutes, if we're lucky."

"And we're never lucky!" Porto said with a flourish, barking a laugh at the end. He was fumbling with the protuberant device, loosening the straps before thrusting the apparatus, which looked like a plastic hump, onto the king's bared belly.

"Turn on your side, Majesty, and let me tighten the straps," Porto said, not waiting for Dalin to respond, but pushing him roughly over and pulling the straps from underneath to attach them to their counterparts on the other side of the hump.

"Now onto your back again," he ordered, pulling the king over until he lay bedridden again.

Dalin's anger at this rough treatment exploded. "What are you doing to me?" he shouted.

Porto froze in mock surprise. "My God!" he said, standing up straight and putting the back of one hand to his forehead. "She does not know! How can this be?"

"I repeat! What are you doing to me?"

Porto ignored the king, bending now to study Dalin's legs, from his ankles up to his thighs.

"Erik, I'll need that . . . *thing* from the case," he said, pointing impatiently at an instrument in the opened metal case, which Erik removed and handed to him.

"Now, this may hurt a bit, Your Majesty," Porto began, turning on the device, which hummed like a happy bee.

"*Wait!*" Dalin shouted. He sought to rise, but found that he was floundered, beached like a huge animal, caught under the weight and awkwardness of the hump attached to his stomach.

Porto switched off the device, just as the hooded-eyed young man's voice called out, "Hurry up, damn you!"

Erik snapped at Porto, "Give him the short version."

Porto, dramatically serious now, bent over to glare

into the king's face and said, "To put it simply, Sire, you are *pregnant*. In about five minutes, you will have a baby, and you will make a good show of it or the men who come in here will raser you and us on the spot. When I say push, you will push with all your might, as if this appendage on your belly had a real child within it. You will give a performance worthy of awards. I will now shave your legs."

Before Dalin could utter a word, Porto had switched on the instrument in his hand back on and turned to use it on the king's ankles.

"Hold still, Sire!" Porto admonished brightly. "I wouldn't want to cut you!"

The razor slid high up the inside of one leg, then the other; Dalin gave two squeals of protest but kept still.

"That's the way, my liege!" Porto shouted. "We'll make a fine woman of you yet!"

Finishing, Porto tossed the razor to Erik, who thrust it into the case, from which Porto now pulled a makeup kit; with deft fingers he applied powder to the king's legs, then a touch of rouge and lipstick to his features.

Porto made a face and said, "Still ugly—but now at least you look female."

"They're coming!" the voice from the doorway warned.

Downstairs, Dalin heard a loud knocking on the door and a high-pitched squeal from the thing with the metal face.

Porto splashed his hands with a red substance and then, as Erick gathered the makeup materials into the case and thrust the case beneath the bed, Porto quickly pulled a gown with bloody sleeves and a high collar from beneath the recliner and climbed into it; placing a bloody cap upon his head, he was instantly transformed into a birth-giver.

"Give me the baby!" Porto demanded, and as something was placed into his hands he leaned over, pushing up and spreading Dalin's legs and shoving the thing in his hands up against the king's privates, which nearly made him yelp.

On the stairs there came tramping, loud voices, the screeching thing's protest; Dalin glanced quickly over to the doorway to see the young man with the hooded eyes step quickly into the room, his face suddenly filled with mock concern.

Porto whispered, "Look at me, moan, and *push!*"

For incentive, Porto took a section of Dalin's inner thigh between two fingers and twisted it.

"Ohhhhhhhhh!" Dalin said.

"That's it!" Porto shouted, shoving the thing in his hands hard between Dalin's legs. "I can see the head! Push!"

Dalin strained, making his face red; suddenly he felt as if he *were* giving birth, and his moans became loud and real, his pushing genuine.

In his effort he could see little; but there were sounds in the room, rough voices, and then a slight glimpse from the corner of his eye of a hard face in a dark helmet, peering close.

"Ugh," the face said, turning away. "Looks the way my old lady did."

"Nothing for us here," the same voice said a moment later, as Dalin continued to cry out and push, his eyes filled with tears now.

He continued to strain, even as Porto's voice, filtering through the pain, said, "It's all right! You can stop!"

The pressure was removed from Dalin's middle; and suddenly he did stop, breathing hard, feeling the flush recede from his face as laughter broke out in the room.

"Behold!" Porto cried, climbing up from between Dalin's legs and holding up the bloodied head of a child's doll, which he manipulated with his clever fingers, making it look real. "I give you the new king!"

Even the dour young man with hooded eyes, who had retreated to his post in the doorway, began to laugh.

Laughing himself, Porto bent back down over Dalin and shoved the severed toy head into the crook of his arm, cradling it there.

"Your child, Sire! Congratulations!"

The king's own laughter blossomed with the others'.

After a moment, Erik approached the bed, smiling his approval, and said, "Congratulations *are* in order, Your Majesty. You *have* given birth today. To your own life!"

14

"It never ceases to amaze me," Prime Cornelian said, "how dank your tastes are."

Sam-Sei, Machine Master, merely grunted.

"You realize, of course, that you are the only creature alive on the Four Worlds who can grunt at me and live," Prime Cornelian said.

Again Sam-Sei grunted, without cognizance of humor.

Prime Cornelian laughed, and now shook his insect's head.

"The driest of the Four Worlds," he said, continuing to chuckle, "and you manage to find a damp place in it. I am astounded."

Prime Cornelian swiveled his head to take in the subterranean chambers where the Machine Master worked. There was almost no light, a bit of natural illumination leaking in through four horizontal slits, one set at the top of each wall, meekly adding to the bare artificial light washing across the high ceiling. This left the damp chamber in levels of shadow. The sandstone walls were driveled with dampness.

The chamber was filled with equipment from five or six ages; some of it looked like museum relics, collections of old beaten metals, ancient parts and dials and switches mingled with sleek field generators, a wall prognosticator, the remnants of failed new technologies and dreams yet unborn. The floor was a tangle of old optical cables thick as wrists, broken parts, rodent leavings. The quiet scurrying of the small animals was just evident, off in the corners.

Prime Cornelian tsked. "As I said, astounding."

"There's nothing astounding about it," Sam-Sei replied after a moment in his gravelly, low, considered, always-serious voice. "It's merely that one of the Syrtis aquifers happens to run beneath this property. The builders did not know it, I'm sure, when this sandstone monstrosity was built."

Prime Cornelian ran a thin fingertip across the wall, making a metallic sound and producing a tiny drop of moisture, which hung off the metal nail before falling.

"And yet you prefer it down here in the bowels of Mars."

"I prefer the lack of attention," Sam-Sei answered immediately, as if the question had been foolish.

"Indeed," Prime Cornelian said. He produced another tiny drop of water from the wall, then flicked his long finger to disgorge it. Immediately to his left stood a rank of thickly metaled cabinets, filled with fluid; in one of them, fronted with thick, now-darkened glass, stood suspended Cornelian's former,

human body, grotesquely twisted in the last throes
of Puppet Death.

The thought of it made something turn sour deep
within the recesses of his mechanical carcass.

"You wish to view it?" Sam-Sei said idly, without malice.

"No," Cornelian answered. He turned his full attention to Sam-Sei, whose back was still to him.
"I'm told you have something to show me."

"Yes," Sam-Sei said simply.

"Show it to me now."

The tone of authority was direct and obvious, and
yet Sam-Sei still took his time in turning around.
Prime Cornelian had yet to decide if the man, who
always acted in this fashion, was entertaining conscious contempt in such gestures, or if his mind was
merely not capable of tearing itself from whatever
problem was in front of him. Prime Cornelian preferred the latter explanation, though he imagined
that at some point in the future he would become
truly angry rather than amused, which would, of
course, end Sam-Sei's life.

Prime Cornelian was about to say something
when Sam-Sei turned around.

His appearance was always startling, and it occurred to Prime Cornelian briefly—though inconse-
quentially, since Prime Cornelian had long ago
given up vanity as one of the weaker vices—that the
Machine Master might act toward the rest of creation the way he did out of self-loathing of his own
image. His thin visage was unnaturally ugly, the

forehead grossly high back to a balding pate of lank,
long yellow-gray hair which always appeared in need
of both cutting and washing. His skin was wan, almost sallow, though more white than yellowish, and
deeply pocked, especially around the eyes and in
the sunken cheeks, with another nest of pit marks
in the hollow of his throat above the Adam's apple.
His eyes were sunk in hollows and were a brackish
color, the whites bleeding sickly into the irises.

But it was his mouth, where the lips had been
snipped away, that made him most grotesque. In
some sense it might also explain his somber tone of
voice, which contrasted so vividly with his perpetual, horrid, bad-toothed, uncontrollable smile.

The rest of his body, now covered with a simple
frock coat, was nearly as horribly maimed, acid-
burned, and grotesque as his face, Prime Cornelian knew.

It had led Prime Cornelian once, and only once,
to ask the Machine Master why he had not changed
his appearance; had not altered it to suit his mood
or—that word again—vanity; had not, in short, performed the same sorts of metallic procedures on
himself that he had performed on Prime Cornelian.

"I have no vanity," Sam-Sei had said, "only
humility."

Understanding neither, Prime Cornelian had let
the matter drop.

"Yes," the Machine Master said now, "I do have
something to show you."

Prime Cornelian raised two of his hands and

brought them together with anticipated satisfaction. "Well, then?"

Sam-Sei turned his back once more, which nearly filled Prime Cornelian with the kind of rage that might make him one day tear the Machine Master limb from limb. But the pause was only momentary, as Sam-Sei hit an ancient switch. There was a pause, and then a thin, rodlike shimmer of light in the middle of the room between Prime Cornelian and Sam-Sei, and then—nothing.

"*Well?*" Prime Cornelian said. He pointed at the long bar of light, stretching six feet up from the floor. "Is this what you have to show me—a bar of light?"

Sam-Sei did not turn around. Finally he said, "Hardly that."

"Then—"

The rod of light broadened and deepened into three-dimensionality. It took on a soft, fiery outline, indistinct hands, arms, legs, two booted feet. The head was oval and smooth, featureless, hatless.

"All right, then," Prime Cornelian said, fascinated but still mildly annoyed. "A *man* of light."

"Not just a man," the Machine Master said. He turned, giving Prime Cornelian that mild shock at his appearance again. He held a thin wafer of metal, something on which he manipulated.

Quick as lightning, the pale fiery figure flew across the room, passed Prime Cornelian, and drove itself into a far corner. In a moment there was another streak of light past Prime Cornelian, and the creature of light stood in its original position, calmly holding four rodents by the tail, two in each hand.

Prime Cornelian clapped his two foremost hands, showing mock joy. "You've done it, Sam-Sei! After centuries of toil by countless thousands, you've built a better mousetrap!"

Unperturbed, Sam-Sei drew his hand over the metal wafer and the creature of light abruptly dropped the rodents.

"Perhaps not. . . ." Prime Cornelian said. But now as the long, thin, pinkish gray Martian rodents hit the floor, crouching stunned for a moment before starting to scurry off into the four corners of the room, the light-man, in four successive motions even quicker than those previously shown, moved into the four corners and then stood quietly back in his original spot.

"I still fail to see . . ." Prime Cornelian said, until he spied that the creature of light now held only the rodents' whiskered heads, neatly severed, in its hands.

"Ahh . . ." Prime Cornelian said.

"They cannot be stopped," Sam-Sei said slowly, in his low voice. "They will fight anywhere, under any conditions, in any weather, and require neither food, water, nor oxygen. They can use weapons, or not. Once given a foe, they will do whatever needs to be done until that foe is destroyed. They—"

Prime Cornelian, inwardly excited now, was scratching beneath his chin with a long metallic finger, showing mere interest. "But will they *obey*?"

Sam-Sei was already turning his back on Prime Cornelian, resting the metal wafer on his workbench top. For a moment he said nothing, as the light-creature continued to stand motionless, waiting.

"Sam-Sei, will they—"

"They will obey," Sam-Sei said. "I can produce a thousand of them with the equipment I now have. With more equipment, I can produce a million. They can be used here on Mars, where you are currently in need, or the equipment can be transported elsewhere, as required."

"Excellent!"

"But . . ." For perhaps the first time ever, Prime Cornelian sensed hesitation in the Machine Master's voice.

"What is it, Sam-Sei?"

There was further hesitation before the Machine Master turned his head, just enough to look straight into Prime Cornelian's face. "I ask only one thing. That you . . . allow me to *interview* Wrath-Pei."

Prime Cornelian could not catch his intake of breath. "You know that is imposs—"

"Nothing is impossible for you," Sam-Sei said evenly.

Feeling almost foolish with his protestations, but still overcome with the enormity of what he had just witnessed and the possibilities it opened to him, Prime Cornelian said, "I thought our agreement was that he stay on the Outer Planets—"

"And safe?" Sam-Sei said.

"Yes, and safe."

"I do not want him safe—any longer."

Prime Cornelian made a face near to an insect's frown. "This is something I will have to consider. Wrath-Pei is currently finding much success on Titan."

Turning his back again, Sam-Sei said, "It is all I ask—*Sire*."

Sam-Sei ran a lithe hand over the metal wafer and the light-creature abruptly winked out of existence. The four rodent heads fell to the floor and lay inert, one of them staring lifelessly, its whiskers askew, at Prime Cornelian, who continued to scratch at his chin, thinking partly at this moment of Sam-Sei's death and how to, one day, make it creative, but mostly of an army made of light. An army of better mousetraps.

15

From orbit, Carter Frolich watched a planet suspended between birth and death.

It sickened his stomach. Venus—his Venus—had been a planet crawling slowly, inevitably, beautifully, toward the realization of a centuries-old dream. A true twin of Earth was what it had been becoming. Not a mock simulacrum of the mother world, like Mars, whose lesser gravity, horribly ferric oxide-rich soil, stubbornly thin atmosphere, and just plain bad luck had reduced it to a lesser version of the real thing. Mars would always be Mars, even with a breathable atmosphere, growing (if thin) vegetation, running (thin again) water. It would always be red dust, pink sky, sandstone buildings. It would always be colonists who called themselves Martians. It would always be slightly angry, different, contrary, a place for certain types of men, men who perhaps *deserved* to be called Martians.

It would always be Mars.

But Venus had been different. It had been like working with the Creator's clay itself, not with a

finished planet that had once, eons ago, lived and
breathed on its own, only to die and then be resusci-
tated by man's terraforming. Venus, unlike Mars,
had never been born, never known the breath of life
that made water run, plants thrive, blue skies fill
the heavens like a bowl of flowers each dawn.

And Carter Frolich had been given the chance to
make that birth happen.

But now it was being taken away.

As the shuttle neared the surface, each sickening
sight was like the stab of a knife point through Frolich's heart. The view of each bright blue plasma
detonation tube was a desecration to the temple of
the terraforming station it was attached to. It had
taken him years to get those feeder stations built,
after years of getting them funded. In actuality, Carter Frolich had spent the entire first half of his life
doing nothing but smiling and asking for money,
pointing to the success of Titan as reason to proceed
with Venus. Titan was the experiment; Venus would
be the crown jewel of the Solar System. Earth's true
twin. In effect, a *new* Earth. After finally getting
that money, from any source he could on any of the
Four Worlds, Carter Frolich had planned to spend
the last half of his life spending it and making that
dream of a new Earth come true.

A potential nightmare now.

"Dr. Frolich, we'll be landing in a few moments,
sir."

Frolich ignored the earnest voice of the earnest
young man standing behind him as here came the

last straw: the sight of the nearest feeder station, the large facility near Diana Chasma, which rose up as they descended, giving him an all too graphic look at the evil blue plasma tube attached to it, looking like an unused booster rocket. If triggered, it would turn the station it clung to into a mass of twisted metal, powdered concrete, and partial planetary death, punching a brown, acidic hole in an atmosphere already ripening with oxygen and nitrogen. If all of those plasma tubes detonated . . .

He turned away in disgust and sat himself heavily in his chair.

"Sir?" the young man, whose face was as earnest as Frolich had imagined under his uniform cap, said. "I'll have to ask that you strap yourself in now."

Looking away from the young man's scrubbed face, Frolich idly pulled the seat belt over his waist and locked it.

"Thank you, Dr. Frolich," the earnest young man in uniform said, and then wisely retreated out of the small, dimly lit passenger cabin and into the crew's chamber.

Taking a heavy breath, Frolich looked down at his hands, which were shaking.

All of it will be gone.

That was not quite true, of course. Venus was still here and would absorb any thousands of plasma explosions that might be inflicted upon it. But without the continuing puff of the feeder tubes, which had been working without pause for twelve years now, it wouldn't be long before the planet reverted to its former state: a super-heated, super-dry, super-dead world with a punishing atmosphere, murderous surface pressure, and a thick permanent blanket of choking clouds that rained liquid sulfuric acid onto the bleached surface.

Not the half-green, birthing world it was today, with shallow lakes and oceans filed with crystalline water and genetically adapted fish, budding forests of fir trees healthier than those in the Cascades on Earth had ever been, orchids grown in natural hothouse conditions on the planet's southern hemisphere, a thousand other bits and pieces that were coming together to make a new world, a real Venus, a new Earth—

And now, possibly back to sulfur and death.

Because of war.

Carter Frolich found himself weeping, at first quietly and then in a full-fledged jag, trembling hands covering his face. This had happened many times recently—at an alarming rate, actually—to the point where he was afraid he was losing his mind. He knew now how any parent who loses a child would feel, and he knew that in his own case he would find it unbearable. Recently he had caught himself staring at his image in the mirror during his morning shave, and suddenly realized that he didn't know who he was staring at. A stranger was looking back at him—someone unknown and unknowable, a ghost whose heart had been ripped out. A week ago he had awakened in a glass tube elevator, a relic in a Cairo museum, from a reverie he didn't remember going into, and had no idea how long he had been on the device or how he had gotten there. Then, for no reason he could fathom, he had continued to take the elevator up and down, from top floor to bottom and back again, until it was time for the museum to close. Luckily, a sympathetic guard, recognizing him, had helped him home.

But all this was something he didn't think about and certainly tried not to show, for the sake of his planet. His Venus. Because he was the only man, on any of the Four Worlds, with a chance to save Venus and make it the Fifth.

Before Council hearings on Earth, in early Senate speeches on Mars before Prime Cornelian's power had coagulated into iron rule, before Titan's Ruling Elect and the City Council on Pluto's budding Tombaugh City, Carter Frolich had tirelessly made his case, at first for continuing with the transformation of Venus (Frolich considered the term *terraforming* a Martian term, a label of failure), and then for the salvation of Venus itself. Even after silence had descended on Mars he had continued his dialogue and, though technically illegal, continued it to this day.

And here he was, back on Venus, with nothing so far but failure to show for his efforts.

While his planet waited to die.

And he lost his mind.

"Sir?"

Carter Frolich came out of this most recent episode and for a moment did not know where he was.

Was he back on that elevator, riding up and down, staring out through ancient, time-etched glass at his world going from top to bottom? Was he somewhere he had never been before, having arrived by a means unknown to him, for a meeting he knew nothing about? Was he in his own bathroom back on Earth, bloodying his hands on shards of his broken shaving mirror after an attempt to make that unknown man staring back at him go away?

No. He was . . . here. On an intershuttle, about to land on his beloved planet—and the earnest young man was back, standing over him, to make sure he was still strapped in, hadn't wandered over to the waist-high window again to stare out.

Carter looked at his hands, which were now resting quietly on the armrests of his chair. They were not trembling, and he was not crying, nor were there any signs of his jag. The tears had dried on his face, and he knew where he was.

He softened his features and looked up mildly at the young man, whose eyes, Frolich now noticed, were light blue under his cap.

"Thank you, Lieutenant . . . Jaeger, isn't it?"

The young man brightened at the recognition from a great man.

"Yes, Dr. Frolich, it is."

"Very good. We'll be landing in a moment, I take it?"

"Yes, sir. The retros are about to fire now. Just wanted to make sure you were comfortable, sir."

Frolich smiled benignly, put out a hand to pat

the young man's arm. He wondered how the young man's parents would feel to lose their child. "I'm just fine, son. Done this a thousand times. Is that a hint of Earth German accent I pick up in your voice?"

"Yes, sir." The lieutenant's smile widened. "Munich, sir. At least my parents grew up there. I was raised in Tripoli, myself."

"Ah."

The young man, still beaming, retreated from the passenger cabin; in a moment the door to the crew chamber, filled with brighter lights than the passenger area, closed.

After another few moments, Frolich felt the thump and then whining groan of the retro-rockets slowing the ship down for landing at Tellus Station.

Ignoring the protesting sway of the ship against gravity, Frolich unlocked his seat belt and stood, making his way to the window.

In the far distance, near the green-speckled horizon, the split tops of the belch tubes at Diana Chasma were just visible, before disappearing behind the rising yellow concrete towers of Tellus.

The ship gave a little lurch to one side, then the other as it settled toward its bay.

Unsteadily, Carter Frolich made his way back to his chair and restrapped himself in for landing.

His hands began to tremble again, and he felt the push of tears into his eyes; but he remembered that man he had seen in his shaving mirror before smashing it, the man he didn't recognize—the man who had so calmly talked to Lieutenant . . . what's-his-name from . . . where? just a few moments ago.

By the time the intershuttle had come to rest, his hands were steady again and his smile back in place, and he remembered the lieutenant's name again.

16

On his wedding day, Jamal Clan finally, reluctantly, sought his mother's help.

"She will not listen to me! And she says she would rather die than marry me!"

Standing outside Tabrel's locked door with her kit of potions, flanked by two guards, Kamath Clan said, "You must leave me with her now."

"No! I will stay with her! I want to see what you do to her!"

Jamal's singsong voice, risen in such panic, made him sound ineffectual and, indeed, unstable.

"You are overly worried, Jamal," Kamath Clan said. She opened her hand, palm up, to show two pale violet tablets. "These will help you to be as you should be on your wedding day."

Wide-eyed, Jamal shrunk back in terror. "No! I won't take your poison!" He looked at the locked door. "And I won't let you give it to her! I've changed my mind, Mother!"

Coolly, Kamath shook her head.

"You've done the right thing, Jamal. I will handle things now."

Kamath made a quick motion with her head and the two guards approached, taking a firm grip on Jamal.

"Help him dress," the queen ordered. "And give him these." She thrust the two pills into the nearest guard's hand, looking sternly into his face.

"Make sure he swallows them."

The guards bowed and began to drag an hysterical Jamal Clan away between them.

"Mother! Please!"

"Don't worry," Kamath said, unlocking the door. "I will make everything right."

"You've greatly disappointed my son," Kamath Clan said. "He may be foolish to have fallen in love with you—but love is beside the point. There will be a wedding today."

"Not without my assent," Tabrel said defiantly.

"That is where you are wrong," Kamath Clan answered in a toneless voice. "The union is legal and will proceed—one way or another."

On the floor, Kamath Clan carefully opened an ancient wooden case. Inside, cradled in blue velvet, were bottles of various make: heavy and thin glass, dull and polished metal. Tabrel saw a smoky green bottle labeled "Obedience," a slim red carafe designated "Truthfulness"; there was a pewter decanter entitled "Affability," and a blackened bottle called

"Death." A clutch of silver syringes were labeled "Sleep."

Kamath Clan withdrew a thin rosy liquid in a clear tube, unstoppered it with care, and held it out toward Tabrel.

"This is a mixture of many things. Imbibe."

Tabrel nearly laughed. "Do you think I'm foolish?"

"No, not at all."

With a movement like a huge cat, Kamath Clan now hovered over Tabrel. The woman's sudden grip was like being caught by a cold iron machine. Kamath Clan's horrid visage filled Tabrel's sight; and now she felt her lips being pried apart, the vial of rosy liquid drawing near.

Tabrel tried to fight, to clamp her mouth shut. But she found she did not have the strength to resist. Kamath Clan pinched the back of her neck, jammed the vial against her opening mouth, and upended its contents.

A thin line of burning cold traced Tabrel's throat.

It blossomed within her, and she felt tentacles of shadow reach out from within and fly to the extremities of her body.

Abruptly, she was not herself.

She wanted to scream, but her lips would not obey, and what's more, they did not wish to obey.

"Now, my dear," said Kamath Clan, "shall we get dressed for your wedding to my son?"

"Yes!" Tabrel's radiant face smiled as she reached a hand that was no longer hers to caress a silken lilac gown, whose folds were as soft as butter, which Kamath Clan, smiling also, held out for her inspection.

It was a wedding such as Titan had never seen.

Bathed in beautiful lights of rose and dim green, the Temple of Faran Clan—the secular philosopher of the end of the twenty-first century, known as the Moral Guide, whose teachings had blossomed with the blossom of colonization of other worlds—had never beheld such a ceremony. It was Faran Clan who had taught the importance of ritual and ceremony: that balance within the soul and body can only be attained by balance outside the flesh; that the human being needs these things for true attainment of peace. After the Religious Wars on Earth in the middle 2100s, his lessons, after a slow beginning, had grown, finding more fertile ground on some settled worlds than on others. It was Faran Clan's own son, Pen Clan, who had led the earliest settlers to Titan, after the beginnings of persecution on Earth and the movement's arid failures on Mars.

And ceremony was in evidence this day. The twin gothic spires of the temple, borrowed from the ancient religions, echoed with the chants of blessing and happiness, some of which the Moral Guide himself had written before his death. The pews were festooned with garlands, the air spiced with fir and pine and spices.

And also—for remembrance—with sulfur, from yellow Io, the Jovian moon.

And Jamal Clan, nervous as any bridegroom, stood fidgeting by the pulpit in front, his mind on fire with worry.

Until . . .

With the swelling of the mixed chant, the Chorus of Happiness, which signaled the appearance of the bride, all his doubt flew away like birds, and he was filled with sudden joy.

"Oh, Mother!" he exclaimed to Kamath Clan, who had made her way silently up the side aisle, provoking whispers and glances as always, to join her son. She nodded to various dignitaries, including Commander Tarn, who occupied a place of honor in the front pew.

For a moment Kamath's heart froze, thinking she had spied Quog among the crowd behind Commander Tarn—but it was only a young boy who had leaned his head sideways to rest it upon his mother's shoulder.

With effort, she resumed her duties of acknowledgment, then stood still beside Jamal.

There was a hush of expectation, and then singing voices rose, filling the vault with sound as Tabrel Kris—head high, face caressed with the barest of veils, her gown magnificent, a living flower, its train trailing like petals behind her—made her way in halting, imperious steps up the center aisle.

Jamal's eyes welled with tears.

"She is so beautiful!"

"This is true," Kamath said, the barest of emotions entering her words. "And finally, the houses of Clan and Kris will be joined."

"Yes!" Jamal said.

A precise three meters from Jamal, Tabrel Kris stopped, lowering her eyes.

Jamal, too, lowered his gaze.

Immediately the chanting stopped, leaving the temple in an echoing hush.

Tabrel raised her eyes slowly and spoke in a loud, strong voice:

"I, Tabrel Kris of Mars, do take you, Jamal Clan of Titan, with heart, mind, and soul, to be my wedded husband."

Jamal raised his eyes to meet hers. His heart was pounding within his breast.

He knew what was expected of him now, but he turned instead to look up at his mother, a sudden fear filling him at the sight of Tabrel's smile.

"Is she mine, Mother?" he whispered fiercely. "Is she really mine?"

His mother looked down emotionlessly. "She is yours. What part of her is not will follow."

Without hesitation, Jamal took a deep breath and stepped forward to lift, with gently trembling fingers, the veil from Tabrel's face:

"And I, Jamal Clan of Titan, do take you, Tabrel Kris of Mars, with heart, mind, and soul, to be my wedded wife!"

With abrupt, choking terror, he knew that something was not right within Tabrel's gleaming eyes. He saw another kind of terror deep within them.

But still, he took her two soft hands into his own, preparing to say, with her, the words that would lock them forever together.

The spices in the air intensified.

And then suddenly the smell of sulfur, a vague, unpleasant backdrop until now, became overpowering.

Vast plumes of yellow vapor roiled up the center aisle in a billowing cloud, overtaking Tabrel and Jamal and expanding to fill the temple. Sounds of choking filled the air.

With a mixture of anger and panic, Kamath Clan strode toward the side entrance of the temple and threw open the large doors. She lurched outside into artificially lit daylight, followed by the rest, all save Kamath wiping at their eyes and gagging.

The queen marched into clear air and looked back at the temple: Its clean, tall lines and twin spires pointing toward the heavens were enveloped in a yellow fog, made ghostly by the bright lights focused on the structure.

"Who dares to interrupt this service?" Kamath Clan roared.

Kamath Clan followed the line of the spires and looked upward.

Her breath caught in her throat.

There, barely illumined by the upward-reaching spotlamps, hung the belly of Wrath-Pei's huge ship. It covered the sky nearly from horizon to horizon, its sleek cone suspended like the hugest of toys on a string.

Commander Tarn, still fighting to regain his breath, staggered past; Kamath gripped his arm and pointed angrily upward. "What is *that* doing here?"

"My God," Tarn said, his jaw dropping open.

"You assured me our shield was inviolable!"

Tarn gaped from the gargantuan ship to the queen's visage. "It *is*!"

"Obviously that is not true!"

"I will go see—" Tarn said, attempting to break away.

"Tarn!" came a nearby voice, even colder than the queen's.

Tarn's knees instantly turned weak, and Kamath Clan had to support him.

Wrath-Pei's gimbaled and cushioned chair drew out of the thinning fog like a floating specter. Kamath knew that it was only a form of sloth that kept him in the chair—though he showed nothing of laziness in his body, which appeared in every way perfect, from the silver mane of hair swept back from his high forehead down through the sculpted cheeks, Roman visage, chiseled features, and commanding eyes, and on through the muscled, tight body, well-advertised through his tight black clothing.

Commander Tarn had turned the color of ash at Wrath-Pei's voice. "Y-Yes, Your Grace?"

Wrath-Pei smiled, lynxlike. "Why haven't you returned my calls? Hmmm?"

Tarn bowed. "I apologize, Your Grace. But with the wedding—"

Wrath-Pei clicked his attention from Tarn to the queen. "The wedding!" he said. "And why wasn't *I* invited?"

Choking back wrath and fright, Kamath Clan bowed and said, "An oversight, Your Grace. My underlings will be duly punished. They must have thought Your Grace was not available—"

"But of *course* I'm available—I'm *here*, aren't I?"

His grin widened, sending Tarn into a near swoon. "And I must say that it was not an easy thing to get here! It seems someone in Tarn's command— an *underling*, perhaps—left Titan's shield on at full capacity! Imagine! But, well—" he said, waving his hand as if in dismissal of unpleasant thoughts, "I'm here now, and that's the important thing. And on young Jamal Clan's wedding day! How glorious!"

He opened his hands in mild benediction in the direction of the temple, which was now becoming visible again through the dissipating yellow smoke.

"But first, before we resume the ceremony, there are a few matters to discuss," Wrath-Pei said earnestly. "You don't mind, do you?"

"Of course not, Your Grace," Kamath said.

By this time they were joined by Jamal Clan, who stood in near shock, staring at Wrath-Pei and his magical chair, and his new bride, Tabrel, who stayed back a step, with no expression on her face.

Wrath-Pei nodded toward the newcomers, yet spoke to Kamath Clan.

"Good. Good. It seems that my old friend Prime Cornelian, who now fancies himself something called High Leader—" Wrath-Pei paused to chuckle, "anyhow, Prime Cornelian has taken it into his head that he would very much like me to return this young lady, here"—Wrath-Pei lifted a finger to point at Tabrel—"to her native Mars. In fact, he's very insistent on this matter."

"No!" Jamal blurted out, earning him the sternest of glares from his mother.

Wrath-Pei laughed. "A boy in love! How charming and rare! However," he continued, his expression thoughtful, "this is what my colleague, the 'High Leader,' demands."

There was silence for a moment until Wrath-Pei blew out his breath softly. "However, I don't believe I'm willing to do that. Because I'm afraid that the High Leader has something nefarious in mind for young Tabrel Kris. And, being a moral man, I don't believe it would be the right thing to do."

Kamath Clan had to restrain her son from throwing himself at Wrath-Pei's feet.

Wrath-Pei showed a slight smile. "Consider it . . . one of my wedding presents," he said.

"Thank you, Your Grace!" Jamal said, breaking out into sobs and stepping back to clutch Tabrel.

"By the way, is she . . . awake?" Wrath-Pei said, studying Tabrel.

"Yes . . ." the Queen said, and when Wrath-Pei caught her eye, he winked.

"I see. . . . Anyhow, I feel we should all get back to the wedding, after I cover one small detail. In fact, I'll need to speak to you about this in more detail privately, Tarn—but that chat can wait until after the ceremonies."

The color drained from Tarn's face.

"The basic point, though, is that I . . . believe we should approach the future security of Titan from a . . . different perspective, if you will. In fact, I believe *I* should be responsible for the protection of Titan from now on."

Wrath-Pei smiled congenially. "Agreed?"

Save for Tarn's gasp, there was silence.

Wrath-Pei clapped his hands. "Very well, then! And now, back inside the temple! There's a young man 'itchin' for hitchin','' as we used to say! But first, my *other* wedding present! Lawrence!" he commanded. "Come here!"

From out of the wispy remains of the yellow cloud limped a young boy. His eyes were masked by a helmeted visor; his arms, which ended in stumps, held a large boxy parcel covered with bright paper and ribbons which sparkled with self-generating light.

"A gift for the newlyweds!" Wrath-Pei said, motioning for Lawrence to deliver it.

When it was handed over into Jamal's arms, Wrath-Pei added, "Please! Open it now!"

After a nod from his mother, Jamal did as instructed. On tearing off the wrappings, he opened the thin metallic case within, then stood looking down dumbly at what appeared to be a human limb: an ankle and foot, shriveled by preservation and swaddled in oiled rags.

"Do you like it?" Wrath-Pei laughed brightly, pointing to Lawrence's left boot, which Jamal now saw was overly large, of a solid piece, lashed to the abruptly ended stump of the boy's lower leg.

"Think of it as a rabbit's foot—for good luck!"

17

On his fifth day as a woman giving birth, Dalin Shar was visited by Erik.

There had been three more visits by the authorities, two in the last day alone, prompting more birthing performances and necessitating that the king remain constantly in bed, ready for another performance at a moment's notice.

"It is no longer safe for you to be here," Erik said brusquely. Dalin had the feeling he was being brusque so that Dalin would not challenge him.

"I can't argue with you, Erik," the king said, patting his prosthetic womb. "I don't know how many more times I can give life to *that*." Dalin pointed to the rubber doll's head, splashed in fake blood, which lay propped on the bed table like a guillotined horror.

To Dalin's surprise, Erik completely ignored his levity.

"It has been decided that you will be transported elsewhere," Erik said, as if the king had not spoken. After a moment he added, "Offworld."

"Offworld! That is impossible! How am I to fight my enemies if I am not here? No—I won't hear of it!"

Erik now looked at him.

"It is not your decision, Your Majesty."

"Of course it is my decision! What you do for *me* is my decision! *I am your king!*"

Erik spoke slowly. "It has been decided that you would be safer in another place, off the Earth. I have been ordered to help that take place."

Dalin's voice rose to an indignant shout. "*Ordered? By whom? Who has decided these things?*"

"I am sorry, Sire," Erik said.

Behind Erik, an unsmiling Porto, along with the dour young man with hooded eyes, whose name Dalin had yet to learn, entered. The nameless man held a hypodermic tube firmly in one hand and now had a wry little smile on his face.

"Do what you must," Erik said, leaving the room as Porto took hold of Dalin's shoulders and held him firmly.

Raising the hypodermic, the dour man said, "Gladly."

Dalin awoke in darkness with a headache and a feeling of weightlessness, which was something he had never experienced. For a moment he panicked until he realized that he must be in the hold of a shuttle.

However, his explorations in the dark did not support this. His first discovery was stubble on his chin, which told him that he had been unconscious for a number of days. He seemed to be dressed in some sort of jumpsuit, which was secured with elastic bands to one side of the enclosure, keeping him from floating free.

After some fumbling he was able to undo the straps, which allowed him to explore his surroundings.

There was not much to find. He was enveloped in a hexagonal box, barely wider than his own height. Four of the six walls were perfectly smooth. One was recessed with what felt like a window covering, but which was impervious to his efforts to open it. The sixth proved fruitful, for it was encased with what felt like a Screen and which proved, indeed, to be just that.

When Dalin ran his hand over the engage strip, the screen blazed into life, blinding him.

"Low light!" he ordered, and the Screen immediately dimmed, giving him his sight back.

Floating before the square screen, Dalin quickly took in his surroundings once more, this time bathed in soothing amber light.

The box really was empty, save for two vents set in one of the other walls, and a lockbox secured in a corner of a second. Dalin was dressed in a common dun-colored jumpsuit, used by maintenance workers on all Four Worlds.

"Raise window," Dalin ordered.

The thin sleeve over the window slid up. Once again Dalin was blinded, this time by outside illumination. He thought he was faced by the sun for a moment, but as his eyes adjusted he soon realized that the blinding object outside his window was the illumined face of Earth's Moon.

"Repor—" Dalin began to say to the screen, but it suddenly came into life on its own.

A man Dalin had never seen before faced him on the screen. He was tall and solemn, dressed as one of Dalin's governors, in tunic and white ceremonial sash, though the emblem of his governorship was unknown to the king. The symbol was circular, with a large white flower, with centered delicate-looking petals.

"Who—" Dalin began, but the other cut him off. It was quickly apparent that this was not a live exchange, but that the other was represented by a recording.

The governor bowed, then straightened.

"Greetings, Sire, from your offworld provinces. I speak to you from the loyal colonies of Luna, who pledge eternal fidelity to your rule and to our planets, Earth and Moon."

Dalin mumbled sarcastically, "Is this where your eternal fidelity put me?"

The governor continued, "By now, you will be awake and, I trust, well rested. I apologize for the methods employed, but believe me, they were necessary for your safety. This will soon become apparent to you.

"By now, you will be in the orbit of Venus . . ."

For a few moments of shock Dalin did not listen

to the governor's words; he swiveled his head to the window to make sure that the Moon was, indeed, outside.

"Wrong world, my colonial friend," Dalin said.

". . . after a rendezvous near Earth's Luna, you were transferred to another cargo freighter bound for Venus. You may very well not be aware of the fact that the tiny colonies on the Moon have remained steadfastly loyal to Your Highness in the current crisis; I hope this provides some comfort to you. You will be transferred from Venus orbit in a matter of hours. If all goes to plan, you will spend the foreseeable future as the guest of our good friend Targon Ramir. When things have . . . quieted down on Earth, you will return to rule."

The governor bowed again. "I hope to speak with you soon in person, Sire. May your days be filled with blessings and peace."

The Screen blinked out to soothing amber once more.

"Wonderful," Dalin Shar said—but barely had the sarcasm left his lips than the blinding white light of Luna was eclipsed.

Dalin turned to the window.

"There's the answer to my question," he mumbled.

Close enough to touch, the blasted hulk of a freighter slid by. It had been hit repeatedly in the belly; gaping wounds showing torn metal, frayed cables, and burned innards speckled the ship's bottom, while the entire engine section floated separately near the freighter's stern, rotating in place as if about to dock. A seared black line marked where it had been cut by massive raser fire.

Floating free, like fireflies circling near a flame, were hundreds of hexagonal containers.

The dead freighter moved slowly past; before long it would slide out of sight, no doubt as Dalin's tiny orbit once again brought his enclosure between it and the Moon, which rose again hot and bright in the window.

"Screen," Dalin ordered, "replay battle events."

"That information is not available to me," Screen responded.

"Why not?"

"I have no recording capability," Screen said.

Dalin said, "Status report, then. Oxygen. In Earth days."

"There is approximately one point two days of usable oxygen," Screen responded.

A cold feeling gripped Dalin. "Is that all? What about reserve?"

"There is no reserve oxygen capability."

"Food and water?"

"There are rations for three meals; water capability is four liters."

Dalin turned to the lockbox, pulled up its lid, and found three meal containers and a medium-sized container of water.

"Screen," Dalin said, "what are rescue options?"

"That information is not available to me," Screen responded.

"Maneuverability?"

"Enclosure is nonmaneuverable. Currently it is in an orbit of point twenty-four days around nearby object. Orbit will decay in one point one days."

"*Decay?* What do you mean, decay?"

"Enclosure will come into contact with vertical area sixteen five three, horizontal area three six twelve, in one point one days."

"What in damnation does that mean?"

"It means—"

"Never mind! Show it!"

On the Screen, an exact model of the crippled ship outside appeared; a target area began to blink, outlined in red, and the view then closed in to show in detail how Dalin's enclosure would strike a sharply studded area just under the freighter's blackened nose in less than a day and a half—just before Dalin's oxygen was depleted and he began to choke on his own carbon dioxide emissions.

"Screen, what is the possibility of enclosure surviving impact?"

As the Screen answered, Dalin was given a visual clue; there was a flash in the window behind him, and as the Screen droned its answer, Dalin turned to see another hexagonal container hit an area near the freighter's broken tail. In a fraction of time, amid a blip of light, it was scattered into a thousand splinters. Almost instantly it was followed by another, which seemed to just brush up against the hull and immediately was torn to bits.

"Shut up, Screen," Dalin said, and Screen instantly returned to warm, comforting amber.

Outside, the dead freighter slipped out of sight. The Moon once more rose; huge, arid Tycho slid into view, its crater walls massively shadowed at this near distance. Barely a hundred miles from Tycho lay one of Earth's two small Lunar colonies. Though he tried, Dalin could not for the life of him remember much of what they looked like. He had been no more than nine or ten when he had last even heard them mentioned by Faulkner. There had been sharply etched pictures of a sharply etched place: jagged, stark whites, grays and blacks under a looming clear dome that stretched halfway to the horizon. The panels were impressively large, framed in thick black octagons. The soil itself looked bleached brown; and, in his studies, Dalin recalled one picture of a man standing proudly beside a single timid row of flowers, thin olive stalks bearing brittle white petals, sad, ugly little things like the one Dalin had seen on the governor's emblem.

Tycho slid majestically away, revealing other, smaller versions of itself: dead, black-etched bleakness, parched basalt, and useless—wasn't that why there were only two Lunar colonies?

Sickened by the Moon's dead whiteness, Dalin ordered Screen to shutter the window.

He was now bathed only in amber light.

Retrieving a food packet and the jug of water from the open lockbox, the king ate and drank, and tried not to think about the coming death that awaited him.

Hours later, Dalin was awakened from a light sleep by the sound of the Screen gently beeping.

Even opening his eyes, the king still felt happily drowsy. It was easy enough to get used to weightlessness; and it was easy enough to feel completely relaxed when one's body had no drag of gravity upon it. Perhaps he would just slip off into sleep, thinking perhaps of Tabrel Kris and that kiss in the garden that now seemed so far away, when this hexagonal box smashed into the nose of the dead freighter, scattering Dalin and his dreams into a thousand pieces.

Finding Tabrel's face in his memory and floating it before his closed eyes, Dalin once more sought to drift off to sleep—but the Screen's insistent beeping became even louder, finally rousing him from slumber to anger.

"Shut up!" he ordered.

The beep ended, but the Screen said, "There is a communications pattern that has crossed my sensors. Do you wish to monitor it?"

Instantly awake, Dalin said, "Yes."

An urgent voice abruptly arose from the blank screen: ". . . deadline has passed, Governor Marsden. Do you think—"

The answering signal was weaker, sounding far away with a slight crackle. It was the voice of the man who had addressed Dalin in the recording: "There is nothing left to think! Acron wouldn't dare follow up on his threat! Even Besh wouldn't stand for it—it violates every treaty ever signed between the Four Worlds! It would mean total war!"

The urgent voice replied: "Everyone's been squeezed into the shelter here, but I'm sure it wouldn't hold—"

"It would provide no protection at all! The shelter here was built to withstand a solar flare and nothing else! Yours is no better." There followed a grim laugh. "You would do better to squat down and stick your head between your ankles."

There was a moment of silence, and then the urgent voice, sounding resigned now: "Good luck, Governor."

"And good luck to you, Frey. Hopefully, this will all pass. That daughter of yours will play dolls with my daughter when we visit next month—"

The reception became garbled and then broke up completely. In another moment Dalin felt his enclosure rocked by a soundless wave, followed in quick succession by three others.

Voice subdued, Dalin Shar said to the Screen, "Open port."

The thin window Screen slid up.

With trepidation, Dalin maneuvered himself in front of it.

The white brightness of the Moon had been temporarily outshone by the remains of four explosion wakes. Two of them, closely spaced, radiated out like thinly spreading fans over Luna's limb. The other two were almost directly below him, beyond Tycho's rim, in the area where the second lunar colony had been. Here, the blast light moved up to the left of Dalin's hexagon, making a brilliant green streak, like a sickly, straightened-out rainbow in space.

Now there were two new craters below, black ugly acne scars, pitted and raw, down on the surface, side by side, smooth as sand within, the crater rim of one breaking into the second. Dalin fleetingly thought of a pair of ancient spectacles.

Where the colony had been there was a double hole.

Gradually, the beams dissipated, like contrails, and only Luna was left, with new scars, to dominate the sky.

Without prompting, the Screen said, "There is an update on our position."

"Give it to me."

The graphic illustration of the ghost freighter returned; the Screen zoomed in on the empty nose of the craft.

A slightly different area was highlighted in a red circle now, still pitted with angry-looking studs which would easily tear his fragile craft apart.

"Analysis of new orbit predicts collision with this section in one point eight days."

"Fine," Dalin muttered sarcastically.

The Screen returned to amber light.

The nearby blasts had knocked him askew in relation to the wrecked ship.

Now Dalin would suffocate before he was blasted to bits.

18

The High Leader was in a foul mood.

It was not the fact that he was forced to do this imminent broadcast, to show himself in every home on the planet. The necessity of that was bad enough—although he accepted its usefulness and was ready to calm the fears of all Martians and assure them that the path he had set them on was the best one, with illustrations of what had occurred at Shklovskii to make his arguments more cogent, of course.

What bothered him was, again, that nagging at the back of his cogitating mind, the itching feeling on the inside of his carapace that something was missing, that there was something out of place that he should be attending to.

But, as he ticked off the various components of his campaign, he found that, at this time, he was exactly where he wanted and hoped to be:

On Mars, the population was on the verge of being completely won over, minus their entire old form of governance and subject to the whims of a

new and seemingly omniscient ruler; with the bonus
of a fanatic core of red-shirted followers, ready to
carry out his cruelest wish and sharing his vision of
a Mars dominating the Solar System; with the added
bonus of a Machine Master so good at his job that
it made Cornelian want to hug instead of strangle
him.

On Earth, another stunned population was under
the rule of a puppet government, ascendant through
coup d'état; their usefulness to Cornelian was
proven by Acron's immediate willingness to use the
Machine Master's impact weapon on his own people
on Luna. Though Besh himself, horrified by the
plan, would have to be monitored, Earth was a vir-
tual nonentity on the stage at the moment; the fact
that Dalin Shar was missing was at best a minor
annoyance.

On Venus, a war was in waiting, with everything
lining up as it should; the one problem would be to
keep the engineer Targon Ramir from blowing up
his own creation. But things were growing toward
readiness.

And Titan.

The High Leader felt a momentary clutch of
anger in his core, a dyspeptic burning in his metal
innards. He had never considered Wrath-Pei to be
much of a threat; when he was a senator, before
his . . . indiscretions forced his ouster and eventual
banishment from Mars, Cornelian had always considered Wrath-Pei a brilliant dandy, more of an
amusement than a danger.

But with distance came boldness, obviously—and now that Wrath-Pei had virtually conquered Titan, and *not* in the High Leader's name (here came that acidic feeling again), he would have to be dealt with eventually. However, Cornelian still could not work up a splendid hatred for the man or take him all that seriously. He was, after all, little more than a creative degenerate. If he was here now, standing before the High Leader, would he act so boldly? Cornelian would grab him with dual pincers, yanking his smirking, lecherous body from his gyro-laden chair, and simultaneously strangle and unman him.

Cornelian took a deep, bellowing breath.

There was, of course, the deeper problem that Wrath-Pei held Tabrel Kris as a hostage. A pawn to protect his own safety. There was some immediacy attached to that problem, some sense of urgency, but the High Leader had no doubt that he would eventually solve that difficulty. For now, it was enough to know that she was safe, even if there had been a marriage to the idiot savant Jamal Clan. The Clan claims that Mars and Titan were now united and that the Clan philosophy had a rightful place on the Red Planet were nonsense. The Martian people, at this point, would not dare to blow their own noses without the High Leader's consent.

No, that wasn't what was really bothering him.

Something else . . .

Something . . .

"Time to go on, High Leader!"

Pynthas's overexcited, doglike visage was in front

of Prime Cornelian, and he couldn't resist knocking
the man off his feet with a casual sideways swipe
of one front limb. The toady's cry of alarm and the
sound of his hitting the floor gave Cornelian a little
of the amusement he craved. Ah, if only there were
two of Pynthas, so he could knock their heads
together.

A technician, less bold than Pynthas, approached
tentatively, then stopped well out of range to ask
meekly, "Are you ready, High Leader?"

Cornelian waved a casual digit, as if to say, *As
ready as I'll ever be*.

Instead he grumbled, "Let's get it done."

"Very well," the technician said. He indicated a
place on a small spotlit stage behind them. "If you'll
stand there . . ."

"Ah . . ." Cornelian brightened, seeing that the
seal of Martian solidarity, the sickle within a circle
of black iron, had been mounted behind him as he
had instructed. He wanted every Martian to see this
emblem and identify it with himself. As they
watched in their homes on their Screens, he wanted
them to—

But that was what he would accomplish now.

"Turn it on, or whatever," he snapped, blinking
the vertical blue black slits of his eyes against the
glare.

The technician made a rolling motion with his
hand and mouthed a silent, *Three, two, one* . . .

He pointed at the High Leader who, even if he
hadn't been told, knew that the broadcast had

begun—he felt the electromagnetic emanations in his own body.

"Martian citizens," the High Leader began, in a calm voice so unlike his own that he felt like bursting into laughter. "I am here to speak with you tonight about the grave crises we face—and to assure you that we, as Martians, will prevail!

"As to the first point of your concern, the dastardly murder of the entire Martian Senate weeks ago, let me assure you that the perpetrators of this craven act have already been dealt with! It has been learned that these cowards, sent by Earth and assisted by Venusian agents, and based in the traitorous city of Shklovskii here on our own fair planet, were sent to foment rebellion and chaos! But they have been punished!"

Cornelian, now warming to his task, allowed some of his own deep spite to bubble up into his cardboard words. He knew that a dram of true hate was worth a liter of talk, and now he would illustrate once and for all, to all of Mars, that whatever they had heard, whatever rumors they had entertained these past weeks, there was only one direction they were all heading, and there would be only one leader taking them there.

"Make no mistake!" he shouted. "The solidarity of Mars will *never* be compromised! We are one people, under one banner . . ." he paused, pointing with true feeling behind him at the sickle within the iron circle, "and no one—*no one*—will ever take from us the destiny that we, as true Martians, hold within our grip. If need be, that grip will become an iron fist! If the other worlds want war, we will give it to them! If it is our destiny to rule *all* the worlds, then we will *fulfill that destiny!*"

He paused, breath bellowing in his body, his slitted eyes afire. He held one clutch of metal fingers up, balling them dramatically into a slow iron fist.

"If they want the taste of iron, they shall have it!"

He could almost hear the cheers of the weak-minded ones out there, the millions living with their rumors and fears all this time, now told that everything would be taken care of for them, that they didn't have to think anymore, to worry anymore— all they had to do was give up their *souls*.

Of course, there were a few who wouldn't go along—but that was what the Martian Marines, and the newly formed Red Police, were for.

"With your help, my friends, my true Martian brothers, we will be victorious in all we set out to do! If Venus wants war, we will give it war! *We will fulfill our destiny to rule!*"

He didn't need a Screen to hear the wild cheers, the anxiety being expunged in communal orgasm. After all, these techniques had all been worked out centuries before; it was like using a formula in a textbook. Soften up a population with terror and uncertainty, innuendo and fear, then ride in to save them. Prime Cornelian was almost bored with the actuality of having to say the words.

"All hail Mars!" he shouted, raising the fist again;

and then the technician, as previously instructed, cut the broadcast, and the chore was over.

It was only then that Cornelian noticed that Pynthas, rather than rushing out to congratulate him on what a fine job he had done, was hiding back in the shadows, pale as sand.

"What is it?" the High Leader commanded.

All the techs—everyone—were as pallid as Pynthas.

"I asked a question. *What happened?*"

With a lithe movement forward, Cornelian caught the nearest technician in his grip and drew him close to his oil-smelling mouth.

"TELL. ME," he hissed loudly.

"A n-newscast from V-Venus," the technician croaked. "While you w-were speaking."

"And?" Cornelian asked murderously. He noted with disgust that the technician had wet himself.

The technician was turning bluish white, his eyes so close to the High Leader's own that he could make out the hair-thin retinal wires deep within them.

Everyone else had shrunk back into the shadows.

"An exp-plosion," the technician squeaked.

"TELL ME!"

"One of the d-deton-nation tubes. On a f-feeder st-staion. They've s-set it off."

Prime Cornelian saw nothing, heard nothing but his own scarlet rage. A high-pitched keening, which he realized much later was the sound of his own voice, filled his head and mouth and eyes.

*   *   *

When he came out of it, when he began to think
again, the studio was empty and Prime Cornelian,
High Leader, was forced to clean up the mess on
his front digits, his hands, by himself.

19

The breathing of oxygen was not an easy thing.

But Kay Free did it, as she did most things, with grace and with an absolute minimum of motion.

She had only been in water one other time that she could recall. And that had been very long ago, at least a millennium, by the human standard. She had not liked it then. But that had been before she had learned many things, most of all patience, which had carried her through nearly everything in her life.

"*Life*—now, there's an interesting thing," Pel Front said, swimming close by. He was inhabiting the body of what Kay Free thought was a rather comical fish, with long horizontal fins and tiny cilia along the top and bottom of its lengthy body, which propelled it along and also kept it in place. Kay Free herself had chosen the body of a flattened sea-thing with both eyes on one side of its brown body, which kept itself nestled into the silty mud at the bottom of this shallow sea. Her amusement at Pel Front's choice must have somehow showed through the lim-

ited expressions available to the fish, though, because Pel Front managed to make his own host form
a passable frown on the wide-toothed mouth below
its undulating whiskers.

"There, there, Pel Front—there's no need for
annoyance!"

"Annoyance at being here at all!" Pel Front answered in a huff. "I question the reason for this
meeting in the first place—"

Before Pel Front could drive himself into further
exasperation, the third of their party, Mel Sent, arrived with her customary loud entrance.

"Ah!" Kay Free said, as the huge carriage of Mel
Sent's host, a whalelike creature half again as long
and wide as the largest Earth whale, with bright
blue and white stripes alternating down its length,
and eyes large and luminously deep black like monstrous, polished stones, reared itself up before them,
disturbing the mud around Kay Free to the point
that nothing could be seen until it settled.

"I am here—finally!" Mel Sent announced.

"Then we can begin—" Kay Free attempted
mildly, knowing the futility of the gesture.

"We can begin nothing until I tell you what I
wish to tell you!" Mel Sent said.

Pel Front's sound of impatience was audible—but
ignored by Mel Sent. Through the settling murk,
Kay Free made out another frown on Pel Front's
whiskered face and secretly smiled to herself.

"I was detained—*forever*, it seemed!" Mel Sent

explained theatrically. "First there were matters to attend to at home, and then—"

"How *is* your mother?" Kay Free offered mildly.

The huge visage of Mel Sent's host turned ponderously toward her and the eyes, if possible, became even larger.

"Mother is Mother!" Mel Sent rumbled. "She always will *be* Mother!"

"I see," Kay Free said.

"And that is besides the point!" Mel Sent continued. "The point is that I was detained—"

"That's all very well," Pel Front snapped peevishly. "And I'm sure we're all very interested. Only we're here for business, and business is what I insist we get down to."

"*When* I say so!" Mel Sent roared.

Pel Front and Mel Sent faced each other silently for a few moments, and Kay Free was about to intervene in the coming argument when the calling came to her and the world went suddenly silent. Her two companions, also, had ceased even to breathe, their host bodies, absent of the movement of fin or cilia, responding in their own kind: Pel Front settling gently to the ocean floor and Mel Sent, buoyed by the air in her host's massive body, merely appearing lifeless as she hung in place.

In the moment of supreme silence, when Kay Free felt everything in existence lifted away from her—the duties of life, thoughts of existence or less weightier thoughts, worries, awareness of self—she felt now, as she always felt at these moments, as free as anything can feel. Free of everything save being itself.

"Yes, my Life," she prayed in an unapprehended whisper.

The moment of freedom extended, to the point that deep within Kay Free, in a place she was not even aware of, rose the vague thought that her host, deprived of oxygenated water, was dying. And in that small place she was alarmed.

And yet the moment of blissful emptiness went on.

"Yes, my Life," she repeated, knowing now that she was waiting for something that had never been said before.

Into her, into the others, came a knowledge, filling the void of bliss.

A kind of gasp escaped Kay Free.

Then suddenly the calling was over and Kay Free was pushed whole back into the world.

The moment of disorientation that ensued was extended.

"Oh, my," Mel Sent said, in an unaccustomed voice; it occurred to Kay Free that if Mel Sent had been hosted by a human creature at this moment, that creature's eyes would be welled with tears.

"Oh, my . . ." Pel Front said, barely audible.

"Yes . . ." Kay Free said.

And then she slowly became aware of herself and her surroundings again. She had been in a shocked limbo, and now when limbo was left behind, the shock remained, though of a newer kind.

Incorporeal, nearly invisible, like waving sheets of pale green-yellow light, like the aurora borealis, Kay Free saw now that she and the others had left their hosts and stood suspended and shimmering in their natural state.

"It's best that we leave this place," Mel Sent said in a somber, low voice.

"Yes, and immediately," Pel Front said.

They rose, curling, filmy, lighted expanses, up toward the undulating gray-green clearness of the ocean top above them. When they broke through, it felt like stepping through a mirror.

But before they penetrated the surface, Kay Free turned her attention a final time to the scene below her: the eyeless burned thing that had been her host; Pel Front's host, skin pulled back over its exoskeleton in a curl of execution, toothed mouth locked wide open—and Mel Sent's magnificent whale-creature, now rolling gently and dead in the current, over onto its burned back, its huge and beautiful black eyes now exploded from within, cavitied depths of nothing.

20

"I don't understand this," Targon Ramir said, studying the report in front of him with furrowed brow. "You say three high-energy sources *left* the planet? We weren't attacked—we were *un*attacked?"

"Something like that, sir."

"Don't call me sir," Targon said to the young security force officer, whose scrubbed face reminded Targon of his own brief stint in Earth's Nature Scouts, where he had learned how to tie knots and contract poison sumac. Targon looked back at the viewer, trying to make sense of the data: the high-energy sources had apparently shot out of Clotho Tessera—which was the middle of a sea. Scanning had indicated that there were no facilities under the water at that location—that there was nothing there but water and fish.

Targon made the data go away with a flick of his finger.

"Right now it means nothing to me; let me know if it happens again."

The security officer saluted sharply. "Yes . . . Mr. Ramir."

Targon scowled. "And don't salute me anymore."

"Yes . . ." the young officer said, properly confused.

"Send Mr. Sneaden in, please."

Fighting both his hand and mouth, the officer turned sharply on his heel and marched out.

In a few moments, Jean Sneaden came into the room, automatically closing the door behind him. He was youth to Targon's age, but Ramir had quickly learned that this young man with the shock of red hair was nearly as infected with enthusiasm for Venus as the old engineer himself was—which explained the pained look on his face.

"It's a black day, Jean," Targon said.

Sneaden nodded. "Black as they come."

"It could get blacker," Targon added quickly; and just as quickly regretted it. Though Sneaden was enthusiastic and loyal, his age sometimes precluded his complete understanding: in short, his lack of years prevented him from seeing the umbrellaed arc of any policy; with his impatience, he saw only the rain on one section, forgetting that the rest of the umbrella was getting wet, too.

"Has there been any response from Cornelian to our ultimatum?"

"No."

"I'm a little surprised. Especially after that speech he gave on Mars. It may mean he's not as ready as we thought he was."

Sneaden's frown was infectious. "It will at least give us more time to prepare."

"Prepare what? Our only weapon is the planet itself. Cornelian knows that full well. We know his shuttle forces have been gathering for the past week. We know the Martian Marines have been mobilized to full strength. We knew the only thing we could do to keep him away was prove that we meant what we said: that if he attacks, he'll win the race but lose the prize."

"*Everyone* loses the prize," Sneaden said.

"Yes . . ." Targon Ramir took a deep breath and turned to stare out the window. Already in the far distance, the brown stain from the detonation of the Aurelia feeder station was drifting high into the atmosphere and westward. The pictures from the sight had been painful enough to look at: the hole in the ground and in the sky. That it was in the most desolate area of the planet, totally unpopulated, made little difference: The thought of the stray animals and plant life alone which were vaporized in the explosion, not to mention the point oh four percent loss in total atmospheric oxygen that had already occurred—a wound which would take five years to bandage and heal—made Targon sick to his stomach. The sight of the poisonous smudge on the healthy skyline brought actual bile up into Targon's throat. He could well imagine the way it made his young friend Sneaden feel.

Or Carter Frolich. . . .

Something like a shiver went through Targon

Ramir. It would be hard to think of his old friend any longer without feeling pain, loss—and, yes, fear. For with Frolich's disappearance soon after returning to Venus, and his subsequent underground missives condemning Targon Ramir to death and proclaiming himself the one true leader of a free and independent Venus, the relationship between master and apprentice had mutated into something horrible, a deadly adversarial duel. Though Carter was thus far seemingly on his own made no difference: His stature alone was enough to make anyone listen to what he had to say, and there had been some grumblings in the lower ranks of the Engineering Corps about why Targon was taking the course he had chosen.

Which had prompted Targon to do something even more painful than ordering the destruction of Aurelia station: releasing the mental health records of Carter Frolich, defining and proving his instability and, in effect, assassinating his character in public.

That the tactic had apparently worked was nearly beside the point; the sour taste in Targon Ramir's throat was almost a constant thing these days.

Targon turned away from the painful scene outside to face Jean Sneaden, who was studying his face, looking for something he apparently had not found.

"Targon, what happens next?" Jean asked.

Targon sighed. "We wait. Hopefully, the Martians will get the message and not attack. The last thing

Cornelian wants is a Venus that is useless to him. He is a patient man, but not that patient—he knows that by the time Venus is cleaned up, he'd be in his grave fifty years."

Jean was silent for a moment; and then he asked the question that Targon Ramir knew he had come to ask.

"But will you really do it?"

Targon Ramir fixed a steady gaze on the young man's face. "Yes, I will, Jean," he said without a trace of hesitation. "Because it would be better to let a future generation fulfill our dream on Venus, rather than let it be realized by a man like Prime Cornelian. This is what Carter doesn't understand. To him, the dream itself is more important than anything. Throughout history, that has been a mistake that mankind has made. Men of vision have all too often ignored the consequences of their discoveries and realizations. What good would this planet do for mankind if it's in the hands of Cornelian? Would it be right to create paradise—if the only use for it is as a more pleasant setting for slaves to live?"

Targon found his passion ebbing into sadness. "The only weapon we have is the thing we love," he said. And though he felt more alone that at any time in his life, he added, "And we'll use that weapon if we have to."

21

On Titan, Saturn was rising.

At the lipped horizon of the world, the sharp thin line of the E ring, shepherded by tiny Enceladus, one of the Lesser Moons, pushed its curve into view, followed by ring G. But these thin lines were only a prelude. Soon F rose, at Titan's distance and without optical aid a flattened band separated by the deceptive black emptiness of the Encke Division. Wrath-Pei was well aware that the Encke Division was filled with millions of tons of material, all ground into tiny dust motes. He also had no interest.

From Wrath-Pei's vantage point outside the open dome of Schumacher Observatory, comfortably seated in his floating lounge chair whose gyros, similar to the ones enclosed in the nearby telescope's guide system, adjusted to his every muscle's whim of movement, the best part of the show was yet to come. For now the partial majesty of the A ring slid up the sky. Now the ring system was beginning to resemble the edge of a huge yellow-white scythe cutting up into the darkness.

"Ouch," Wrath-Pei said, smiling to himself, shifting sinuously in his chair, thinking of what the imagery meant.

Wrath-Pei's interest heightened as the smooth wide darkness of the Cassini Division rose into view.

"Is that it?" Wrath-Pei said.

"Yes, Your Grace."

"Good. And we'll be able to see it when?"

"In four minutes and fifteen seconds, Your Grace."

"Excellent."

Lawrence, standing beside him, dressed in black to his eyebrows, bowed slightly, keeping his eyes to the inside float-Screens of the visor he wore. He was no more than ten, but had not seen anything without the aid of his visor since the age of three.

"Three minutes and thirty seconds, Your Grace."

"Very well."

Wrath-Pei's palms began to sweat with excitement.

The Cassini Division was broadening into the sky now. Already the rings had eaten nearly twenty-five degrees of night, and the giant planet had yet to bulge into view. By then, of course, the real show would be over.

"Time?" Wrath-Pei said.

"Just . . . three minutes, Your Grace."

Wrath-Pei made an impatient gesture, shifting in his chair, which whirred imperceptibly to accommodate his uneasiness.

"When will the Screen kick in?" he asked, already knowing the answer.

"At one minute and thirty seconds, Your Grace." Anticipating the next question, the boy announced, "We are now at two minutes and forty-five seconds."

Impatience metamorphosed into the thrill of anticipation, and Wrath-Pei suddenly hit the armrests of his chair with his balled fists, unable to contain his hunger. The chair gimbaled forward like an animal bucking its rear legs, nearly throwing him to the ground before instantly settling back again.

"Ohhh, I can't *wait*!" Wrath-Pei said. "Ti—"

"Two minutes and ten seconds, Your Grace."

Now the B and C rings, wide and bright, were nudging the Cassini Division broadly up into view. Soon the faint D ring, barely visible from Titan, would pull the planet's limb after it.

"You're sure about all this?" Wrath-Pei suddenly snapped, last-minute fears, as always, besetting him.

"Unquestionable," the boy said instantly. Arms straight at his sides, black sleeves ending in the knobby stumps of fingerless hands, the boy stared straight into his darkened visor, head moving in slight circles as he studied his private data.

"One minute and fifty seconds, Your Grace," the boy announced. After ten seconds of silence he said, "One minute and forty seconds."

Now Wrath-Pei's excitement grew exponentially with his attention. He rocked gently forward in his chair, staring hard at the deep wide black of the Cassini Division while at the same time trying to anticipate the point at which his close-up view, gratis the Schumacher telescope, would pop into space before him.

"They said I would be able to see something before—"

Ahead in space, off in the center of the black band, Wrath-Pei saw a tiny flash of light.

"There!"

"Yes, Your Grace," the boy announced. "That is exactly—"

He immediately broke off and said, "One minute and thirty seconds."

Before Wrath-Pei's eyes, the night burst open into an invisible Screen. Wrath-Pei thought he heard the gyros of the giant Schumacher telescope behind him wheel slightly, sharpening the focus of the picture hanging in air before him: a slice of space deep inside the Cassini Division, a jumble of tiny bright stones and faint cloudy flows of dust. And, in the exact center of the view, a spacecraft.

"You should be able to detect the partial impact of a moment ago, Your Grace," the boy said.

Wrath-Pei leaned farther forward, squinting.

"Yes . . ."

There, on the front right nose of the craft, was a crushed spot.

"That's what I saw? The flash?" Wrath-Pei asked.

"Without doubt," the boy answered.

"And . . ."

"Fourteen seconds to total impact, Your Grace."

"Audio?"

"In . . . three seconds, Your Grace."

With held breath, Wrath-Pei waited.

"Now, Your Grace."

Then Wrath-Pei heard them, the dying men, trying desperately to avoid their fate and change their
course. A jumble of shouting voices—all four of
them, Wrath-Pei detected—mixed together, but
Wrath-Pei easily picked out Commander Tarn's
loud commands as he tried to shout his underlings
down. Vaguely, Wrath-Pei could hear the hiss of
escaping oxygen from the first hit the craft had
taken.

"Just do what I say!" Tarn shouted. "Try to turn
the forward sta—"

"Two seconds, Your Grace."

Tarn's voice turned into a sudden scream, louder
than the others.

"The window—!" someone, not Tarn, shouted.

Then there was a glancing flash of light, and the
object they fast approached, which was artificial,
fired a beam of pencil-thin violet light which cut
the spacecraft into neat slices, starting at the stem
and continuing to the stern.

There was a final burst of audio screams which
abruptly ended, though Wrath-Pei could follow the
suitless men's twisting agony as they flew away from
the cut wreckage and writhed out their last moments in the airless space between two beautiful
Saturnian rings.

One of the bodies, still moving, floated too near
the smooth orb of the defensive satellite that had

attacked the spacecraft, and the artificial orb fired another thin line of fire that cut the man in half.

Looking closer, Wrath-Pei was pleased to see that it was Commander Tarn.

Sated, Wrath-Pei leaned back in his chair. "Off," he said.

Instantly the close-up view before him went away, replaced by the sight of Saturn's yellow, fat, banded bulk rising in the wake of its ring system.

Wrath-Pei yawned and, with the aid of the chair, stood up.

"It is very pleasing to me that you were able to calculate that performance so well," Wrath-Pei said to the boy. "How could you know that the first object, the . . ."

"Ring particle, Your Grace. It was approximately a half meter in diameter."

"Yes, ring particle. How did you know it would be in exactly that position, to give them that initial blow, alert the defensive satellite, and rupture their hull?"

The boy said nothing.

"You may be flippant, if you like," Wrath-Pei said.

"I see no other way to answer the question," the boy said. "The ring particle was there . . . because it was there. It was always meant to be there."

Wrath-Pei yawned. "Whatever. You did well, Lawrence."

The boy's head bowed slightly, and his lipless mouth, just visible in his black hood, opened slightly in satisfaction.

"And now, to bed—" Wrath-Pei began.

"There is a transmission, Your Grace," Lawrence announced, his eyes studying the inside of his visor.

Wrath-Pei waited.

"It is Prime Cornelian, Your Grace."

Wrath-Pei said nothing for a moment, then snapped, "Put it on."

Again the Screen flashed into view before Wrath-Pei's eyes. Only now instead of the satisfying picture of Commander Tarn's bisected torso writhing out its last moments of life, Wrath-Pei was faced with the horrid anomaly of Prime Cornelian, or, as Wrath-Pei called him privately, the Bug.

"Prime Cornelian," Wrath-Pei said, bowing.

The insect nodded its head a fraction in greeting. "I . . . need to ask a favor," Prime Cornelian said.

Guessing already what the favor was, Wrath-Pei said in a munificent voice, "Ask away!"

"I need you back on Mars."

Amused, and not able to completely hide it, Wrath-Pei said, "Oh?"

"Yes," Prime Cornelian said. "And I need you to bring the young girl, Tabrel Kris, with you."

"Ah . . ."

That had been the favor he had been anticipating.

"But Cornelian!" Wrath-Pei said. "She is now a happily married woman! I could not possibly leave her husband behind!"

"Then bring the simpering idiot with you!" Cornelian snapped.

Enjoying the Bug's discomfort, Wrath-Pei made a

show of tapping his chin in thought before answering.

He finally said, shaking his head decisively, "I'm sorry, Cornelian—I mean, *High Leader*—I couldn't possibly leave Titan at the moment. So much to do."

"I'm *ordering* you back here!" Cornelian raged.

"Oh? A moment ago you were asking a *favor*," Wrath-Pei cooed.

"Call it whatever you want! But do what I say!"

Wrath-Pei made a great show of yawning and deliberately let the High Leader see him reach to disconnect the transmission.

"Wrath-Pei! Wait!"

Wrath-Pei arched an eyebrow in faint interest. "Yes, *High Leader*?"

Showing his remarkable ability, which Wrath-Pei secretly envied, of utterly concealing his true feelings, the Bug offered, "I . . . may be able to get you an audience with Sam-Sei."

Wrath-Pei could not hide his astonishment.

"I thought you would be interested," Prime Cornelian cooed. "In fact, Sam-Sei has indicated to me that he may want you . . . to visit him, here on Mars."

"Splendid! When—"

"Soon, Wrath-Pei. He is still a bit . . . hesitant. But if the word is given . . ."

"Yes, yes," Wrath-Pei said, "of course I would be on my way immediately. And I'll bring the girl, if that's what you want."

"Good. And as a measure of your good faith in

this matter, I should like you to do a tiny favor for me at this time."

"Anything!" Wrath-Pei said, suddenly impatient to be rid of the Bug, to give his thoughts over completely to returning to Mars—to unfinished business with Sam-Sei.

"What is it?" Wrath-Pei asked.

"A small thing. I should like you to relay a recording, which I will transmit to you after our chat, to the new bride. It is from her father. Let's call it . . . my wedding present to her."

"Fine!" Wrath-Pei said; and before the Bug could chatter on, Wrath-Pei severed the transmission, leaving open a link for the promised recording to be relayed. He would screen it himself later on, but at this point, he had no interest in it whatsoever.

Sam-Sei . . .

A mixture of heated emotions roared through Wrath-Pei. He sat for an indeterminate time staring at the space where Saturn was, but seeing only the horribly deformed visage of the Machine Master.

At his side, his hands flexed and unflexed, finding purchase finally around the handle of the ancient tool he wore there, holstered like a gun.

Wrath-Pei brought the aviation tin snips up to his eye level and ran his gaze lovingly over the two sharp blades.

Pulling the handles, he brought the blades slowly together in a razor-sharp, finely oiled lock.

"Lawrence," he said sweetly, knowing that the

boy still had three toes on his left foot to attend to, which Wrath-Pei had been saving for a moment such as this, "I believe it's time for us to go in!"

22

Suffocation.

Dalin Shar knew the word intimately now. He was nearing the place where he was almost begging for annihilation; each slow orbit of his soon-to-be coffin brought him achingly closer to the freighter wreck. He could now make out close details of the docking studs below the ruined front cabin, and had made a kind of tepid game out of trying to guess which of them his hexagonal craft would hit, less than an hour after his air was gone. It was a futile exercise, of course—he would be already dead—but the diversion was welcome. He had decided on one particular rust-colored knob, but his last slow orbit, showing him sadly pocked Luna and then the incrementally closer nose of the freighter—whose name he could now make out: *Ad Aspera*—had nudged his craft slightly away from that impact point, and in line with another, equally deadly, stud.

Any diversion was welcome. . . .

He had stopped counting time. For the first two days he had contented himself with conserving

movement, breath, and food—and with following
the course of his own countdown to death. Then
there had come a point where he had decided that
rescue by any means was better than suffocation
and had attempted to get the Screen to develop
some sort of transmission. This, of course, had
failed.

Finally, sickening of the Screen's calmly irritating
tone, Dalin had told it to shut down completely,
leaving him in darkness.

Darkness . . .

In this semi-womb, with his food gone, his air
turning stale and bitter-tasting, and only the sights
of his porthole to divert him, it was easy to think
of Tabrel Kris. Somehow he knew she was safe, for
the moment. He wondered if she thought of him,
of their brief time together that would have to suf-
fice for all eternity.

If there was such a thing as eternity.

He knew that his mind was becoming poisoned.
The oxygen content of the air was lessening with
each breath; Dalin could almost hear the air purifi-
ers and tiny oxygen pumps shutting down one by
one, as the thin tanks wafered between the walls of
the hexagon let out their own last breaths so that
he might have his. . . .

And there it came: the looming nose of the *Ad
Aspera,* so close now that he could count the attachment locks on the surface of the rusty stud that
would smash his little pod to bits on its next go-

around. It was close enough to touch now; and if he just reached his hand right out, perhaps he could—

Suddenly the docking stud pulled away from him. Impossibly, it now stood a good hundred meters away. In fact, Dalin could no longer make out anything but the studs themselves, in a cluster, and the smashed front cabin of the *Ad Aspera*, whose name was no longer readable.

"What in damnation?" Dalin said wonderingly.

Suddenly his empty stomach lurched as the hexagon spun entirely around before coming to a dead stop.

Dalin heard two dull thumps followed by a solid clang before darkness descended on the inside of the pod.

"Screen! Give me light!"

But Dalin's voice was now so weak that the command was not even heard. Here he was, on the point of salvation, and the time had run out on his oxygen, and he was pulling air in that wasn't air, weakly heaving like a fish out of water, but too weak to flop on any deck—

More sounds were followed by a bang, and he felt his body, already floating off, bounce once and then become still.

Tabrel, good-bye, he thought—

—and then air was rushing over him, breaking like hard waves.

For a moment he could not breathe, because there was too much air. His lungs seized; and then he was coughing, his hungry alveoli pulling in as much as they could get, flooding his system with richness. The air tasted like cream.

Then, gaining strength, he looked up, and there were two figures standing in front of him, one of them holding a long piece of iron, and one of them said:

"Cripes! 'Tain't nothin' in here but a fella— nothin' of use a-tall!"

Dalin knew immediately they were pirates, but, not knowing all that much about pirates, he decided immediately to play on whatever hospitality they might possess and keep his identity to himself.

Which proved a wise choice, because a fight immediately broke out between his two benefactors over how best to dispose of him.

"I say whack 'im now!" the one with the iron bar, some sort of prying device, suggested. For emphasis, he brandished the bar over his own head.

"No, no, Enry! Tha' won't do a-tall!" his friend said, though he did not dissuade his companion from flourishing his iron weapon. His was obviously the voice of reason. "He mi' be useful—and if he ain't, you ken whack 'im later!"

"All ri'," his friend said sullenly, lowering the iron and using his boot instead to kick Dalin.

"Ge' out!" he shouted, and Dalin complied by crawling out of the opened hatchway, remaining on all fours as further blows were rained upon his buttocks and ribs.

"He's a soft 'un, ain't 'e?" The conciliatory one laughed.

"Yeah, ri'," the other said, landing a particularly effective kick to Dalin's midsection, driving out most of the sweet air that had so recently invaded his lungs.

"Who are ye?" the hard one said, poking his iron bar at Dalin to make him roll onto his back.

Dalin could not catch his breath, nor answer.

"Dumb, is 'e?" the iron-bearer said, raising the weapon again.

But the other one once again intervened, lowering his greasy face to within inches of Dalin's own.

"Naw, 'e can speak," he said, smiling, showing off his scarcity of teeth. "Can't ye, mate?"

"Y-yes," Dalin croaked out.

"Awww," the iron wielder said dejectedly, lowering his weapon and walking away.

Amazingly, they both left Dalin alone.

Behind Dalin came a loud whishing sound, and a hexagonal box identical to Dalin's own was pushed through a lock, bumping Dalin's forward. He was just able to roll out of the way in time to avoid injury.

"New 'un up!" the bar-wielder shouted, and went about prying open the hatch of the new hexagon with serious intent.

Suddenly he stopped, eyeing Dalin ominously before turning to his companion.

"Hey, Ralf—ye don' think there'll be another of 'im in here, do ye?"

Ralf shrugged. "If there 'is, you can brain 'im, all ri'?"

"Ri' as rain," the other said happily, as he bent to his task of opening the box.

In another moment the hatch had been popped free and the two pirates stood peering into the interior.

"Al ri'!" the bar-wielder shouted.

"Heaven above—ye can say tha' again, Enry!"

"It's a veritable golden one, it 'tis!"

"Hurrah!"

For the next ten minutes, Ralf and Enry tore metal crates and packages from the hexagon, pulling them open like children on a holiday morning. There were a variety of goods within—everything from viewer Screens to wearables to a box filled with tiny round objects with tufts of hair on them that none of them, including Dalin, recognized. After studying these gewgaws for a minute or so, Ralf said to Enry, "We'll sell 'em to the Clanners!" Which produced a big laugh from both of them.

The celebration went on until a vague sound announced the arrival of a new pod. Suddenly Ralf and Enry, knee-deep in open packages, jumped aside as another hexagon was pushed through the lock, bumping forward those in front of it. By now, Dalin had moved out of the line of fire and stood witness as Enry's crowbar once again went to work, eliciting a new round of excited exclamations when the door was popped open to reveal new riches within.

Tiring of watching the antics of the two pirates, Dalin turned his attention to his latest prison. It was little more than a badly lit storeroom of vast dimensions. Dalin was at first curious as to why he would have the run of it unsupervised; but this question was quickly answered when it became apparent that there was nowhere to go. There were literally hundreds of meters of aisles, all of them lined with packed shelving from cluttered floor to high ceiling, and all of them backed against smooth walls. It was like a library of booty; Dalin had never seen so many goods in one place in his life.

When finally he did locate the single door in the storeroom, it proved to be sealed tight, employing a security system that seemed an amalgam of two or three technologies, some of them ancient. There were fingerprint coders, facial sensors, and a quaint keypad with symbols on it that were unknown to Dalin. For good measure there was an antique tumbler lock, which, Dalin mused, might actually be worth quite a bit of money as a dealer's curiosity.

Bored, his recent brush with death already fading in his mind, Dalin wandered back to the lock. The hexagon he had come in had already been pushed far into the room and looked forlorn without a scatter of broken crates around it.

A new pod had now been broken into, and Enry and Ralf were displaying anew their obviously bottomless sense of delight in pillage.

"May I help?" Dalin said.

Both pirates looked at him, startled.

Ralf suddenly grinned, showing again his nearly toothless smile.

" 'E wants a job, does 'e?"

He turned to his companion.

"What do ye think, Enry? Shall we give 'im a job?"

"Put 'im to work!" Enry roared, picking up his crowbar to shake it.

Ralf's grin widened. "Clean up!" he growled, spreading his hands to indicate the mess of opened boxes surrounding them like a small mountain.

"Grahhhh!" Enry said for emphasis, oscillating his iron in rough humor.

Dalin looked around for place to start—but the shock of an empty crate hitting him in the chest, sending him sprawling and sending the two pirates into convulsions of laughter, gave him an incentive and a point of departure.

"Clean it all, or we'll eat ye fer breakfast!" Enry laughed, showing his prodigious and dirty teeth to his companion, who whooped.

Dalin bent to his task, but before he had gotten more than an hour or two into it, most of his time spent in trying to decipher the two pirates' filing system, he was summoned back to the latest pod to enter through the ship's capture lock.

Work had ceased, and Ralf and Enry sat resplendent on a tall hill of unopened crates, which had been scooped from the belly of the salvaged hexagon.

"Hey, Nub! Come on up, then!" Enry called in

a distinctly friendly fashion, waving to Dalin. His companion, also, was motioning for Dalin to maneuver his way up, which Dalin did, both cautiously and suspiciously.

At the top, he found the two pirates lounging in a man-made nest, surrounded by numerous empty bottles and even more numerous unopened ones.

"Titanian champagne!" Ralf said happily, holding a bottle out for Dalin's inspection before tilting its mouth up to his own.

"Tons of it!" Enry cried, spreading his hands to indicate the mountain they resided on.

Ralf wiped his mouth and belched. "Them Clanners may be ti' butted and grim, but they know their grape!"

"Huzzah to tha'!" Enry said, tossing an unopened bottle to Dalin. "Si' down, Nub! 'Elp us celebrate our fortune!"

The two pirates watched Dalin's attempts to open the champagne container with increasing amusement. Finally they broke into snorts of laughter at Dalin's fumbling, and Enry snatched the bottle from Dalin's hand, pressing the tiny switch on the neck which released the protective cage; then with a twist and pull the cork flew toward the ceiling and the wine was released.

Enry pushed the bottle back at Dalin.

"Now drink it!" he said, his voice a mixture of humor and command.

Shrugging, Dalin tilted the container up to his lips. Feather-light bubbles trickled down his throat.

" 'E likes it!" Ralf snorted.

"Then let 'im have another!" Enry said and, to a chorus of his friend's cheers, quickly retrieved, opened, and shoved another bottle of champagne into Dalin's hands.

Soon, Dalin sat between the two pirates, participating in toast after toast. There was a lopsided grin on his face; and the world itself became increasingly soft around the edges.

"To Nub!" Enry said, holding his current bottle aloft. Finding it empty, he tossed it down the side of the hill, where it broke into pieces at the bottom.

"I'll clean it up later!" Dalin laughed.

His companions roared approval.

"Tha' you will, Nub!" Ralf said. "Tha' you will!"

"To Nub!" Enry said, resuming his toast to Dalin with a newly opened bottle. "Our very own slave!"

"Ri'!" Ralf said. "Our very own slave!"

And Enry added, his eyes as bleary as Dalin had ever seen on a human being—though if Dalin had been able to see his own at that moment he might have been forced to alter his assessment—" 'E makes us laugh, so we'll let 'im live!"

23

From high orbit, Venus looked no different than it did on a Screen.

In fact, the High Leader preferred to study the Screen; the detail enhancement was better, and one could not close in on a real-time image without goggles.

Pynthas, though, was in a near rapture, and Prime Cornelian found that he had to physically threaten the toady to keep his mind on the business at hand.

"Maat Mons is magnificent—nothing like the pictures!" Pynthas marveled, as Venus' second highest peak glowed with morning mist beneath the floor portal. At the volcano's base spread a scattering of shallow lakes and the beginnings of a forest; already the vegetation greens were deeper than they ever were on Mars; one could almost taste the water in the atmosphere and on the ground.

"Stunning!" Pynthas cooed.

"Would you like to see it close up?" the High Leader whispered into Pynthas's ear with a hiss.

Lost in rapture, the toady began at first to nod, but his demeanor turned to one of dread as the truth of Cornelian's message registered in his brain.

"You'll have a wonderful view," the High Leader continued, "as you hurtle down toward the surface without a space suit—would you burn up or implode first, do you think?"

Pynthas came to trembling attention, though his eyes wanted very much to stray to the view below them. "What may I do for you, High Leader?"

"As much as you ever could—nothing," Cornelian answered. "But you might as well check with communications and make sure the ring will be complete by tomorrow, as I was told."

"Yes, High Leader," Pynthas said, and was instantly gone from Cornelian's sight.

The High Leader glanced briefly down through the floor; the vista meant nothing to him, but his eye was caught by the flash of another of Sam-Sei's drones locking into place below him and off to port. A ring of such craft, forming an anklet around the planet, would soon be in place.

Uneasy with the view of reality, the High Leader turned from the floor, commanding that the window be shuttered. Instantly it was.

Cornelian moved to the nearest viewer, mounted high on the wall of the ship behind him.

"Sam-Sei," he said to the Screen, and a moment later the Machine Master's den filled the view. Sam-Sei himself was absent.

"Damnation—where is he?" Cornelian said; and

a moment later his vertical eyes blinked, showing surprise, when the Machine Master stood before him, where he had apparently been all the while.

"What did you do?" Cornelian said, half intrigued and half angry.

Sam-Sei shrugged, his ruined face regarding the High Leader with its perpetual, horrible smile. "Something I have been tinkering with. A filter of sorts."

"You will keep me posted, of course."

Again the Machine Master shrugged. "As you wish," Sam-Sei said in his ponderous tone. "Though perhaps nothing will come of it."

"I wanted your reassurance that our little surprise on Venus will be successful."

"I do not give reassurances," the Machine Master said. "If everything was done as I directed, the results will be as I predicted."

Cornelian tamped his own anger. Always, when dealing with this man, there was annoyance! It was like keeping a snake happy.

"I wish to know," Sam-Sei asked, "when Wrath-Pei will be returned to Mars."

"Ah," Prime Cornelian said, momentarily caught off guard. "That is . . . something I am working on."

"It is not in process?"

"No," said the High Leader, trying to think of something to placate the Machine Master. "There is no possibility of his return before this Venus business is completed."

The Machine Master looked for all the world like

a cadaver standing and talking to him; his wan complexion, the scarred pits around his sunken eyes, the tuft of greasy yellow hair high up on his forehead, made him appear anything but alive. Not for the first time, the High Leader wondered just how alive the man was, save for his work and his burning passion to face Wrath-Pei once more.

"You will have no trouble on Venus. I wish Wrath-Pei to be brought home as soon as possible," Sam-Sei said.

The High Leader had heard the words of assurance he had sought; now he let anger flow into his voice. It was time to poke the snake with a stick. "It will happen when I command it," Prime Cornelian snapped.

Seeming to ignore his ire, the Machine Master said distractedly, "Perhaps I will have something that can aid you in his retrieval."

Cornelian began to speak, but the Machine Master had disappeared; the ghost of his outline was barely visible, like a soap bubble's edge.

"Sam-Sei—speak to me now!"

But there came only silence from the Machine Master's underground chambers. And now the High Leader could see nothing of Sam-Sei at all, only the track of dust motes caught in a beam of sunlight from the high slit of windows, which fell across the flanks of ancient machines.

24

"Tabrel?"

Through the gauze of what reality had become to her, Tabrel Kris heard her father's voice.

It was not a strong voice—as his voice had always been strong. It was weak, like a bent reed, hollow and wispy—but it was him nevertheless.

For the first time in a week, she had been left alone. That in itself had lessened, the tiniest bit, the constant pressure exerted on her by Kamath Clan's drugs. Being in the presence of the queen, as she had been during her "ministrations," and more horrible yet, being in the constant company of Jamal Clan, whose annoying voice, continual whining, and perpetual state of anxiety drove what little there was left of her own personality to distraction, had only made the drugs' powers more effective. In some sense even welcome, since it made the pain of her being on Titan more endurable. It had almost been with sorrow, then, that she had witnessed the recent reduction of the dosages, which had come at Jamal's insistence. Claiming that Tabrel's love for him was bound to flower and that the potions would soon no longer be needed, Jamal had finally convinced his mother. Tabrel had wisely chosen to mimic the same air of obeisance with the reduction, even though it meant that Jamal's clinging, in his belief that her feelings for him were truly growing, had become all but unbearable.

Even now Jamal Clan stood outside the door to her chamber, proclaiming loudly that leaving her alone was a mistake. The boy was like a dog; and his true feelings for her were pathetic in their earnestness. At least he had a sense of chivalry, which had spared her from his bed. Proclaiming that he would not have her until she would have him without the aid of his mother's methods, he had left her to her own bedchamber, even on their wedding night. Still, she had not passed that night in peace, listening instead to his pathetic sobbing from the room next door.

But now here she was alone, feeling almost herself again.

And here was her father speaking.

So he was alive—though barely. On the Screen he looked as if he had aged ten years since she had seen him last. Which had only been . . . two months ago? Three? Inside, where there was still something of herself left, she wept for him, seeing him this way.

He sat on a thin chair, but looked as if his bag of bones had been set into it. His hands trembled, as did his lip, though his eyes were still strong and clear.

"Tabrel?" he said again, and it was only now that she realized he was not speaking to her on the recording, but to Prime Cornelian, whose vile voice was heard, though his visage, thankfully, remained unseen.

"Yes, Senator," Cornelian said, "we are speaking of your dear daughter Tabrel. Would you like her to come and visit you?"

"No!" her father said.

"Are you sure, Senator? Are you afraid she wouldn't like to see you this way?"

"I've told you, Cornelian, that you will never get near her!"

"Now, now, there's nothing to get excited about." One of Cornelian's horrid metallic limbs stretched into the picture, patting her father with Cornelian's thin metal simulacrum of a human hand. The hand withdrew. "How do you think she'd feel if I told her that I would spare your life, restore your property and title, and nurse you back to health if she would only agree to come?"

Here Senator Kris broke down completely, a shaking, sobbing bag of bones.

The Screen, mercifully, went blank.

In the darkness, Tabrel Kris felt something she had not felt since Queen Clan's ministrations had begun—a tear of her own, on her own face.

Though she knew that Prime Cornelian had manipulated her into feeling exactly what she was feeling at the moment, she didn't care.

She would go to her father.

That evening, as the lights of Titan dimmed to darkness and the stars moved aside like a folded blanket from rising Saturn's majesty, Tabrel Kris stole from her own bed and went to the room of Jamal Clan.

The Titanian prince slept with the pale glow of Saturn-light on his face; his mouth was open distastefully, his breathing loud, and Tabrel thought fleetingly of her first view of him. How handsome she had thought him. A shiver ran through her; but even so, she made her hand touch his face lightly, to bring him awake.

"Mother?" he said apprehensively, sitting up. Then his eyes lit on Tabrel. "My princess!"

Fighting through the layers of Kamath's potions, Tabrel put a finger to his lips.

"Be quiet. And listen to me . . . husband." The last word stuck in her throat, but the drugs in her helped her to continue to smile.

Delirious with joy, Jamal put a hand on her arm. "You have come to me! And on your own!"

"Yes," she whispered. "And I wish to be with you. But not until I am myself again."

Dismay crossed Jamal's face. "My mother! Damn her interference!"

Tabrel nodded. "I have been fighting to be myself

since her first ministration. It pushes me into myself and makes me who I am not."

"I will *kill* her!"

Tabrel set her hand lightly on his face. "No. But you must help me stop her. Do you know where her potions are kept?"

"Yes."

"Can you get to them?"

Jamal became thoughtful; finally he nodded. "She makes her rounds tomorrow. The room will be accessible to me."

"Good. Then you must bring the potions to me so that I can switch them with something harmless."

"I will switch them for you, my bride!"

"No, you must let me do it. If your mother asks you later, you must be able to tell her the truth, that you did not exchange them."

Jamal thought a moment, then nodded vigorously, caught up in the plan. "I will do whatever you ask!"

"My father is very ill."

"Then we must help him! Perhaps Wrath-Pei—"

"There may be a way," Tabrel said. "If you are willing to help me."

He scrambled out of the bed and knelt before her. "I would do anything for you, my bride! I would *die* for you!"

Though she was thinking *That may be necessary*, Tabrel only forced herself to lay her hand gently on his head—which made her think once more of him as a dog.

Leaving him there in rapture, she padded back to

her own room, slept all that night, and late into the next morning.

Jamal's knock upon her door found her already awake and dressed.

He had brought the case, as she had prayed he would.

She took it from him and said, "Now go outside and make sure no one bothers me."

Immediately he left.

Tabrel turned her full attention to the case of potions. From its blue velvet cradle she drew out the green bottle labeled "Obedience" and the slim red carafe designated "Truthfulness." The blackened bottle called "Death" she slipped into her tunic, after making sure it was tightly closed. She also withdrew and hid the clutch of silver syringes filled with "Sleep."

She emptied the carafe containing "Truthfulness," refilling it with water. She did the same to "Affability."

"Jamal!" she called, and when he had returned, she put into his palm the opened bottle of "Obedience." "Drink, and see if I have done well!"

To allay any suspicion, she drank from the carafe of Truthfulness.

"I have replaced them with water!" she said.

Eager to please, Jamal tilted the green bottle to his lips and drank deeply.

He lowered it almost immediately, his eyes growing heavy. "Oh . . ."

"You will follow my every command," Tabrel said. "You will not disobey."

Dreamily, in his singsong voice, Jamal said, "Yes."

"You will use whatever power you have while your mother is away. You will feign emergency. You will book passage for me offworld on the fastest and most untraceable ship possible. You will do everything in your power to get me home to Mars."

Jamal nodded.

"You will do all these things for me, Jamal Clan, and you will tell no one; no knowledge of these things will ever leave your heart."

"Yes . . ."

She put her hands on him and turned him to the door. "It is time to go."

He opened the door obediently and walked straight into the monstrous form of Kamath Clan. Behind her, lounging in his chair, which floated on the air like a suspended bird, sat Wrath-Pei, looking languidly amused.

"Hooray for us!" he said to Kamath Clan. "We were both right! I guessed *why* they'd do it, and you guessed *how*! I'm shocked that Cornelian thought something so crude as that transmission to the girl would work! The Bug must be losing his touch!"

"Mother . . ." Jamal said.

Kamath pushed past him into the room, brushing Tabrel aside to gather her bottles. She turned to Tabrel and held out her hand.

"Give them to me."

Wrath-Pei chuckled while Tabrel, refusing to

move, was roughly searched by the queen, who produced the bottles and syringes. Kamath Clan's face darkened at the sight of the bottle marked "Death."

"You would have used this," she said.

Tabrel said nothing, but stood defiant.

The queen said, "My mistake was to reduce her dosages. I should never have listened to the boy."

Wrath-Pei eyed Jamal with interest. "Perhaps if you let me *interview* the prince . . ."

"No!" the queen said. She quickly added, "He needs my care now."

Wrath-Pei smiled and shrugged. "Ah, well."

"You must leave me alone with the children now," Kamath Clan said. "There are measures I must take to assure this doesn't happen again."

"Of course," Wrath-Pei said. "We can't have anything happening to our little princess. She seems to be so valuable to Cornelian." He continued, "Lawrence found an amusing reference to her situation in the ancient literature. It's a pity her name isn't Helen."

Kamath Clan looked at him blankly, but he did not elaborate.

"When I am done here, I will come to you," she said. "There are two matters we must discuss."

Wrath-Pei nodded. The boy Lawrence, barely visible behind the chair, nudged a mechanism with the stump of one hand, and the chair slid back smoothly and began to turn.

"Don't be long."

The queen assented, and then, behind closed doors, began ministrations in earnest.

For some reason, Wrath-Pei had decided to install himself in the residence of the late Commander Tarn; though Kamath Clan knew there was irony in this, she did not see amusement.

Tarn's residence, like his office, was in the Ruz Balib section. The Sacred Grounds always gave her a measure of peace, though today she found herself too preoccupied to find this repose. Using the central walkway of the tree-lined quadrangle, she passed the late commander's offices and walked on. Soon the drab colors of office buildings turned to brighter shades of residences; and, behind the guarded gate of Tarn's property, the orange-red of the house's ornate front for a moment arrested her. Though she had never been here, she had assumed from Tarn's bureaucratic demeanor that his home would be as boring as his office or himself. This did not appear to be so.

She was further surprised by the interior, which was stuffed to overflowing with trinkets and furnishings from the Four Worlds. Tarn, it seems, had been either a secret collector with a private income or an embezzler of state funds. Some of the items, such as a tea service of nineteenth century Earth and a painted tarp of early twenty-first century Mars, were museum pieces even to the queen's barely trained eye. The rooms were spacious and airy, in vague Martian style; and, on closer inspection, the home itself seemed to be built of Martian sandstone, a luxury in itself.

Thus, perhaps, Wrath-Pei's interest in it.

"Hello!" Wrath-Pei's torpidly cheerful voice called. At first she could not locate it. She stood at the midpoint of five branching rooms, a Martian architectural style; all were filed with abundant and cleverly hidden artificial light and more booty—including, in one, massive pieces of Titanian furniture, finer even than that in the palace.

Queen Clan was clutched with anger and felt now that perhaps Tarn's method of disposal wasn't so extreme, after all.

"Please! Come in!" Wrath-Pei's voice called again. Now the queen caught sight of the hovering chair and its occupant. It resided in none of the five rooms but beyond one of them: an enclosed patio which led to an open area even more brightly lit than the indoor rooms.

Kamath Clan made her way through the patio, noting more antiques and treasured pieces: a painting by Carvan-Shay, a Titan landscape long reported stolen from a nearby gallery.

The queen passed through an open archway into brilliant light resembling that of Earth's Sun. For a moment her memories came flooding back: the fields under brilliant blue sky, the warmth like toast on her skin. . . .

But the artificial sky in this domed room was pink and the light not quite as bright as she thought, more Martian than Earth, but still blinding, by Titanian standards.

"Sit down! Join me!" Wrath-Pei offered.

His chair floated over an artificial pool of water—one of the largest such amusements the queen had seen on all of Titan. The pool, shaped like a human kidney, was illuminated by hidden lights which brightened the pink dome with reflected light and played on the gently lapping blue of the waves.

The image of Wrath-Pei's chair hanging still over moving water was unsettling.

"Do you like what I've done with the place?" Wrath-Pei asked.

"I've never been here," the queen answered.

"No? I wish you had; you wouldn't recognize old Tarn's hovel." He gave a slight wince. "It looked like a barracks before I took it over."

"So all the furnishings are yours?"

"Of course! Some of these pieces looked lost in my ship. But here . . ." Wrath-Pei gazed around lovingly.

So Tarn had been guilty of nothing but being in the way, after all.

"Would you enjoy something to drink?" Wrath-Pei asked, and it was now that the queen caught sight of the nearly invisible Lawrence, standing still in one corner of the pool room, like a potted plant. There *was* something vaguely vegetablelike about him, his stunted limbs like short roots, his black clothing, the short-toed boots unmoving, perhaps seeking to suck up the rogue droplets of water splashed onto the nearby tile from the pool.

Wrath-Pei was still waggling his own glass, which held a bright red liquid. (Blood? No . . .)

"No, thank you."

"Perhaps you'd enjoy something else? A . . . ministration from . . . Quog?"

At the potioner's name, Kamath Clan went cold inside, and Wrath-Pei smiled over his cocktail.

"Don't worry, my queen. It will be our little secret. Am I correct in guessing that you've just given your daughter-in-law and your son their initiation into that particular fraternity?"

How does he know? How could he know?

Queen Clan found herself saying, "Yes."

"Ah. Then they should be much easier to . . . manage. Old Quog is an interesting fellow, is he not?"

"You've visited him?" the queen said, almost in horror.

Wrath-Pei's smile widened. "Only . . . in the line of duty. I followed you there this morning. An interesting follow, as I say. But old, very old. I hope he isn't near death?"

The queen fought panic. "He is . . . not well."

"A pity. But we must do what we can for him."

"Yes . . ."

"Good. Now, what was it you wanted to discuss with me?" The incremental smile widened another notch.

"I . . ." Fighting the clutch of anxiety in her

throat, Kamath Clan forced herself back to rigid control. There was a way to handle this—there was always a way.

"I wanted your thoughts on what Prime Cornelian's intentions are."

"His intentions toward Titan?" Still Wrath-Pei's smile had not left.

"Yes."

"He intends to have it."

A blink was the queen's only show of surprise.

Wrath-Pei continued, in a slightly more serious tone, "Oh, surely, he means to have it all. Earth, Mars, Venus, Titan, Pluto. All of the worlds. But as for Titan—not yet."

"We are safe?"

"For now, yes. His immediate goal is Venus. That, of course, is the true prize. And before long he will possess it. But Cornelian having a prize and keeping it are two different things. The Bug will never feel safe—or content—until all the worlds are in his orbit."

"Is there nothing we can do?"

"Hmmm?" Wrath-Pei looked as if he had been distracted from his thoughts. "Oh, yes," he said, still distracted, "there is much we can, and will, do. Cornelian will find that the rose that is Titan has a very long thorn. I was just thinking . . ."

"Then you have no intention of forming an alliance."

"What? Of course not! My only alliance is with *you*, my queen. But perhaps a . . . nonaggression pact, for the moment. They are useful. By now, Cornelian knows that he will have to contend with us sooner or later. Later will serve his purpose, as well as ours. We are quite safe from his tinkering, for the moment. But . . ." Again Wrath-Pei was preoccupied.

"Is there something else on your mind?"

Slowly, Wrath-Pei turned his gaze back to the queen. His smile had returned, widening. With barely a flick of one finger in Lawrence's direction, the hovering chair moved over the water toward Kamath Clan. The queen looked at Lawrence; the boy had not moved a muscle, but there had been a flit of red light across his visored face.

Wrath-Pei's chair stopped a precise meter from Kamath Clan. The two were face-to-face, Wrath-Pei's smile locked in place as he lowered his drink to a holder, which ratcheted out from the chair's base, above the holster where the ever-present clippers reposed.

Wrath-Pei leaned slightly forward, arms resting on his knees. His sculpted face and lionine hair framed his beautiful eyes, which stared intently into the queen's own.

"I was thinking of our own alliance."

The queen, completely humorless in such matters, and who had been contemplating a similar gesture, said, "That was the other matter I came to speak with you about."

"Ah . . ." Wrath-Pei said.

Kamath Clan strode forward and lay her thick hands on Wrath-Pei's knees. The chair rocked

slightly down, its gyros whinning, bringing it instantly back to level.

Kamath Clan looked into Wrath-Pei's amused
eyes.

The queen said, "It has been some time since I
took a mate—but I have not forgotten."

With a smooth motion she began to undo the
fasteners of Wrath-Pei's lower garment; her eyes
never leaving Wrath-Pei's smiling face.

Her wrist was caught in Wrath-Pei's viselike fingers, which held it fast.

"I was thinking," Wrath-Pei said, his voice filled
with the same constant amusement as his eyes,
"more along the lines of what I asked you earlier.
About your son."

25

"It doesn't make sense."

From his outpost set into the side of Sacajawea Patera, in what had been planned as a tourist haven with one of the most stunning views on all of Venus but which now served as a command center for what had so far been a phantom war, Targon Ramir tried once more to make sense of a senseless situation.

He felt helpless, and almost foolish. Actually, more than anything, he felt that he didn't belong here. Not only was he not a military leader—but he felt divorced from his area of true usefulness. Back in Tellus Station, he was an engineer with his hands on the controls. Here, he was a tourist with a pair of binoculars, playing war.

He had to admit that Jean Sneaden had been right to choose this place for reconnaissance. If the Martian attack came—*if*—then this was the place on Venus to monitor the situation. The Sacajawea Center was nothing more than a giant room with a view. But what a view. Like an eagle's nest, the center, known appropriately as the Piton, jutted outward nearly a hundred feet and was tapped into the extinct volcano only four hundred feet down from the summit. The effect was like hanging in midair. One actually had to crane one's neck to catch any glimpse of the peak itself—there were other stations on the patera for mountain sightseeing—and if one had any sense of vertigo at all, it would emerge here. Large sections of the floor were of quartz glass, giving an unrestricted view of the floor of the patera, a rocky glaze of sparse vegetation, and a lazy ribbon of blue river, seven thousand feet below. Now and again a crane would glide by, below one's feet and above a thin finger of cloud.

And the view to either side, and straight ahead, was more than magnificent. A mostly clear horizon dotted with paradise in the making. There was no other place on Venus where so much of the progress that had been made could be seen at once. Lake Clotho Tessera, the widest waterway as yet, was a blue glint to the east; at its shores was the budding community of Lakshmi Planum, where a few hundred early colonists augmented a worker's colony which would someday blossom to tens of thousands. Even now, in the midst of crisis, some defiant soul was plying the shoreline in a sailboat, its bright red sail a promise of possible summers to come.

It was when looking at things like this that Targon Ramir most understood Carter Frolich's descent into madness. To think that all this could be pushed back a hundred years, two hundred years . . .

Other communities were spread like benevolent
rashes in the middle distance; and close by, almost
in the shadow of the volcano, stood Frolich, larger
even than Tellus Station, whose citizens had insisted on the name over Carter's violent objections.
It was destined to be the planet's largest city, a true
metropolis, and already was the center of finance
and trade on Venus, as well as the home of a dozen
transplanted industries from Earth and as many
more from Mars.

With his binoculars, Targon traced the empty
streets, the abandoned construction sights; a swirl
of dust resolved itself in the instrument's autofocus
into a lone little girl, gliding back and forth on a
swing set in her flat backyard, empty beside its new
house save for a single tree and the toy itself. Back
and forth.

She looked so lonely.

Targon moved the binoculars to the perimeter of
Frolich and studied the near battalion of security
forces and batteries of raser cannon, their thin barrels like a row of ancient cigarettes, pointed at the
blue sky.

Pointed at what?

What war?

This was what disturbed Targon most—not knowing. Though he could give a signal from the room
behind him and destroy every feeder station on the
planet, he had no idea if and when—or why—he
would have to give that order. The fact that there
was only one feeder station visible to him—and that

one far off, at the base of another volcano, Sif Mons—made him nervous, but he knew well enough that if he gave the command, the sky would instantly be filled with the brown ugly stains of their destruction. There were no more personnel near any of the stations, and even Tellus itself had been abandoned save for a skeleton crew to monitor the system. They would be safe from the initial blast in their underground bunker—though they would have to abandon the site within a day to avoid residual exposure.

But why would he have to give that order?

The fact was, there were no Martian troops in orbit around Venus. No Martian Marine transports had popped into nearby space, and all intelligence indicated that there were no troops en route. In fact, the most maddening bit of espionage, both electronic and human, that resided in Targon Ramir's Screen indicated with certainty that the Martian Marines on their home planet were currently at stand-down, and many of them were on furlough.

This was insane!

And yet Venus had now been ringed by the Martians with a string of flat metal satellites: too thin to hold troops; too restricted to hold full-scale plasma weapons, which would not get through Venus' shields, anyway; too large to hold raser cannon, which would be ineffective from that orbit.

What was Prime Cornelian up to?

And nothing Targon Ramir's own advisers had been able to come up with was of any help. Were the satellites communications blackeners, old nuclear weapons set to go off simultaneously and form an electromagnetic blanket around the planet, destroying communications? Was this just the first step in Cornelian's invasion? In any event, all defensive units had been given individual instructions in the event of some such an occurrence. But there were no radiation sensor readings from the flat packages, and while it made some sense for Cornelian to destroy Venusian communications, it made not very much, since Cornelian would then hamper his own communications on landing.

Were they decoys? Some sort of new weapon?

That was what made Targon go cold and why all the feeder stations had been kept on highest alert since the first flat box had zipped into orbit five days before. That and the fact that apparently Prime Cornelian himself was in orbit along with the orbiters, while all his troops stayed back on Mars, playing cards and on drinking binges.

It just made no sense.

"Have we heard from every station?" Targon said to Jean Sneaden; he realized that he had been staring at the little girl on the swing while his thoughts wandered.

"Yes," Sneaden said. The red-haired young man held the same preoccupied, worried look he had held for days.

"I should speak with Colonel Hexon myself."

Sneaden nodded and turned to activate the Screen which dominated the center of the room.

And to think they should be serving steins of beer and handing out tourist leaflets here, Targon thought.

Hexon's face filled the screen. He wore his new uniform, and position, well. Former head of Venus security, he was a born military man. Some men were like that, Targon knew; as he had been born to lay his hands on machines, so had Boran Hexon been created to fight. That Hexon had had the misfortune (for him) to be born on Earth as Sarat Shar was bringing peace to Afrasia was his bad luck; he had been one of the first to volunteer for duty on Venus, and over the years had steadily marched his way up the ranks to head Targon's security team. He was sober and tenacious, a rule reader, a prig—just the kind of man for the present situation.

"Sir," Hexon said, bowing curtly and unsmiling.

Targon was about to chastise Hexon for his use of the word *sir*, but under the circumstances he thought better of it. He was wearier of correcting people than he was of the use of the word; and, whether he liked it or not, he was in charge.

"Colonel," Targon said in greeting.

Hexon's uniform looked freshly pressed, the creases as sharp as his eyes. He was not a tall man but appeared tall, and his close-cropped hair made his head look like an ancient bullet.

"Everything's as ready as we can make it, sir," Hexon said, anticipating Targon's question.

"Thank you. I . . . hate to be single-minded about

this, Hexon—but do you have any idea what those orbiters contain?"

"Electronics, and nothing more. There's a lens system, approximately two meters wide, in the base of each one, but that may be to capture reflected light for power. My guess is still that Cornelian is in the early stages of his invasion and that these orbiters are nothing more than communications devices." Hexon's face showed the slightest sour grin. "Anyhow, he's not answering any of our queries— or your ultimatum to leave Venus orbit."

"Not that we could do anything to back that up," Targon said, mostly to himself.

"It was a necessity," Hexon said immediately, and humorlessly. "He knows it, and we know it. Conventions one four eight of the Four World Treaty called for it."

"They also call for Prime Cornelian to remove his orbiters and himself from Venusian space immediately," Targon replied dryly.

Still without humor, Hexon nodded. "And he'll pay for it."

To himself, Targon said, *We'll see*.

To Hexon, he said, "Carry on, Colonel."

"We'll do that, sir. And may I say that I'm proud to have this opportunity to serve."

"Thank you, Colonel," Targon said.

With a snapping salute, Hexon was gone from the Screen.

Targon turned to Sneaden, who was hovering

nearby. The man looked ready to break apart at the seams.

"Have you slept, Jean?" Targon said, putting an arm around the young man's shoulder.

"Not for a while."

"Why don't you get some rest now? If anything happens I promise to wake you."

"I'd . . . rather stay awake," Sneaden said.

Ramir was touched by the young man's gesture.

"All right," Targon said, "then why don't the two of us get some coffee?"

As they approached the coffee server, the room exploded in light.

For a moment Targon thought there had been an attack on the outpost or that Sacajawea Patera, which enfolded them like a cupped hand, had somehow become active again. He braced for a physical sensation, but it was only his eyes that had been affected. Immediately, then, he thought of a power surge; the room was filled with blinding light emanating from the copious banks of Screens trained on Prime Cornelian's orbiters and the areas of land directly below them.

"What in hell is happening?" Targon snapped.

But in a moment he saw for himself.

The world outside the Piton was filled with thin rods of brilliant light piercing the sky, stretching from the atmosphere to the ground. Targon quickly followed one upward and saw no end; it looked like a physical thing, a luminous, sharp line tracing into the highest clouds.

Through the din around him, Targon turned to Sneaden and shouted, "Are they the same as those three energy bursts we monitored a week ago—the ones from the middle of Lake Aurelia?"

Sneaden glanced at a monitor and looked back, puzzled. "They're different. These shouldn't have gotten in past our shields."

A cold feeling gripped Targon. "Could they be some sort of elevator system—a physical phenomenon?"

But even as Sneaden was answering in the negative, the brilliance subsided. The gleaming light rods disappeared as quickly as they had come.

There was a momentary rush of relief throughout the command post—but almost immediately a Screen monitor announced with alarm, "Mr. Ramir, sir, you'd better come see this!"

This plaintive call was followed by ten others.

Targon moved to the nearest screen and saw what looked like a mass of blobs on the ground, made of light, formed into neat rows.

"Where is this—where am I looking?" Ramir snapped.

The monitor said, "Lavinia Station, sir. From two kilometers up."

"Move in on it!"

"Yes, sir."

Instantly the picture zoomed closer to the ground. There was the Lavinia feeder station, and there to one side of it, in a clearing where a second station had been planned, were ranks and ranks of lights, seemingly man-sized.

"Can you get any closer?"

"Yes, sir. *Zoom.*"

The picture zoomed in, onto the roof of the station.

"Move it out into the clearing, dammit!" Targon snapped.

The Screen moved over the clearing.

Targon Ramir held his breath; around him, there were gasps.

The man-lights were soldiers—booted, uniformed, light-shrouded soldiers.

"Are they human?" Ramir said loudly.

From another monitor came, "No, sir! They're . . . energy-based."

"My God," Targon said.

He stepped back, his mind racing, and took in information from the other Screens around him. There were light-soldiers everywhere—in Aurelia, in Lakshmi Planum, in Clotho Tessera, Sif Mons, in the streets of Frolich itself.

Ramir thought fleetingly of that little girl on her swing.

He strode to the window and looked out. There, far below at the base of Sacajawea, were a formation of light points making their way toward the base camp.

Targon spun around and ordered, "Blow the feeder stations!"

There was a freeze of movement.

"Did you hear me? I said blow them!"

For every man and woman at every terminal, it was the death sentence for Venus they had been dreading to hear.

Sneaden, white-faced, was suddenly beside Ramir.

"Targon, we have to talk about this."

Ramir's face was livid. "There's no *time* to talk about it! We have to blow them now or we won't be able to!"

"Those soldiers are not human; they may be only decoys. Or a scare tactic."

"We have to act *now*!"

Sneaden took a deep, shuddering breath. "Targon, I'm afraid I'm going to have to relieve you of command."

Targon Ramir stood immobile, uncomprehending; he was still thinking of the sequence of events he had set in motion: the plasma tubes would be blown, and then there would be a planned exodus from the planet. He would leave Cornelian with the ruins of his own ambition and send him back to Mars empty-handed.

And Venus would be safe, healing her wounds, for a hundred years or more.

Targon barely registered the two guards who now flanked him; neither did he feel the solid sound of the security device activated over his wrists, which had been pulled together in front of him.

He shouted, *"This is the only chance we'll have!"*

Breathing heavily, his eyes focused on Sneaden,

who stood with bowed head before him, and on the others in the room, who stood momentarily oblivious to the chaos on their Screens and would not meet his eyes.

"*What you're doing is madness!*"

Jean Sneaden said quietly, "We can't give up what we've done here."

"I've explained all this to you a hundred times!"

"We took a vote," Sneaden explained, "and decided it was better to fight for Venus than to damage it."

"You're wrong!"

Targon studied the room, looking for a pair of eyes that would meet his own, that would contradict what this foolish young man with red hair was saying. He suddenly felt like weeping.

"Then you'll lose everything," he added.

"We don't think so. We believe Hexon can hold off anything Prime Cornelian can throw at us. We'll fight in the streets if we have to. We'll fight hand to hand if we have to. But this is our home and we won't destroy it."

Wearily, Ramir said, "Is Carter Frolich behind this?"

Jean looked hurt. "This is something we decided on our own, Targon. Frolich is . . . mentally disturbed."

It was the slightest relief to know that they had done what they had done out of conviction and not because they had fallen into Frolich's demented web.

"God help you all," Targon said, suddenly empty.

A kind of peace came over him, knowing that it was out of his hands. He looked for a chair, found one, and sat down. He felt suddenly old, like a tightly wound spring suddenly snapped. Wearily, he looked up at Jean Sneaden and gave the young man a slight smile. He realized suddenly how much Sneaden reminded him of himself forty years ago.

He was so tired, now.

"I understand, Jean," he said quietly. "I understand what you've done. You're wrong, but at least you believe in what you're doing."

Sneaden took another deep breath, as if a great weight had been lifted from his own shoulders, and said, "Thank you, Targon."

"Don't thank me for anything," Targon said. Suddenly all he wanted to do was sleep, and dream. Perhaps dreams would be better than what he saw on the nearest Screen.

He pointed the view out to Sneaden. A swarm of light-soldiers was occupying the Tellus Station, setting up defenses around its perimeter. A group was on the catwalks around the plasma detonators; by now they would have begun to disarm them.

He glanced at the Screen beside it, which displayed a short battle at one of the outer defenses of Frolich City. A strict line of light-soldiers advanced on a raser cannon battery. The battery opened fire. The raser fire went right through the advancing soldiers, who overran the battery without losing their step-march. Suddenly there were three quick flashes of light. Three light-soldiers disappeared from the precise line, appearing a moment later behind the lines, where they caught up to the defenders, who were now attempting to retreat.

There was a blur of motion—then the three light-soldiers were back in formation. The entire line marched over the now bisected bodies of the defenders, which still twitched on the ground, leaking blood.

Targon Ramir's tired eyes met Jean Sneaden's suddenly frightened ones.

Targon said, "What you should be most worried about, Jean, is who let those things get through your shields."

26

This was the moment Boran Hexon had waited for all his life. A fierce fire roared in his belly; he thought of all the ancient tales in his family, which claimed to trace itself back to the ancient Picts who once inhabited a place on Earth now part of the Lost Lands, called England. He had relished the tales of their bloody fights, their conquests, and even their defeats, for they had been a proud breed of men, who had set a goal and then never flinched from pursuing it.

All his life he had wanted to be that kind of soldier—that kind of man. Now he was getting his chance.

However, he didn't quite know what he was fighting yet.

"Report from Sector Five," he snapped to the leftmost of the Screens mounted in front of him.

Nothing came back.

"Sector Two—report," he snapped to the next.

A soldier's face appeared—but not that of Captain Keep-Nel, who was in charge in that area.

"Who in hell are you?" Hexon growled at the scared young face.

"Poston, sir," The soldier made a half-hearted salute, glancing behind him as he did so, and Hexon made a mental note to have him disciplined later on.

"Poston, where the hell is Captain Keep-Nel?"

"Dead, sir."

"And what about the rest of your officers?"

"All dead, sir."

"Look at me when I speak to you, son!" Hexon roared, as the young man once again looked over his shoulder. There was a commotion there, which Hexon could hear but not see.

Poston turned back, looking very scared.

"I'm sorry, sir—" Poston's mouth went wide in pain, and he hissed out something before a bright flash subsumed his image.

Suddenly Hexon was faced with an oval, featureless, helmetless visage made of light. Hexon had the feeling he was being studied.

The Screen went blank.

The main Screen below the others blinked on, giving him the face of young Jean Sneaden.

"Colonel Hexon," Sneaden said without preamble, "you are hereby promoted to the brevet rank of major general."

Hexon's chest swelled with pride. "I will live up to your expectations, sir."

Sneaden nodded, but Hexon picked up the fear on his face.

"Don't worry, son," Hexon said, in as soothing a voice as he could muster. "We'll beat 'em back to Mars."

"So far, nothing has stopped them," Sneaden said.

Hexon answered, "They haven't hit our main defenses yet. I have concentrations of troops in the center of every city and town. The outlying districts we've already had to concede, and they now control the feeder stations, which they went after first. But no matter." Hexon felt his bravado swelling. "They're not us. They're just a bunch of light beams." He gave a grim smile. "Maybe they'll just run out of juice."

"If you could knock out their orbiters—"

Hexon shook his head. "We tried that immediately. After our shields went down and they beamed those things to the surface, the shields went back up again. But there's an eyehole in the frequency they're feeding those things with."

"Can't you jam it?"

"We tried, but no luck. And our cannon can't get through the shields. What I'm hoping for now is something here on the ground to neutralize them where they stand."

"And if you don't come up with something?"

Hexon froze the grim smile on his face. "We'll come up with something."

Sneaden's worried visage blinked out, and Hexon immediately called for an orderly and stood still while a set of general's bars was affixed to his collar.

We'd better come up with something. . . .

*   *   *

In the center of Frolich City, little Amie Carn
saw the beams of light, like beautiful yellow strings
falling down from the sky, and stopped her swinging. Her father had built her swing set for her himself, with expensive wood from the nearby Thin
Forest, where he worked as a conservationist. It had
taken him nearly six months to collect enough cast-
off pieces of good quality to make the swings, but
after the wood was gathered, it had taken him only
two days to construct the swings. It had made Amie
by far the most popular girl in the neighborhood—
though today there was no one else out to play with.

And she shouldn't have been out, anyway. Her
mother had made her promise to stay in her room.
But it had been so boring in there, with nothing on
the Screen but bulletins and warnings. So she had
waited until her mother took a nap, late in the day,
and then she snuck outside.

And now this show in the sky! There were so
many strings that they looked like spaghetti going
into a pot. Some of them had looked like they were
falling straight at her, where she sat still and openmouthed in her swing—but at the last moment they
had begun to fan out away from her, hitting the
ground like fireworks blocks away. There was a fizz-
ing sound as they fell and hit—and then suddenly
things were back to normal.

Amie began to swing slowly again, keeping her
eyes on the sky in case more fiery spaghetti fell. But
things were just as they had been before.

Silent. Still.

Boring.

And then the sirens went off.

Instantly Amie stopped swinging and ran for the house. There was one thing every boy and girl in Frolich knew, and that was to obey the sirens.

Her mother, eyes wide with surprise and sleep, met her at the back door.

"Wha—?" her mother said, grabbing at Amie but looking with wonder at something behind the little girl.

Amie turned around and saw a man made of fiery light; he was crouching as if he would jump.

Then there was a blur, and the man was not there anymore. Amie felt a singing on her skin and grabbed for her mother, but felt only a vague burning in her hands.

She looked up and saw the man of light staring down at her with his blank yellow face.

And her mother was not there.

The man made of light lifted her and carried her away, kicking and screaming.

And now, through her hysterics, Amie saw the doors of other houses opening, and men of light were marching out with Amie's friends in their arms, Bil Mart and Fin-Del and little Jay from next door, who had only started to walk.

Amie twisted her head around, crying, and looked back at her own house, where something that looked like two parts of a real human were laying in the doorway, not moving.

＊   ＊   ＊

"We have reports of high civilian casualties," Major Lent-Kel, who was even more of a soldier than General Hexon himself, reported tersely.

Hexon stared at him, waiting for Lent-Kel to elaborate. They were on one of the last transport shuttles out of Sector One, flying at mid-altitude. The first shuttles to attempt a retreat were fired on from orbit; the shields had been dropped completely now and Cornelian's own ship, manned with raser cannon, had picked off two of three of the first retreating craft. The next two, flying at treetop level, had been downed also, one by ground raser and the other by, incredibly, a leaping light-soldier, who cut the tail from the ship.

"Apparently," Lent-Kel said, "the plasma soldiers have been programmed to kill all adults."

Hexon blew out an angry breath. "What I'd give for just a minute alone with that Martian insect Cornelian." He turned his hard attention back to Lent-Kel. "What about the children?"

"They're being gathered."

"Have we been able to save any of them?"

Without blinking, Lent-Kel said, "Whenever we have, the plasma soldiers go right for that area and wipe out our men." His own frustration and anger was barely held in check. "*Why can't we fight them?*"

"Because they're not human," General Hexon went on, as if amazed at what he was saying. "Three hours, and it's almost all over. Eighty-five percent casualties—almost all of them fatalities." He looked at Lent-Kel. "You've heard the term lightning strike?"

"Yes. Twenty-first century Earth. From an even earlier term, blitzkrieg."

Hexon nodded, pleased. "You know your history."

"I grew up on it. My father was a historian—and he also fought in the Afrasian War."

Hexon said, "I missed that war by three years." He snorted in frustration. "But I got this one. The Afrasian War lasted four years. This one will last four hours."

He shook his head. "*Blitzkrieg* isn't a good term for this."

"Not fast enough," Lent-Kel said, and General Hexon almost laughed.

In the distance, the peak of Sacajawea Patera steadily grew. With a little luck, they would reach the Piton in a half hour. Every available shuttle from every sector was concentrating on this one goal. At the Piton, they would make their final fight. There was little else to do. With most of their men gone and nearly all of their equipment confiscated, it made a grim sort of sense that they would all go down the drain together.

Hexon's greatest frustration, besides the fact that he had been unable to stop or even impede the plasma troops, was that so many civilians had been sacrificed and he had been able to do nothing about it. But someday, he vowed, knowing that it would in all probability not be by his own hand, Prime

Cornelian, the mass-murdering arachnid, would pay
for what he had done—

They did not see the shot that hit them. Hexon
was watching the scenery drag by—a cool-looking
lake surrounded by a scattering of new structures,
including what looked like a boathouse and the beginnings of a dock—when his eyes detected light all
around him.

Uttering a curse, Hexon stiffened his back and
went out proud. He had lost, but had given the
fight everything he had—even though that had been
almost nothing. In the flash before annihilation, his
thoughts were of his ancient ancestors, the Pict general, no doubt, among them who had seen the Iron
Age men swarming down on him in the final fight,
leaving him nothing but pride.

Benel Kran was alone now, he knew. The last
pullout had been more than an hour ago, which
meant that he had had to hide under a table to
prevent being dragged along.

But he had been successful in his quest for soli-
tude—not because he wanted to desert and not because he wanted to be alone, but because he knew
in his gut that he was twenty minutes away from
beating the plasma soldiers. *Twenty minutes.* But
that wasn't a twenty minutes anyone would give
him—not Sergeant Morrin or anyone above him. If
Cast-Prin had survived, he would have understood
what Benel was talking about, because Cast-Prin
had been the only other physicist within a thousand

miles. And now Benel Kran was probably the only physicist left on the planet Venus.

Tentatively, Benel crawled out from under his table and glanced around. Yes, he was surely alone. In the far distance, he could hear occasional battle sounds—sounds which had become increasingly infrequent over the last hour or so. But every *flit* of a raser cannon still made him flinch, and each noise outside the building made him hold his breath.

He stood shakily and realized that his vision was blurry. Closing one eye and then the other, he discovered that the corneal overlay on his left eye had peeled off and been lost. If only he had gone for implants or the even cheaper alternative of eye replacement; but the thought of someone pulling his eyeball out and putting another in its place—the thought of anyone messing with his body parts at all—made him queasy.

So, keeping his left eye closed, he could see what he was doing.

He turned to the equipment on the top of the bench—a scatter of digital analyzers, CompScreens, even a few very old-fashioned loose wires and test leads—and tried to pick up where he had left off. The solution was to merely mirror the plasma entities' energy. In effect, turn them on themselves. When faced with their own "anti-soldiers," the plasma troops should just . . .

Disappear.

He had been on the verge of demonstrating this when the pullout had been ordered. And now all he had to do was activate this circuit . . . *here*, and find a willing subject.

Cradling the miniature aiming dish and humming tubes and boxes, which were difficult to carry (he would have to get one of the engineers to cram all this stuff into an elegant case—that's what engineers were good for), he wandered out of the barracks building, still seeing through one eye.

Outside, a troop shuttle flew low overhead, making the hairs on the back of Benel's neck prickle. It pulled up in a steep sudden angle before flattening out again; in a moment it was gone.

Close by, though, Benel found what he wanted.

At a range of perhaps fifty meters, a plasma soldier was making its way, its back to Benel.

As the plasma trooper sensed him and turned in his direction, Benel pointed the aiming dish in the creature's direction.

For a moment he thought he had achieved instant results, when the plasma soldier disappeared. But then he realized that he had overlooked one facet of the creatures' abilities: their quickness.

Without turning, Benel felt the hairs on the back of his neck rise once again.

He knew the plasma soldier was standing behind him.

"Uh-oh—" he managed to get out, before dropping his equipment in a heap at his feet.

For three hours, Jean Sneaden had been bothered

by the sight of Targon Ramir all but lashed to a chair, following the proceedings like a prisoner.

Now he ordered the older man freed.

There were some surprised looks, but Sneaden repeated the order and it was carried out.

For a moment Targon remained seated, rubbing the spot where the security device had been. Then he rose and walked stiffly forward to the Piton's jutting, windowed end and stood, with his hands behind his back, still gently massaging his wrists.

Sneaden approached him.

"I imagine you consider me little threat now," Targon said gently. He did not turn around to face the younger man.

"That's true," Sneaden said. "And I need your help."

"I would have given it to you tied to that chair," Ramir answered. There was a slight, sad smile on his lips.

"Thank you, Targon," Jean said.

Ramir said, as if the young man had not thanked him, "But it's already too late for all of us."

"Yes."

Ramir nodded toward the outside view. "It would have been a beautiful place someday."

"It still will be," Sneaden said.

"But not for us."

Sneaden was silent.

For a moment the two men stood, not talking, but listening to the increasingly violent sounds of a battle raging in the rooms behind them. Soon, they knew, the defenses of the Piton would be breached, and their own battle would be over.

"I want you to negotiate with Cornelian," Sneaden said.

"He hasn't answered any of your communications, has he?"

"No."

"Then what makes you think he wants to negotiate at all?"

"Perhaps he'll listen to you."

After a moment's pause, during which there were loud exclamations behind them, Targon said, "I'll do what I can. Perhaps we can save the civilians, at least."

Sneaden said, "Cornelian's light-soldiers have been killing everyone but the children."

"The children, then."

"That's what I had in mind."

Ramir looked at Sneaden with comprehension. "You have a daughter, don't you?"

"Yes."

"I'll do what I can."

There was a great rush and blast of light behind them; Sneaden and Targon Ramir turned to see plasma soldiers rushing into the opened doorway at the back of the Piton, their forms still and then flashing in quick movement as they cut down the remaining technicians and Screen monitors in the room.

"My God—" said Targon.

There was the slight punch of air being displaced,

a whiff of ozone; and then Jean Sneaden gave a small cry at Targon's side and was cut down where he stood.

Ramir waited as the last technician was slaughtered, and a ring of plasma soldiers now stood vigil around him.

Oddly, the engineer in him wanted to reach out and touch one of them, to test their corporeality; but he stayed his hand.

Targon took a deep breath and put his mind at peace.

But the end did not come. Rather, there came a loud noise at the rear of the Piton, as someone bustled into the room, followed by more plasma soldiers in formation.

Targon Ramir now knew who had engineered the break in Venus' shields, allowing Prime Cornelian to beam his plasma troopers to the surface.

"Hello, Carter," Ramir said.

With quick strides, Carter Frolich strode toward Targon. The ring of plasma soldiers broke to let the two men face one another.

For a moment the two men's eyes met, and Ramir saw the madness swimming in Carter's mind.

Then Carter said, loud enough for anyone else in the room to hear, if anyone had been alive, *"Now Venus belongs to me!"*

27

Dalin was beginning to fancy the life of a pirate.

It beat working—or running a planet. The hours were flexible; and if one didn't feel like working, one didn't work.

Which encompassed most of Ralf and Enry's philosophy. Dalin could not recall ever meeting a more slothful pair of men in his life. Even his Earthly ministers couldn't compare for lack of initiative. It turned out, in fact, that the scavenging expedition which had brought Dalin into their circle had been the first real work the two had done in months.

"Mostly we *drift*," Enry explained, days after Dalin's arrival—and after their gargantuan drinking jag, which had finally rendered Dalin unconscious and ultimately all three of them with epic hangovers. The two pirates, in fact, had all but turned the running of the ship over to their protégé, whom they now termed a full partner.

Which gave Dalin one-third of . . . what?

For it turned out that the acres of stored goods in the ship's hold had been there for months and

that there was little chance of moving any of it any-
time soon—or making a profit.

"These things 'appen, they does," Enry continued,
explaining their situation from the bow of the
freighter, where Enry and Ralf sat nursing their latest hangover. Dalin had learned from his first experience with Titanian champagne that it was
powerful and stealthy stuff: a froth of bubbles with
a kick like an Afrasian elephant. He had since all
but refrained—though he had to make a good show
of keeping his glass filled, just to be sociable.

The maximum glare shielding was down over the
fore windows, making the stars dull blue points; this
was a necessity, to spare Ralf and Enry's latest
headaches.

" 'Appens ev'ry once in a while, it does," Ralf
piped in. "The lines o' commerce get blocked, an'
nothing gets moved. 'Appened in '21, an' again in
'25. This time could be a bad 'un, with the 'appen-
ings on Venus, and the situation on the Four
Worlds."

"It's a bad 'un, indeed." Enry sighed, comforting
himself by filling his glass with champagne and sip-
ping at it—which made him wince but didn't stop
him.

"It's li' this," Ralf said, holding up the index fingers from his two hands a few centimeters apart.
"Things need to go from point A to point B." He
folded one index finger. "But when point B ain't
there no more, things has t' stay where they is."

"So true." Enry sighed, again sampling his wine.

"So the war is holding you up?" Dalin said innocently.

"Oh, it's great f'r business!" Ralf said. "Wif war you get explosions and such, an' battles, and things get left around for the pickin'. Like the load you came in on, f'r instance. Trouble is, you can't sell it so easy. So you've got to sit on it awhile."

"Yeah, sit on it," Enry said.

"Things'll get better, though," Ralf said with conviction. "They always does. Just li' in th' ol' days, afore Wrath-Pei was runnin' things, when Shatz Abel was king o' the pirates."

Enry smiled. "Now, tha' was a pirate, ol' Shatz Abel! Tear y'r 'ead off wif one hand if y'crossed him, 'e would!"

"But 'e was fair, 'e was," Ralf added.

"Yeah, he was fair enough, all ri'. Unless 'e didn't li' you, an' all."

"An' 'e kept things runnin' pretty much regular, he did. Point B 'ardly ever shut down wif ol' Shatz Abel at the 'elm. But then Wrath-Pei comes along, an' being Martian and all, 'e drives ol' Shatz Abel off, an' plants 'im on Pluto by 'imself, where it's all cold and such, wif tha' little SunOne giving a teeny bit o' light an' a little teeny bit o' heat, and such—"

"A bad break for ol' Shatz Abel, that was."

The two of them sighed, lost in sad, nostalgic thoughts.

"So you're convinced things will eventually get better?" Dalin asked.

Breaking out of his reverie, Ralf said, "Once

Wrath-Pei figures out wha' he's up to, things'll get ri' back to where they was."

"Gravy an' onions!" Enry said hopefully.

"Ri' enough. Gravy an' onions. But ri' now, ol' Wrath-Pei hasn't quite settled his score with that bug Cornelian on Mars, so point B is closed down. You follow?"

Ralf gave Dalin a serious look, and Dalin nodded.

Ralf nodded with conviction. "I knew you would. You're a smart 'un, you is."

"Smart as a pin," Enry said. "You'll make a dandy pirate, wif us as your teachers."

"Ri' enough," Ralf said. "I could tell ri' off that ol' Nub here has had Screen-book learnin', and such. It won't help much in piratin'—but it can't 'urt."

"Can never 'urt," Enry said, filling his glass again and offering his two companions a fill-up. Though Dalin had not meant to imbibe, he now found that he had emptied his glass while listening to these two talk and was ready to empty it again; the light, airy bubbles were spreading through him like a warm bath from the inside out.

"Yes, sir, Screen-book learnin' is a useful thing t'ave. I been wondering, young Nub," Ralf said, slapping Dalin on the knee good-naturedly, "where did you ge' all that learnin'?"

"On Earth," Dalin said brightly. The smooth warmth of the champagne was spreading through him, and he felt himself smiling wider than usual— his glass had been emptied and filled again, as had those of his companions, whose own smiles had grown in proportion. "I grew up in Afrasia! In a palace!"

"A *palace*! Oh-ho!" Ralf said. "And wha' was our little Nub, here—some sort of page or courier?"

Enry was laughing now, spilling as much champagne on himself as he managed to get into their three glasses.

"No!" Enry said. " 'E's the king 'imself! Dalin Shar, 'e is!"

"Ha!" Ralf said, slapping his knee before downing his glass. "Imagine tha'! Wouldn't tha' be somethin', if we was entertainin' Dalin bloody Shar!"

"Ho-ho!" Enry said. "Wouldn't tha' be grand as 'ell!"

Dalin, laughing along with them, took another refill, knocked it back in one swallow, and then heard himself say, "It's true!"

His two companions broke into gales of laughter; Enry quickly uncorked another bottle of champagne and said, "This calls for a toast! The king 'imself!"

Another round was taken, and then another; Dalin felt himself buoyed on champagne and goodwill. Suddenly he was grabbing the two pirates by the arm and proclaiming, "No, it's really true! I *am* Dalin Shar, King of Afrasia and Ruler of Free Earth!"

The two men gave a gulp of laughter.

And then suddenly Ralf caught Enry's eye and the two men stopped laughing.

"Say tha' again?" Ralf asked Dalin soberly.

But Dalin was smiling now, boastful and full of

himself, and he proclaimed with pride, "You *do* have the king himself on board your modest ship! I am Dalin Shar!" Dalin took the bottle from Enry's hand, poured himself and the others a round, and drank off his own.

He saw that his companions hadn't joined him. Abruptly, they looked very serious and sober.

"Say, Nub," Ralf said slowly, "is all this true about you being King Dalin Shar and all?"

"Certainly!" Dalin said, lost in champagne. And then he told them the story of his escape, exaggerating his own exploits, finishing with his arrival in their cargo hold on the verge of death.

"Well, I'll be a Martian monkey," Enry said in wonder.

"Yeah, me, too," Ralf concurred. "And 'ere I thought we was lucky just findin' all tha' champagne. Turns out we 'ad a treasure ri' under our noses and didn't know it."

"We know it now," Enry said, all business.

"Ri'," said Ralf.

Dalin heard all this through a haze of alcohol and laughter. The laughter was his own, and he barely felt it when the bottle and glass were lifted from his hands, and when he himself was lifted bodily and carried from the foredeck to the cargo hold.

"Time to work?" he asked, his grin creasing his face, and he began to giggle so hard that his two companions had to stop and lay him on the ground until the fit passed.

"Not work. Not for you, exactly, Nub," Ralf said.

The two pirates once again lifted him and bore him to the hexagonal cargo holder which had borne Dalin into their midst.

It was only when he woke up with a headache eight hours later, sealed within what had so recently almost been his coffin, that he realized perhaps he was not to be a pirate after all.

He lost track of time. He was not treated badly; but neither was he treated with the comradeship he had so recently enjoyed with Enry and Ralf.

Enry brought him his meals twice a day; but there was no more champagne, and Enry would not meet his eyes and only grunted when Dalin tried to talk to him.

Dalin knew they had gone into phase drive, because he felt the emblematic shiver and rush—but where they were heading he could only guess at—which began to fill him with a growing fear.

He spent his time thinking of Tabrel Kris.

When, on the fifth or sixth day, Enry brought him his first meal of the day, Dalin finally said, "Is this a matter of money, Enry? Because if it is, I can work something out. Whatever you're being paid for my capture, my people on Earth will double, when the time comes."

Enry grunted.

"They'll murder me, you know, if you turn me over to Cornelian or to his Afrasian traitors. I won't live for ten minutes after you hand me over."

Again, Enry grunted.

"Don't you have any feeling at all? Any pride, or patriotism?"

"I wouldn't know abou' tha', Nub," Enry grumbled, before closing the door.

But on the other side, Dalin heard Enry say, "An' it ain't like we 'ave a choice, Nub. Sorry and all."

The days passed. And passed.

And then suddenly they pulled out of phase drive. There followed nearly a whole day of inactivity; and then Ralf was there at mealtime, only he did not bear a meal but rather a grim visage.

"Time to shove off, Nub."

Dalin said, "You'll pay dearly for what you're doing."

Ralf said, "You don't qui' understand, Nub. We got 'earts, and all. Truly we do. We ain't turning you over to no Martian or Earth scum. Almost as bad and all—but not anything we could do anything abou'." Earnestly he went on, "We could 'ave 'id you, but in the long run 'e would 'ave found out and cut us up like fresh meat. He's quite a pirate, 'e is, and 'e knows everything." He put his index fingers up, wiggled one, then the other. "Our choice was an easy one, Nub. Either get kilt or turn you over from point A to point B. You was one o' the only moveable commodities on the market these days."

He lowered his eyes. "Sorry and all, Nub. Truly I am."

Two strangers had appeared behind Ralf and
waited for the pirate to move out of the way before
pulling Dalin out of the capsule. They were dressed
in black, including boots and gloves, though they
appeared fingerless and wore visors which covered
most of their faces. Between them, though, they
had enough strength to hold Dalin between them
and propel him forward, out of the ship's lock and
into another, docked vessel, where other black-
suited strangers waited.

Dalin looked back and saw both Ralf and Enry
looking at him dejectedly; Enry managed a tiny,
grim wave.

Dalin was pushed roughly forward toward the
waiting black figures.

He guessed he was planetside. The gravity was
different—substantial, though less than Earth's. He
guessed he was either on Mars or, more likely,
Titan.

He had been blindfolded with a blank visor almost immediately. He was offered neither food,
drink, nor conversation, and his own questions had
gone unanswered.

But the trip had been short enough. When he felt
the bump of either docking or landing, he guessed
the latter; his evidence only mounted when he was
taken out of the ship and smelled what must be
atmosphere, thin and sweet, nothing like the dry
canned oxygen of ships.

A short trip in what felt like a ground transport

followed, and then a short march into a building, his forced sitting in a chair, quite comfortable, to which he was bound.

And now?

Suddenly the visor came alive, making him gasp. It was like the blind finding sight. The dimensional image registered on his retinas, flowed up to his brain—

He gasped again, cried out.

"Tabrel!"

It was her: Tabrel Kris, whose features over the last months had stayed sharp in his mind: Tabrel, whose very existence had kept him alive, continued to fill him with hope. She was sitting on a chair in a barely furnished room, staring out through a window at a landscape that must be Titanian: a lush hill rolling to a blue lake in the middle distance, under an eerie clutch of lights that brightened the clouds in a blackened sky. It was like staring at a strange photograph.

"Tabrel!"

"She cannot hear you, King Shar," a voice chuckled, very near.

The image blinked out.

Someone pulled the visor from Dalin's face, making him blink and gasp again.

The voice said, "I am Wrath-Pei."

A figure was there, leaning over him from a gyro chair anchored beside Dalin's. He was beautiful and repugnant: a man like a statue, perfectly featured but chilly as white marble. A mane of silver hair

flowed back from his high forehead; he was dressed
in silver and black. In his hand he held something
like an ancient machine: two open blades flowing
back to sculpted ebony handles. Dalin smelled the
scent of oily lubrication. The man's fingernails were
perfectly manicured, polished.

Dalin suddenly realized that he could not move
his head, not a millimeter. The man did not blink,
but leaned out over Dalin's face, his free hand deli-
cately grasping the edge of one of Dalin's eyelids,
pulling it away from Dalin's eye as if he were about
to remove a rogue lash.

The clippers rose up into view.

As Dalin began to hear his own screams, the
man's gentle voice lied, "Now, this won't hurt a bit."

Blind, once more.

Weakness made Dalin unable to move. There was
a band of hot pain across his face, as if he were
wearing a visor heated to searing temperature. He
felt something soft pressing against his eyes and was
able to reach gently up to tap at two bundles of
soft, gauzy material held in place with a thin metal
strip that encircled his head. He could not remove
it and did not wish to; whenever he moved his face
in any way, the band of hot pain shot from side to
side like a poker laid across the bridge of his nose.

He felt an overwhelming urge to close his eyes—
but even when he slept, which was fitfully, he was
unable to indulge this compulsion.

Always, he felt the tender touch of those gauze pads against his naked eyes.

By meals, he was able to count two and a half days before he felt, with a shiver that made him want to scream, the knock of Wrath-Pei's chair bumping against his own. He felt the monster's clement touch over his eyes, heard Wrath-Pei's coos of solicitous attention.

"There, there," Wrath-Pei said, patting Dalin's arm. "It won't last more than a day longer. You'll feel much better come tomorrow."

With a chuckle, the monster was gone.

Only to return the next day, while Dalin dozed. Dalin awoke to feel Wrath-Pei's hands on him, peeling back the gauze with care, making those loving sounds. . . .

The world brightened. He saw the monster's grinning face hovering over him, the eyes probing this way and that.

"How do you feel?" Wrath-Pei asked.

Before Dalin could answer, the monster had placed something in front of the king's face: a mirror, with which he could regard himself.

Dalin screamed at what he beheld: a human face with a skeleton's sight: round lidless eyes bulging, always to be open, never able to close.

Laughing, Wrath-Pei drew the mirror away. "Splendid! Thank you! Splendid!"

"Why have you done this to me?" Dalin cried.

Wrath-Pei chuckled. "I'm afraid your troubles have only just begun, King Shar. To Prime Cornelian, you are of no use at all. If he had you, you would be dead now. You are of no use to me now, but you may be later. So I'm afraid you must go to a safe place, an out-of-the-way place."

Wrath-Pei's chair moved back away from Dalin's; the king beheld a black-dressed boy without fingers, who guided it from the room. He felt his own chair move forward, following Wrath-Pei's, through corridors, out into the deep, cool darkness of Titanian night. They entered two transports, and after a short journey, Dalin's chair once more followed, as Wrath-Pei entered a spacious building whose outside dimensions Dalin gauged as huge. They were sped through hallways, and then Dalin was thrust ahead of a waiting Wrath-Pei, whose chair had been pulled to the side of an open entrance, into which Dalin's own was pushed.

And there was Tabrel Kris, in the flesh, sitting quietly in her chair staring sadly out at the night.

Overcome with the sight of her, forgetting his circumstances, Dalin screamed "Tabrel!" while trying to urge his chair forward from where it had been stopped in the center of the room, meters from the window and from Tabrel Kris.

Slowly, Tabrel turned from the window. She stared at Dalin with unfocused eyes. For a long moment she looked confused, as if her mind were traveling back from another place.

Then, slowly, she turned back to the window.

"Tabrel, it's me! Dalin Shar!"

Tabrel made no movement.

Dalin covered his face with his hands, tears beginning to flow from the corners of his ruined eyes.

To the sound of Wrath-Pei's laughter, Dalin was taken from the room and returned to the waiting transport.

"I should have told you, King Shar," Wrath-Pei tittered, "that she's married! I can't tell you how amusing it was to me when Queen Kamath Clan discovered through her . . . ministrations that our little princess was in love with you instead of poor Prince Jamal. Though by her reaction to your current appearance she may rethink her relationship to her hubby—unless, of course, due to the potions she didn't even recognize you." The titter built to a full-throated laugh as Dalin was pushed into the back of the transport and the door closed on him.

"Off we go!" Wrath-Pei said, and when Dalin's tears began to dry he was once more on board a ship in phase drive, on his way to a place he could not imagine.

28

_____

"Magnificent!"

Prime Cornelian, High Leader, could not keep the delight and satisfaction from his voice. Though he knew that most, if not all, of what he now beheld had been staged for his benefit (especially since he had given the directions himself), there was nevertheless a part of him that relished the moment in terms beyond the purely theatrical.

There was, after all, a part of all humans that relished spectacle, was there not? Did not the ancients have their victory celebrations?

Bread and circuses—didn't someone once write that that was what the public craved?

And staged and theatrical though it was, the public surely seemed to crave it.

Lowell City—and Mars—had never seen anything like it, of this the High Leader was sure. Even in the early days of the republic, when the first prefects marched on foot to preside over the first Senates, Prime Cornelian knew that there had not been such a turnout as this. For those early parades had been mere celebrations of government, a public display of civics. This was something much grander, and much more conducive to hysteria: a planetwide banquet hailing the subjugation of another planet—and, of course, the man who had accomplished it.

Had any such thing ever occurred anywhere on the Four Worlds? The High Leader doubted it. Even the Earth ancients of Rome—who had, after all, named Mars after their god of war—could not approach this spectacle in elegance and magnitude, never mind sheer length. Here came the High Leader himself at the head of the pageant, riding upon an armored float forty meters high (shielded of course); its lighted bunting pleasantly hurt the eyes, even here in broad daylight, of the thousands who lined the thoroughfare, fifty deep in places. From his perch the High Leader tried to find guile or hidden treachery on their adoring faces, but could find none. Oh, how the people loved a winner! Weeks ago he had been vilified in secret, no doubt plotted against; his only ally had been the iron fist and the absolute will to use it. How long ago had he ordered the annihilation of one of his own towns—and then blamed it on off-planet intervention, not expecting anyone, most of all Martians, to believe it? How recently had they hated his every move; his suppression of liberties, even basic ones; his outright murder of their elected officials; his threat to destroy any of them, at any time, merely because it suited his purposes? But today—they loved him! Pynthas had reported that the Red Police

had arrested only *ten* people in the last three days—
and seven of them for plotting victory celebrations
in Prime Cornelian's honor that were so grand as
to be dangerous! The High Leader had immediately
commuted their sentences.

They *loved* him!

This was something that Prime Cornelian had yet
to fully understand. He knew it was possible; as a
student of history he understood the phenomenon
well. But these adoring, wildly happy, tear-stained
faces to whom he had merely brought a victory he
had expected all along—this was something new
and unknown to him. And he found that he was
. . . enjoying it.

Waving now to the endless crowds, lifting two
and sometimes four limbs in acknowledgment, to
the extent that his joints began to ache for an oil
bath (oh, how good that would feel later!) he had
to admit that it was much better to be liked than
hated. Not quite as good, or useful, as being
feared—but it could take second place.

And to the horizon, to either side of the grand
thoroughfare which had been built by the early Martians to celebrate their independence and their democracy, he saw only Martian faces, filled with love
for him.

For the briefest moment, his own heart felt something like love for these, his people, to whom he
had brought greatness for his planet.

Proudly, he stood up on his rear limbs and waved
high to the crowd, knowing that they would enjoy

the rest of what the day held in store, the rest of the victory parade.

Behind Cornelian's armored float came another display, at eye level. As the ancients had done, so, too, now marched, in the modern equivalent of chains, the vilified loser of the recent conflict: Targon Ramir, lately Venusian leader, now conquered and humbled.

And behind the prisoner and the mile of sharply dressed, crisply marching Martian Marines, a veritable circus of wonders: miles of captured goods already imported from Venus: carts filled with fruits and vegetables; expensive fishes and animals rarely seen on parched Mars, not even in zoos—otters, seals, the massive, tanked sleek body of a tiger shark swimming angrily and ceaselessly, a *penguin* (all but extinct on Earth, a quick failure at Mars' north polar cap, but thriving in the doctored southern wastes of Venus' growing ice shelf)—and tomatoes as large as big fists, cabbages like leafy gods, red peppers the size of heads, bananas so yellow they hurt the eyes. All of these were wonders to the thin Martians. And there were other goods as well: trees, sequoia breeds pulled up at the root and transported whole, displayed on trailers like fallen rockets; they would make expensive houses and be worked by Martian craftsmen into marvelous carvings. Indeed, there had been a time on Mars when wood itself had proved better barter than precious metals; these days, it was merely pricey and rare. There were carvers out in that crowd, Cornelian knew, who now wept with joy and thanksgiving. Feeling their eyes on him now, he made his wave even more imperious.

There came caravans of Venusian equipment. Though much had been left on Venus to aid Carter Frolich in his continued work, much had been stolen away to find new uses on Mars. The prize of the lot: a feeder station, whose parts, now displayed, would be reassembled in the Syrtis region and aid in Mars' own continual renewal. It represented the finest in all the Worlds, and though Frolich had been loath to part with it (not that he had had much choice), he had contented himself with Cornelian's promise of aid to build even bigger and better facilities. At this, Frolich's eyes had nearly washed over with grateful tears.

My, my! Cornelian thought. *Everyone loves me these days!*

And then came eight massive plasma detonators; their tubes, bluer than any ocean or sky, straddling three trailers each. They made the sequoias look like toothpicks. But here they were, serving a threefold purpose as testaments to Targon Ramir's failure, as spoils of war, and (though no Martian was aware of it) as useful weapons on the home front.

If any of these adoring millions, traveled here today from say, far-off Argyle Planitia, should plan open revolt in the future . . .

The High Leader smiled to himself: so many weapons! So many ways!

And on and on came the parade, the miles of goods, the nearly endless stream of booty that made Wrath-Pei's pirating look puny by comparison.

Wrath-Pei . . .

For a moment the High Leader's demeanor darkened, as all of his remaining problems lined up in his mind: Wrath-Pei, who would be dealt with in the future; Kris's daughter; and that infernal boy Dalin Shar, apparently still alive, though inconsequential; and then that other problem. . . .

There it was again—-that tickle at the back of Cornelian's mind that he could not scratch. What was it? From the beginning of the enterprise, there had been this feeling of something else, something hidden. . . .

What was it?

What the devil was it?

The High Leader came back to himself, realizing that, for a moment, the grand parade had stopped and that he stood, frozen and angry, roaring like a metal lion on his high perch. Down below him, the crowd stood suddenly mute and frightened. As well they should be. Cornelian could imagine how he looked: the depths of terror he was capable of instilling, as well as beneficence.

Loosening his iron fists, allowing his mouth to relax from its bellow of anger and frustration, he showed a kindly face and said, "Proceed!"

Instantly, the fear turned once more to cheering, and the procession continued: the child-slaves from Venus, hundreds and hundreds, in ranks of fifty and files of a hundred, in their new red uniforms, the new Martian Youth who would someday return to Venus, thoroughly indoctrinated, and run it in Mars'—in Cornelian's—name.

Oh, such a day!

Such a spectacle!

But here they were, already at their destination! The high, pink sandstone facade of Olympus Stadium already loomed before them. To either side of the massive gates, which had been opened wide to accommodate today's procession, spectators were massed to gain entrance to their seats. Cornelian could see the frenzy in their eyes.

Not to be missed! Not this!

And then Cornelian was passing beneath the portal, his head nearly touching the crown. There was the cool darkness of the entry tunnel—and then they burst out into sunlight, and the bathing roar of cheers that greeted the High Leader as he was slowly borne into the high, deep bowl of the structure.

Oh, the green of the field—greener than any lawn on Mars, sprinkled with precious water day and night for days to bring it to succulent thickness! And then, how carefully it had been clipped! As the High Leader regally looked down, the *smell* of that grass reached his brain, and he nearly swooned with delight! Here was something nearly unknown on Mars—*the odor of cut grass*!

Magnificent!

And finally, his armored float, now a dais, was

moved into place at the far end of the stadium, and the crowd hushed as one, the gasp of their silence an audible sound, as they waited for his words.

The High Leader paused for a moment and drank it in: the green grass, with its waiting gallows gantry in the center; the ring of stiffly standing, raser rifle-bearing Red Police circling the perimeter of the field; the seats packed with expectant faces all the way up to the high lip of the stadium; the flags of the three worlds—Earth, Mars, Venus—flapping in the languid breeze high above that lip: the new Martian flag—a black sickle in a black circle, in a field of crimson—in the center and higher than the other two. The blue-green of Earth's flag, and the yellow of Venus', seemed to stand in subjugation and gratitude to Mars—*to the High Leader himself*.

He gripped the edge of his platform with his front digits and looked out over them.

And then he spoke.

He spoke, and shouted, and waved his fists, and their cheers rose, higher than his dais, higher than the lip of the Olympus Stadium, and higher than the yellow and blue-green and red flags.

He screamed at them, told them of their power and destiny, how they were made to rule. "Yes! Yes!" they screamed back; it was their fate to rule, and it was their joy for him to lead them!

He went on and on, for an hour and nearly two, until twilight came and dropped into darkness; until the stadium lights took over for the departing sun; until his voice was dry and his fists tired of beating at the air. And then suddenly he turned from them, at the height of their ecstasy, and the lights went out, except for one brilliant spot which fell on the gallows gantry in the center of the stadium.

And the lone figure who was bound to the top, as fires were lit beneath.

Targon Ramir fell asleep three times during Cornelian's speech. He knew that whenever he awoke, he would be able to tell exactly what the so-called High Leader was saying. The harangue was such a mishmash of ancient rhetoric, such a theatrical display of jingoism, worldistic blather, and twisted patriotism that it literally put Targon to sleep. There were sections of it that had been lifted whole from other such speeches of the past.

When the chemical fires were lit below him, however, Ramir came fully awake. He knew what would follow. He had expected Prime Cornelian to at least offer him a good drugging to dull the searing pain to come, but he should have known better.

Luckily, he had been able to devise something himself (thank you for those chemistry tutorials back in his early days with Carter Frolich!) from the various putrid meals he had been fed (cocoa, distilled from the rancid substance the Martians called *krint,* had finally done the trick), and now he was well on the way to feeling little when the fires reached him.

No doubt the insect was out there somewhere in

the darkness, licking his metal lips over the show to come.

The gantry's metal had been treated with a layer which allowed the flames to creep upward, growing as they rose. Targon had heard that Cornelian had even considered using some of his precious stolen Venusian wood to stoke the fires, but Sam-Sei had been brought in instead to simulate a wood burning and thereby save money.

Targon almost laughed at the thought.

Targon's last days had been philosophical ones. The obligatory torture had taken much of his outer existence away, leaving him only with private thoughts. He decided he was a good man, and so could go to his death with pride—even if his body no longer looked very appealing.

Whatever sadness he had left he had saved for Venus—the planet itself, and on what it would now become. The stolen children, which would have been Venus' legacy, would still be that, though in a horribly mangled form. Perhaps there was one or two among them who would resist the indoctrination to come and hold hope in a secret place. . . .

The heat was beginning to grow—to the point where, even with the drug, Targon could not ignore it.

Targon thought of Carter Frolich and found that he could no longer find hatred for the man. While Targon was about to taste hell and then pass on to whatever else there was, Carter had made his own hell and would live in it until Prime Cornelian had

no further use for him. That Frolich did not realize
he was in hell made him only that much more
pitiable.

There—a hint of high heat now, making breathing difficult. It was like that moment in the dentist's
chair when all his potions fail and the laser hits a
still-sharp nerve.

Targon knew that the end was near. He would
mercifully suffocate before he burned. His body, as
unappealing as it was now, would be quite unattractive roasted to a cinder.

The stadium's cheers were beginning to fade.

Flames were licking at Targon's legs. The drug
was working, at least for the moment. He began to
gulp at hot air, fighting with the flames for oxygen.

"*God help Venus!*" he cried out hoarsely.

And then he felt himself rising. It was as if he
were being lifted on a column of heat and cloud.
There was pain, but it was distant—as if the dentist
had done his work.

All at once he felt a surge of hot memory and
saw himself back in his early life, on a street in
Delhi, on a golden day when a man saved him from
himself and the entire future of a planet opened up
to take him up on golden wings—

29

Beyond the outer reaches of the Five Worlds, beyond their outermost world, in a region of darkness but not emptiness known as the Kuiper Belt, Kay Free met with her two companions once more.

Again, Mel Sent was last to arrive, with blusterings and lack of apology.

"So much to do—always so much to do! There was *Mother* to attend to briefly, and then once again . . ."

She went on, but there was an undercurrent of melancholy to her complaints that Kay Free both understood and mourned.

"*I* was here when requested—as always," Pel Front snapped.

Mel Sent began to defend herself, making Pel Front even more waspish.

Kay Free said nothing, though normally she would referee and find contentment in the act. But her mind was on other things.

"You've both attended to your other duties?" she

asked when finally the sparring between Mel Sent and Pel Front ended on its own.

"Yes," Pel Front said shortly.

"Mother was not happy—but, yes, of course."

"None of us is happy," Kay Free said.

"True," Mel Sent said, and even Pel Front did not disagree.

"Then we are agreed that the calling was not a false one," Kay Free said.

"Agreed." Mel Sent sighed.

Pel Front nodded.

"Very well," Kay Free said, with a sense of finality.

There were no creatures here, no life-forms to inhabit. Kay Free herself was but a whisper of pale light, a shimmer on the border of the visible and infrared spectrum. Seen by an optical telescope, she would be all but invisible, a scatter of particles excited by the faintest of solar winds. With the aid of an instrument studying the infrared band, she would appear more substantial; in a radio telescope, she would give evidence as a blot of the faintest noise.

For some reason, perhaps sadness, Kay Free wished that she was embedded in a life-form at the moment. She sensed the same in the others. In her mind's eye, she still saw the bloated, blackened dead thing she had shared in the water; and now she knew the source of her despondency.

"I wish this were not so," Mel Sent said; and if she had been in a life-form capable of tears, she would show tears at this moment.

"Wishing will not make it go away," Pel Front said, his peevishness muted.

"There is work to do," Kay Free said, seeking to break the spell.

The others acceded; and work was done.

Kay Free thought of farming. Or, specifically, of harvest.

She had studied farming once, early in her days here, had studied it with the fascination she held for all life. On the third planet, where she had begun her study, she had first been drawn to the regularity of it: rows of planted things, cultivated with almost worshipful diligence, because, to these creatures on the third planet, this cultivation meant life itself. For a brief time she had studied the hunt—but had quickly lost interest, because hunting was only the extension of the end of all life: death. Death did not interest her, except as a process; it was the struggle of life *to stay alive* that she found fascinating, and elegant. *Noble* was a word she had favored.

Pel Front had argued, and persuasively, that the growing of crops was only another form of hunting: that one form of life, vegetation, was raised with care not out of love but only to sustain another form of life. "It's the same as the raising of livestock," he had said, "only vegetables don't moo."

His reasoning had been persuasive, and yet it had not won Kay Free over; to her, vegetables, though life, were not in any way sentient. They were more a hybrid of life and nonlife; even a cow could think, on its own terms (she had once inhabited a cow, just to test this theory), but a vegetable was nothing more than response to stimuli.

But this was all play: what really interested her was the excitement that the end product of farming engendered in the farmers themselves. The harvest was, on the third planet at that time, an actually mystical experience—something that would later be called religious. There were festivals to the natural world, to water and earth, blessings for rain and temperance of climate, worship of the star that gave the farmers, and their crops, warmth and needed sustenance.

"Hogwash," Pel Front had said—pointing to these same primitive farmers beating in the skulls of rival tribesmen when in the least threatened, when Kay Free had tried to argue their nobility. "They just do what they do to stay on their mudball as long as possible, before turning back to dust."

But Kay Free had kept her thoughts and had always taken a kind of schoolmarmish pride in the witnessing of any harvest, be it a row of fat kale in Mesopotamia or the first hydroponic tomatoes, tiny and pallid, on Mars.

And here, now, was a different kind of harvest.

While performing her task, something unknown to her dropped over her like a shroud. In all of the millennia of her existence, she had only felt doubt once or twice. Always, it had dissipated almost before it was sensed.

This time, it rose into her thoughts and stayed.

Instantly the calling came to her.

It came to the others, also. A light-year to her left, Pel Front stopped his task; and a hundred light-years beyond him, Mel Sent did the same. Without living bodies to inhabit, they became merely particles frozen in space. It was more a silence through their being than an outer silence here, where there was no sound.

As always, everything was lifted away from Kay Free: All thought and awareness were gone; she was freed of everything save being itself.

Without thinking or speaking, she said, "Yes, my Life."

Blissful nothingness filled her, drowned her doubts, washed her clean.

"Yes, my Life," she repeated.

As instantly as it had come, the moment of calling went away.

Kay Free sensed in her companions, also, a removal of doubt and a cleansing.

No longer did she wish for a living thing to inhabit, in order to produce tears. There was still a sadness—but with it now, making it whole, was understanding.

In a little while they were finished.

In the gathering place, they pushed their chosen fragments off into the appropriate orbit.

Kay Free once again thought of harvest; the chunks of ice, planetary detritus, had been selected with care from the farm that the Kuiper Belt was; they had been pulled out of their rows, ripe and fat, and now they would perform their appointed task.

One after another, the fragments, some as large as ten kilometers, were flung in a precise arc, dropped out of their farm and downward. Soon the warmth of the star would warm them, and they would grow tails. Some of the ice and gases on their surfaces would melt away behind them, making them beautiful for a while to behold.

They would become comets.

And, when they reached their destination, something else.

30

Wrath-Pei's ship was the biggest Dalin had ever seen. In the brief glimpse he'd had of it before being transported from the ground shuttle which had brought him to orbit, he estimated its length at at least one kilometer. Perhaps more.

It was a veritable city inside—though Dalin saw little of it, save the "cutting room," as Wrath-Pei called it, to which he was immediately transported. The room was identical to the one on Titan in which Wrath-Pei had cut off Dalin's eyelids; there was an identical gyro chair, silver and menacing, the sight of which brought acidic fear up from Dalin's stomach.

But he was not bound to the chair for another operation. Instead, two of Wrath-Pei's black-suited henchmen, this pair possessing all their fingers but walking with a curious, clubfooted gait produced by the absence of most of their toes, soon appeared, bearing a thermal garment and a reentry suit into which Dalin was forced.

In the middle of this procedure Wrath-Pei appeared, the faint whir of his chair audible before it appeared in the doorway, a slight and cruel smile, as always, on his lips.

"You will find it uncomfortable, to be sure," Wrath-Pei said as the two black-suited men lowered the quartz-plated helmet over Dalin's head. Already he felt the cramp of the tight outfit; he knew that once the helmet was in place, he would look like an Egyptian sarcophagus with a porthole over his face.

Wrath-Pei scowled. "They really should do something about the style of these things," he said. "But I suppose function comes before form, in this case. Ah, well."

He stayed to watch while one of the henchmen activated the suit's pressure system and attached an oxygen line.

Inside the suit, flat on the floor, Dalin felt even more uncomfortable; despite the tightness, he now felt itchy all over.

Wrath-Pei grinned. "Oh, yes, it will be quite uncomfortable. But it won't be for long. Out of—" he yawned, "mercy, I'll see that we get to our destination as soon as possible. I've had your body functions slowed down, so you should nap through the entire trip. And lest you find the thermal garment too warm—trust me, you'll thank me for it later. Try to be patient."

And then Wrath-Pei was gone; and so were the two henchmen, turning out the lights as they club-footed their way out of the room.

To his relief, Dalin found that he could sleep—
though his eyes remained, as ever, opened.

And then mercies continued, and they were at
their destination.

Dalin had not eaten, but the suit's reduction of
his metabolism had ensured that he didn't need sustenance. His skin, though, felt like it was crawling
with cold things. He felt sluggish and dull, yet what
he really wanted to do was tear the thick metal suit
off with his bare hands and scratch the bottom of
his right foot.

Just at the height of his discomfort, when he felt
that he could no longer stand it, the two henchmen reappeared.

Dalin's oxygen line was removed; he heard the
hiss of the suit's internal supply tank taking over.
Gradually his body functions were brought back up
to normal—which only made the itching worse.

He was placed on a flat gurney and transported
to one of the ship's airlock chambers, where Wrath-
Pei waited for him.

"Splendid!" Wrath-Pei said, giving the suit a rap
with his fist, stopping it before him. He leaned over
in his gyro chair and looked through the thick
quartz faceplate.

"Just wanted to say farewell, King Shar!"

Dalin's wide, lidless eyes stared up at him.

Wrath-Pei said, "I also wanted to tell you that it
may be a bit irritating on the way down, since I've
had your suit adjusted just a wee bit from normal.

You may feel a bit of heat. But not to worry—you'll survive. And if you get hot . . ." he chuckled, "you'll cool off, soon enough." He rapped on the suit again, making a dull faraway clang to Dalin's ears. "Farewell!"

Without another word, Dalin was put into the airlock; and after a moment the outer door was opened and he was propelled into space.

His body was rammed violently inside the tight confines of the suit by the ejection. Then he was floating free. He felt both weightless and helpless. His eyes filled with a splash of bright stars.

Then the tiny retrorockets on the reentry suit fired and he was moving.

The suit angled around, blurring the stars like a fast-rotating night—and then froze in place.

His sight was filled with what looked like a bright, compact star off to one side. Partially eclipsing it, and nearly filling his sight directly in front of him, was a dull blue world, like a cracked, ugly glass marble.

The rockets fired again, like two quick kicks on his back.

He began to fall.

He screamed. And yet his terror was nearly subsumed by fascination. The blue marble gradually widened beyond his vision; but before doing so, he saw at its limb the faintest of atmospheres backlit by a light source on the far side.

The light source was SunOne.

The planet was Pluto.

He fell faster now.

And then the heat began.

The edges of the quartz faceplate reddened. Heat seemed to leak in around it, like a filament slowly warming, until he felt as if he were being cooked alive.

And still he fell faster. Through the porthole, he watched Pluto grow larger and more menacing. Details began to resolve. He saw below him a chain of icy mountains, bordered by a massive, vicious chasm, as if an ax had been taken to the world.

Inside, the suit pressure built and now threatened to overwhelm both his fright and the heat. He fought to move his lungs, screaming in bursts to make himself breathe. Now the quadruple forces of burning alive, unbelievable pressure, boundless panic, and lack of oxygen nearly made him burst from within.

Just as he felt he could take no more, a marvelous sight rode briefly by his faceplate: a city of lights and ice that tore away from him in the distance.

And then there was a popping sound behind him, even as the blue icy world rushed up to slap him, followed by a jerk. The parachute had opened.

The heat was gone. The reddened faceplate cooled as he drifted down. It was as if he were on a cloud. He beheld wonders: the thick fingers of mountains pointing up at him—and, directly below, a flattened plateau, edged out over a shallow canyon, all covered with swirling snow.

He dropped into a squall of ice crystals, which

beat against his faceplate like tapping fingernails. He could see nothing. Again he felt claustrophobia try to take him—but then there was a blow of wind, clearing his vision.

He saw the place he would land.

An ice shelf, a hundred meters from the edge of the cliff, pushed up at him.

He hit the planet.

Again ice crystals gathered around him as the re-entry suit fell by design over onto its back. Dalin heard snaps and clicks of mechanisms working.

And now the suit opened; the top rose away from him on hinges, like a coffin, and the cold reached him—

Assaulted him.

Freezing, he tried to pull the reentry suit back down around him. It would not budge. Shivering, he scrambled from its confines and stood up. The thermal suit Wrath-Pei had provided for him was bare protection; already the sting of ice crystals cut his face. He pulled the hood tighter around him, but it was scant help.

There was a constant low moan of wind.

As if on cue, it stopped snowing. And now the planet spread out around him in true icy splendor. A cliff of ice blocked his view to the east and south; to the north, a hammered plain of blue-white spread out flat like a plate, melding gradually into the mountain ranges westward. The sky above was inky black, mutely lit by the glow of SunOne, just edging below the horizon; trailing it was Charon, Pluto's moon, a dark circle of shadow.

And in the midst of overhead stars, Dalin saw the impossibly far away Sun, barely a star, and then, to the east, something blue.

At first he thought it was Earth. A pang went through him; it seemed as if he had been forever torn from the place he belonged. A flood of memory and longing rushed through him. He saw Minister Faulkner, and felt his own father lift him high into the air, calling him Little Prince; and then he abruptly smelled roses, thick and sweet, and he was back in the gardens of his palace, under the unimaginably bright sun, its gentle warmth like a gift on his skin.

Tabrel was there, kissing him, telling him, "Forever . . ."

But the blue world, he realized, was only Neptune, Pluto's nearest neighbor.

Earth was somewhere far distant, a tiny unseen dot.

Dalin Shar, king of a world, cried out, hearing a faint echo of his own anguish against the distant ice come back to him. He was more alone than he had ever been; more alone than he could imagine being. He might as well be Charon, or any other rock floating in space—he was now truly torn from everything he loved or had ever known.

Shivering, teeth chattering, he fell to his knees, beating his hands in the snow; and then he turned his lidless eyes to the heavens and uttered a vow:

"I am Dalin Shar, king of a world! I will get back everything that is mine!"

He clenched his fists and held them up to the heavens. For a moment the stars twinkled, and he thought of portents. He shouted again, in anguish and resolve.

But it was only the thin clouds regathering overhead into another weak storm.

Soon it began to snow again and Dalin could not see his own hand in front of his face.

The cold assaulted him.

On all fours, he crawled until he found the shelter of the open reentry suit. But it was half filled with snow and would not close to protect him.

Fighting with it, Dalin began to lose his battle with the snow and biting wind.

"Damnation!"

Shivering uncontrollably, he lay in the open suit, curled like a puppy.

Perhaps, he though, he would be better off if the cold took him.

His sight dimmed. . . .

A huge shadow loomed over him.

Shivering, barely conscious, Dalin stared up weakly into an unseen face. He tried to speak but could not. He was easily lifted, felt himself pressed against warm fur.

Again he tried to speak, but his body, on the verge of surrender, would not let him.

He tumbled down into unconsciousness.

And awoke to blinding whiteness, and singing.

It was not a good voice. Deep and rich as a cold

stream (the image of cold made Dalin wince), it was nevertheless just flat enough to be almost painful.

Dalin wanted to beg the voice to stop singing.

The blinding white hurt his sight.

He tried to move, but found himself still too weak to so much as lift his hand to shield his lidless eyes.

But he was warm—surrounded by white warmth.

"Ah!" the deep singing voice said, ending his singing on a particularly flat note. "Our king awakens!"

Slowly, Dalin turned his head even as the singer's face hove into view: a huge face to go with the huge voice, bright eyes, reddened, hearty cheeks—and the fiercest, fullest, richest beard Dalin had ever seen on a man.

Weakly, Dalin said, "How did you know . . . I am . . . a king?"

"You said so yourself, out in the blasted snow! King Dalin, of Earth!" The beard split into a grin. "You vow with the best of them!"

Dalin nodded weakly. "And you are . . ."

"Me? I'm just your humble servant—and a man who used to steal from you whenever he could!" The bear of a man made a mock bow. "Shatz Abel's the name!"

Dalin nearly fainted. "The *pirate*. Oh, no . . ."

The grin grew even wider. "You've heard of me! I'm overwhelmed!"

"Ralf and Enry . . ."

"Enry and Ralf! Those rogues!" For a moment the man's visage clouded. "They owe me money." Again the grin returned. "But no matter! What I'd like to

know is, how did you get here, Your Majesty?" The
voice deepened. "From the look of your eyes, I fear
I already know."

"Wrath-Pei."

Now Shatz Abel's face flushed red with anger. He
said nothing, but a fierce light unlike anything Dalin
had ever seen rose into the man's eyes. Now, as
Shatz Abel's fists clenched, Dalin saw for the first
time just how powerful he was; his closed hands
the size of earthly hams, his muscled arms hard as
mahogany logs, his chest bulging beneath his tunic
like two barrels stove together.

The anger slowly passed, until Shatz Abel said in
a basso hiss, "*Wrath-Pei . . .*"

"Yes," Dalin said weakly.

Suddenly the king was lifted into Shatz Abel's
arms. Too weak to protest, he was carried across
the white chamber, whose walls appeared made of
metal, to a huge window fronting one end. It was
apparent from the rocky sill framing the window
that the structure they were in had been cut into
the side of a mountain.

Outside, the blue-white storm raged. But now
once again one of the strange silences came over it.
A swirl of snow gave way to a clearing sky.

Up above, the stars momentarily glinted.

Cradled in one of Shatz Abel's arms like a rag
doll, Dalin felt oddly at peace.

With his free hand, the pirate pointed. "There,"
he said, softly.

Dalin looked hard, but saw only a black area near the distant starlike Sun. "I don't see anything."

"But it's there, Your Majesty. Earth."

Dalin's heart quickened.

"And I now make a vow of my own, to return you to it, and to your rightful place. Just as I vow to turn Wrath-Pei into jelly, for the things he's done."

For a brief moment Dalin felt himself tightened in Shatz Abel's grip, until the huge man's anger passed.

"Let me stand," Dalin said.

He was lowered gently to the floor and now felt his legs hold him with their returning strength.

The two stood side by side, staring into a clearing night.

"Yes," Dalin said.

Soon he could see the tiny blue dot he sought.

Here's a Preview of *Journey*
Book Two of *The Five Worlds*

Gilgesh Khan, ruler of no empire, was, nevertheless, descended from one. On the wall of his office on icy Europa, at the base of monstrous Carlton Cliff, was hung a duly signed and witnessed document containing a sliver of Lexan enclosing a minute particle of genetic material attesting to such fact that Gilgesh, mild and small, weak and inoffensive manager of the "Greatest Attraction in the Solar System," was, nevertheless, a direct descendant of the feared and hated Earth Khan known as Genghis. It was a matter of great pride to Gilgesh (it had cost enough) but it gave him no comfort on this day, when the ancestor himself might be needed.

"What in Rama's name could Wrath-Pei want with *me*?" he sputtered nervously, fussing with the instruments on his desk, turning to tap the tilt out of the framed and sealed genetic testimonial.

To his right, the side wall of his office was nothing short of a full window, giving a view of the lower portion of the cliff. As Gilgesh turned nervously toward it, a customer fell into view from the sheer icy white heights above, flailing as they all did until the auto-chute opened, bringing the rider up short a few meters from the ground. The rider kicked happily and touched down, running a few strides before turning back to gaze wonderingly at the wall he had just descaled. The trip down had taken nearly twelve minutes—an "Eternity of Thrills," as the advertisements spread over the Four Worlds so hyperbolically, and nearly accurately, claimed—and by the end the thrill seekers who took the plunge at the top were over-whelmed. It was a common reaction—and one Gilgesh had often wished he could charge extra for.

But such pecuniary thoughts were far from his mind today. "Why *me*? Why *now*?" he whined, to no one in particular, being as the office was empty. On learning of the Titan tyrant's imminent arrival he had sent his crew of four scrambling home, and prepared to close the at-traction for the day.

There came a knock at the outer air lock, and Gilgesh for a moment froze, thinking that Wrath-Pei had already arrived. But that was impossible—the madman's ship had not yet been detected by Europa's sensors, and Wrath-Pei himself had declared that he would be extending his stay on sulfurous Io before traveling on to Gilgesh's hum-ble amusement ride.

"There's nothing else *on* this frozen rock!" Gilgesh pro-tested, before activating the lock on the outer door and running to the porthole to see who was there to waste his time.

Two figures shrouded in visored climate suits con-fronted him; the larger of the two began to raise a hand in greeting before Gilgesh cut him off.

"Go away! We're closed for the day!" he snapped.

The two, obviously stupid tourists, did not budge.

"Are you deaf? I said leave! Go to the hotel and sit by the fireplace! Spend money in the gift shop! Come back tomorrow!"

Still they stood staring at him, faces unseen.

A brief chill ran through Gilgesh Khan, making even his ancient Khan's blood freeze: could these two be ad-vance guards for Wrath-Pei himself? To find out: "Don't you know that Wrath-Pei is due here today? We're closed, I tell you!"

That got a reaction, and a good one, from the pair: instantly the larger one turned, pulling the shorter one after him, and they made their way out of the lock, leav-ing it open behind them.

Though secretly pleased at their alarmed reaction, Gilgesh was also angry: "Stupid tourists! No discount for you tomorrow!" he shouted after them, activating the closing of the lock from where he stood. No one had any common courtesy anymore. . . .

But even as the lock closed, Gilgesh Khan turned from the door to fret once more over the items on his desk, and to tap again at the ever-so-slightly askew testimonial on the wall behind his desk.

"Why *me?* Why *now* . . . ?"

Halfway between the icy beauty of the Europa Hotel and the precipitous majesty of the Carlton Cliff, Shatz Abel reached out a hand to stop Dalin Shar in his tracks.

"We don't have much time," Shatz Abel said grimly.

"Why?" Dalin answered. Though he couldn't see the pirate's eyes through the darkened visor, he nevertheless turned in the big man's direction. "And why didn't you ask Khan's help?" A note of sarcasm crept into the king's voice. "I thought you two were 'tight as tigers' in the old days."

Ignoring the king's tone, Shatz Abel answered, "We were tight, but Gilgesh is about as seaworthy as a sieve. If he knew we were here, Wrath-Pei would soon know it, too." The answer that surfaced when Shatz Abel articulated Wrath-Pei's name was evident.

"But what about his ship? I thought—"

"There are other ways to secure a ship," Shatz Abel said. "And the sooner we get to doing it, the sooner we get off this waste of a moon."

Without another word Shatz Abel turned toward the hotel once more; in a moment, Dalin Shar, throwing up his hands in resignation, followed.

Still fussing with his office bric-a-brac, Gilgesh Khan was startled to hear the audio monitor on his wall Screen come to life.

"Is anybody home?" a voice said lightly.

"Who is that!" Khan shouted back into the monitor; at the same time he ran to the window, straining to see up the sharp face of Carlton Cliff. "Don't you know the ride is closed? Get out of there immed—"

The last word turned into a gag in his throat as he caught a glimpse of a monstrous wedge-shaped ship, as long as Carlton Cliff was high, hovering over the top of the ridge.

Wrath-Pei's chuckle filtered through the Screen's audio. "Why, Khan! Is that any way to greet an old friend? Do come up and say hello."

"Yes, of course," Gilgesh croaked out. Already he was fumbling for his climate suit, climbing into it backwards before discovering his mistake and pulling it off to try again.

All the while muttering, "Why *me* . . . ?"

The ride up was not pleasant for Gilgesh Khan.

The ride's owners had insisted that the elevator to carry customers to the cliff's summit not only be spacious but that it be nearly invisible. Made of quality quartz glass, the elevator was little more than a soap bubble in which its passengers felt as if they were riding on air.

Most customers loved it; but Gilgesh, being afraid not only of heights but of upward movement (two facts which he had judiciously kept from the owners, since he very much needed the job at the time) hated the elevator with a passion. This hate was only superseded by his loathing for the ride itself; he made sure that his hirelings did as much of the maintenance at the apex as possible, leaving Gilgesh to fret about the much more important matters of cash receipts and promotion—two endeavors which could be carried out very easily at ground level.

So tightly were his eyes closed, in fact, that Gilgesh did not even realize that the elevator had reached the top of the cliff until he felt a gentle hand on his shoulder and snapped open his eyes to peer into the crystal clear visor of Wrath-Pei's climate suit and see the delightedly smiling face of Wrath-Pei himself.

"Khan!" Wrath-Pei said, releasing the proprietor from his grip one uncurling finger at a time before settling back into his gyro chair. "So nice to see you again!"

As always, Wrath-Pei was dressed with impeccable, if chilling, taste: his climate suit, jet-black, was form fitting and seamless to the tips of his gloves; his helmet save for the clear faceplate was ebony also, and sculpted to mimic Wrath-Pei's swept back leonine mane of silver hair: the effect was startling.

Trying not to shiver, and trying most of all not to stare at the holster secured at the side of Wrath-Pei's gyro chair like a scabbard, Khan bowed at the waist and stuttered, "And n-nice to s-see you, too, Your G-G-Grace!"

Wrath-Pei clapped his hands in delight. His protegé Lawrence, standing a few paces behind the chair, took a tentative, creaking step forward before resuming his silent position. Gilgesh noted that the boy was somewhat shorter than at their last meeting; bile churned from his stomach into his throat when he saw the blunt lines at the boy's thighs that delineated real flesh from artificial limb.

"H-How may I serve you, Your Grace?" Gilgesh Khan said, wanting only for the interview to be over.

Wrath-Pei, still immersed in delight, turned his eyes from Gilgesh to take in the land and skyscape around him. Hypnotized like a cobra, Khan's eyes followed. Beyond the profile of Wrath-Pei's ship, outlined against the diamonds-on-black-velvet of starry space, sat Jupiter like a fat red pumpkin. The horrid crimson swirls of its Great Red Spot were just hoving into view, surrounded by a thousand other variegated storms and fault lines. At the horizon, the contrast of ebon space with white ice was startling; a far line of cliffs smaller than Carlton stood like blunt teeth biting at the deep heavens. There had been vague talk about developing those other cliffs into further amusement rides, or the possibility of the exploitation of Europa's huge ocean, sixty feet below the icy surface. . . .

Suddenly Gilgesh Khan was filled with excitement: could this be why Wrath-Pei was here? Could this be about *money*?

Gilgesh's confidence replaced his fear in an instant. Now he was on terra firma. If there was cash to be made, Khan would be involved. Perhaps Wrath-Pei had taken over the present ride, and had come to introduce himself as the new owner. Or perhaps he really was here to present new plans—for new amusement rides, a new hotel, even a theme park! Oh joy! Oh *money*!

"Your Grace, are you here—?"

"I am here for two reasons," Wrath-Pei said, with sudden detachment. The tyrant's sight had fallen and stayed on the line of auto-chutes lined like obedient dogs at the edge of Carlton Cliff. Beside them was the tall credit machine, the lone sentry of commerce, which allowed customers to release one of the chutes from its locked mooring, don it, and leap from the titanium ledge perched like a pirate ship's plank against the top of the cliff. Exactly eleven point eight minutes later the chute would automatically activate, ending the ride.

"Is it . . . fun?" Wrath-Pei asked idly.

"I wouldn't know, Your Grace," Gilgesh said, impatient to discuss the tyrant's plans and reasons. "I've never been down."

"No?" Wrath-Pei said, turning to study Khan.

"As to your reasons—"

"Yes, my reasons for being here," Wrath-Pei said. "As I said, there are two. First and foremost, I need this ice-ball as a defensive station against Prime Cornelian. I am therefore claiming it in the name of . . . me, and closing your facility, including the hotel, forthwith."

Shock replaced both fear and anticipation in Gilgesh Khan. "But Your Grace—"

"Second, and also important, I am looking for an old friend of yours, Shatz Abel, who I'm sure has come to you for help."

Gilgesh Khan, dumbfounded, and beginning to feel fear again, sputtered, "I have not seen—"

"I'm sure he has come to you. I know he is on Europa, and there is nowhere else for him to go. He had an impudent pup who fancies himself King of Earth with him."

"Dalin Shar?" Khan said in wonder.

"Yes. When did they come to see you?"

"But they have not been here! They have not—"

"In the old days," Wrath-Pei said, "I overlooked your alliance with Shatz Abel because it did not matter. Suddenly it matters."

"But I assure you—!"

"Lawrence," Wrath-Pei said, turning slightly in his seat to confront his ward, "please secure an auto-chute for Khan."

Walking like a man on stilts, the young man went to the credit machine; in a moment there was a loud click, and one of the auto-chutes unsnicked from its mooring and flipped onto the ice, waiting.

Wrath-Pei looked at the chute. "Put it on, Khan."

Gilgesh, quaking with fear, said, "Your Grace, I implore you!"

"Don't implore. Just do what I say."

Trembling, Gilgesh retrieved the auto-chute and secured it, pulling the straps tight across his front. It occurred to him that though he had helped countless foolish tourists with this procedure, this was the first time he had ever actually mounted one of the devices himself.

"Now jump," Wrath-Pei said, indicating the titanium plank jutting out into nothingness.

"I cannot!"

"Of course you can, Khan," Wrath-Pei said.

In a moment the tyrant's chair had whirred into motion, and Wrath-Pei hovered beside Khan, at eye level. A gentle hand was once again placed on his shoulder, urging him forward.

"Jump," Wrath-Pei said.

"I canno—!"

The murderously cold look on Wrath-Pei's face spurred Khan into action, and he stumbled forward, moaning, to the plank's beginning, and then, step by edging step, to its end, where all of Europa seemed to hang below him, in dizzying white splendor.

"Ohhhhh . . ."

"Now jump."

After giving Wrath-Pei the briefest look, Gilgesh Khan did so.

He fell, into splendid nothingness—

And found, to his amazement, that his vertigo was gone!

A thrilling ecstasy filled Gilgesh Khan. Behind him, the vertical face of Carlton Cliff glided slowly past, as if in a dream. The wall was pocked with ridges and icy depressions which resolved themselves into pictures. Gilgesh had sold 3-D Screen views of these anomalies, but had never appreciated their beauty: the Smiling Clown, its face naturally etched in ice; the Rocket, a natural formation in the shape of a Martian cruiser; the Infant; and all the others.

And here now were other marks on the ice—manmade graffiti etched by clever parachutists working vertically in a deft fight against gravity: "Mark Loves Ang-Frei," "Choi Lives!" and "Lem-Jarn Was Here."

As mesmerized as he was by his slow-motion fall, Gilgesh turned to face away from the cliff.

He felt suspended in space. There was the Europa Hotel in the distance, its green spires rising like emerald fingers from a blanket of white ice. And beyond it, all of Europa outlined now against the massive limb of Father Jupiter, King of Planets, its red, orange, and creme bands like a dream in the sky!

How could he have missed this wonderful attraction, this marvelous ride, for so long?

Each day, from now on, he would begin with a ride down Carlton Cliff, the "Greatest Attraction in the Solar System," to renew his sense of wonder!

And now Gilgesh looked down, and saw the ground rising slowly up to meet him. How long had it been? Six minutes? Eight? In only a matter of minutes now he would reach bottom, the slow journey down nevertheless having imparted enough velocity to his mass to crush him like an egg but for the opening of his chute . . .

His chute—

It was now that Gilgesh Khan, long-separated descendant of Genghis Khan, who had proof of that blood bond, remembered what he had seen in that last brief glimpse back at Wrath-Pei before he had leaped.

What he had seen?

Wrath-Pei, re-sheathing his razor-sharp snips in their holster next to his chair.

And, in Wrath-Pei's other hand, the severed straps of Gilgesh's auto-chute; while, on the ground, the packed mass of the chute itself lay unrolling.

To confirm his fate, Gilgesh Khan reached around to feel nothing strapped to his back.

The flat shelf of ice at the bottom of Carlton Cliff rose inevitably up.

Gilgesh opened his mouth to scream—but something far down and ancient in his genes stayed his terror and steeled him.

He glared at the approaching ground with defiance.

And Gilgesh Khan, ruler of no empire save his approaching death, opened his arms wide to meet it as that other Khan would have. . . .

🅁🅞🅒 BRINGS THE FUTURE TO YOU